All Roar
And No
BITE

CELIA KYLE
NEW YORK TIMES BESTSELLING AUTHOR

chapter one

Van wondered if killing a wolf would start a blood war. Just one. Not the whole pack. Not even the Alpha. Nope, he had his sights set on the Redby Beta, Morgan.

He leaned against the brick wall, cell phone pressed to his ear, as he focused on the cars entering and leaving the gas station parking lot. He'd stopped for a cup of coffee. Five minutes, in and out. Except his quick break turned into a fifteen minute phone argument with the wolf.

"They're twenty-five days over the limit," Morgan growled and Van's inner bear responded to the low threat.

His beast took orders from one man—Ty—his older brother and Itan of the Grayslake bear clan.

"And as the Grayslake Enforcer, I'm telling you to give them additional time," he snarled in return, keeping the sound low.

Humans strode past him left and right and it was illegal to expose themselves to non-shifters. Sure, a handful of older humans knew of them, but it was important to keep a low profile.

"The order was twenty-four hours for singles and forty-eight for families. It was issued by *your Itan* over three weeks ago."

1

Fuck. Van wondered if Ty realized the cluster fuck he started by agreeing to work with the wolves. It wasn't the Itan dealing with logistics, organization, and finally punishment, if his orders weren't followed. No, that fell to him and the hardheaded asshole on the phone.

It'd been hell since Ty swept into a nearby town, Boyne Falls, and ordered the hyena Alpha and ruling circle killed while also demanding *all* hyenas leave the area. The Alpha had been involved in the kidnapping of Ty's adopted son and, as a result of the hyena participation, Ty's mate Mia had been injured and nearly murdered.

Van didn't disagree with the punishment—hyenas in general were a nasty breed. The werewolf alliance, however, caused his bear to bristle and balk at following Ty's directives.

"I'm aware of the order. As you said, it came from *my* Itan. That doesn't change the fact that leniency is necessary for those in the *hospital* who need assistance vacating the town. Helicopters capable of life-flighting someone to another hospital don't materialize out of thin air and some patients have specific medical needs." Van's fingers tingled and warmed, a sure sign his bear was annoyed by the wolf.

One on one, the beast could take the smaller male and his animal was ready to prove it.

"The order is—"

"Oh, fuck the order. I'm telling you they get enough time to ensure they don't fucking die on the helipad." He held onto his control by a thread, his whole body trembling with the effort. "Leave them the fuck alone."

"The order—"

Van closed his eyes and banged his head against the brick wall. "Seriously? I don't know how it is with wolves, but bears have common sense with a lot less hardheadedness."

Not a sound came over the line for several seconds and Van wondered if Morgan had hung up.

Unfortunately, the man spoke. "Are you challenging me?"

"Fuck me," he grumbled and ran a hand over his face in frustration. "No, I'm telling you to leave the patients in the hospital—along with their families—until arrangements can be made. Go be an asshole to everyone else, but quit messing with the injured and ill."

Another moment of silence.

"I will speak with your *Itan*." On Morgan's lips, his brother's title sounded like a curse rather than a position of respect.

Van's bear bristled at the insult. He opened his mouth to ask when he wanted to meet in the pit, but the rapid beep of his phone indicated the call had ended.

"Son of a bitch," he growled through clenched teeth and a low *crack* sounded in his ear. He pulled the phone away and glared at the hunk of plastic, metal, and glass. The damned screen splintered, lines marring the surface, making the damn thing useless. "*Fuck.*"

Screw it. Van finished the job by crushing the device. Taking a little help from his bear, he squeezed until the phone was nothing but jagged bits of its former self.

A soft throat clearing pierced his focus, but it wasn't until the newcomer spoke that he pulled his attention away from the phone.

"Um, Officer Abrams?" Van recognized the speaker. One of the clan guards, but he was also a Grayslake police officer like himself. "Everything okay?"

He reached for a nearby trashcan and uncurled his hand, letting the pieces tumble into the receptacle. "Just fine." Van turned toward the other cop and didn't miss the cautious step the man took in retreat. "Just fine."

"Sure, sure."

3

Damn it. He took a breath and released it in slow increments. It wasn't the man's fault the wolf pissed him off. "Sorry. Everything's fine. How are patrols this morning?"

Van wasn't just another cop, he was the clan's Enforcer. If bad things, illegal things, happened within the clan or affecting the clan, he was the one who carried out justice. He did the heavy, bloody lifting. Which was why he was saddled with handling the issue in Boyne Falls.

And normally, Isaac would be around, waiting to patch up their asses when they needed a Healer. But Isaac… he wasn't going to think about Isaac. Not at the moment, at least.

"Good, good. Pretty quiet, considering."

Considering the clan had lost four men due to the machinations of Ty's mate's family and hyena interference. "How's everyone feeling? We got any hotheads?"

That was the last thing he needed. The clan was already hurting. He didn't want to make it worse by punishing someone for letting their beast free and going after the hyenas themselves.

"No, sir. Upset—angry—but we all know you and the It—" A human walked by and the officer coughed to cover his near slip. Damn humans were everywhere. "We know you and Ty are handling things the way they need to be. The wolves, though…"

Van didn't care for the wolves either, but he couldn't bad mouth them to the clan. Not when the peace was so tenuous. Fuck, he was gonna get his ass reamed over how he'd spoken to Morgan.

"I understand. Trust in Ty, though." He raised his eyebrows, waiting for the man's agreement and it was quick in coming.

"Yes, En— Officer."

The cop's radio, clipped to his shoulder, squawked and their dispatcher's voice crackled over the speaker.

Van listened, keeping his mouth shut while the woman rattled off the information.

Domestic disturbance. Rich side of town. Humans, no shifters involved.

It paid to have a werebear in the dispatch office.

"Excuse me, Officer Abrams." The man spun and stepped off the curb, intent on getting to his cruiser.

"Let 'em know I'm right behind you."

He looked at Van with bewilderment clouding his features. "Sir?"

"I'm coming on the call. I'll be behind you." It was what he needed—to help someone, get his mind off the asshole Beta and back onto his town.

"It's, uh," he looked around and leaned into Van, "it's a human call, sir."

The man's confusion brought him up short. He was well aware of the altered incident codes used by their department. He knew it was a human call, no shifters involved. "And?"

Another squawk of the radio and tension vibrated in the male. "Sir, you don't do human calls. We all understand." He rushed out the words. "I don't want you to think we don't, but… we know how you feel. You're dedicated to the clan and we appreciate it."

Van's mind whirled as he flipped through call after call he'd been assigned over the years. He went on human calls… hadn't he?

"Tell dispatch I'm coming." Van headed toward his car. Was he that much of a dick when it came to humans?

He knew he'd given Ty shit about mating Mia. For a while they'd thought she was one-quarter werebear which was as good as human when it came to wanting shifting cubs. When he'd met her, all he could think of was how Ty being with Mia would impact the clan and the line of succession. Everything was always for the clan.

They now knew a human and a bear could have shifting cubs as long as they were meant to be together. *Fated mates.*

He tugged on the door and just before it thumped closed behind him, he heard four words screamed across Martin's radio. Words that made him realize he *had* been a huge dick about humans. *"He's coming as backup?"*

* * *

Lauren threw her beat up pickup truck into park before the thing even came to a halt. Metal grinded and squealed in objection while gravel flew through the air. There were more important things to worry about than her transmission or the state of her friend's driveway.

She didn't bother tearing the keys from the ignition, leaving it running in case she needed a fast getaway, if it came to that.

The 911 operator kept talking, asking her questions, but Lauren didn't have time to deal with the woman. She'd given the address and told her what was happening, hadn't she?

Adrenaline filled her, sending her heart rate soaring while anger warred with worry and fear. Her hand trembled as she tossed aside her cell phone and reached for the bat under her bench seat.

A panicked scream came from the house in front of her. On the outside, it looked like any other mansion in Grayslake. Big. Gaudy. Ugly assed white pillars and wraparound porch.

No one knew about the hell it was for her friend Anna. That the walls were soaked with pain and some places were red with Anna's blood.

Another scream got her moving. Who knew how long this beating had been going on? The woman next door called her, telling Lauren to hurry. Part of her cursed the old lady for not calling the cops, but

6

people had their reasons. They all had something to lose when it came to ratting out the mayor of Grayslake.

Lucky for Lauren, she didn't give a damn.

Gripping the bat tightly, she ran across the pale gravel, her boots crunching the white rocks as she raced to the bright-red front door.

Red, like blood.

How much would be covering Anna?

No, she couldn't worry about that. She had to get her best friend safe first.

Lauren didn't pause in her approach. Nope, she sped up. She might hate her ass and big thighs any other time, but now it was extra weight to throw against the door. She braced herself for the coming collision, preparing her muscles for the impact.

It took one great crash to bust the panel from its frame, the wood braces and small lock no match for her. If they didn't want fat chicks breaking in, they should have built the damn thing stronger. Her boots slid across the marble floor, slipping out from under her and she stumbled, rolling until she thumped against the wall. Not the most graceful entrance.

She heaved herself off the ground, knocking over some random, shiny, expensive-as-hell vase. Anna's pretty prison was filled with glitter and gilt, things meant to salve her bastard husband's conscience.

Another yell, followed by a sob, had Lauren heading down some fancy hallway, past the formal dining room. She jogged through the sitting area and came to a stop in the kitchen.

Fucker.

Anna's husband, Bryson, loomed over her, hand raised, ready to strike her again.

"You bitch." The man's voice was cold, deadly. "I told you to have—" That arm descended, aimed right for her friend's face.

She spared a glance for Anna, taking in her swollen black eye, split lip, and dear God… was that a burn?

"You asshole!" Lauren screamed at the man in his perfectly pressed suit with his perfectly styled hair and his fucking perfectly shined leather shoes. "Get the *fuck* away from her!"

Bryson whirled around, giving her a good look at the man she was ready to kill, ready to bludgeon to death if she could. He wasn't going to hurt Anna ever again.

"*You.*"

"Fuck yeah, me." She tightened her grip on the bat, holding it steady, though her arms trembled. She talked a good game, but delivering was going to be interesting. "Why don't you take on someone your own size, dickhead?"

It didn't matter that he had eight inches and seventy pounds on her, she was a hell of a lot bigger than Anna's tiny body.

"Lauren, no." Anna held out a hand toward her, as if asking her to stop. "Don't."

Bryson whirled. "Shut up, you bitch."

"Hey, fuckhead!" Lauren needed his attention on her, not Anna.

Bryson slowly panned back to her, rage flashing in his eyes. Well, she was pissed too. "Bitch."

"Can't complain if it's the truth." She brought the bat a little higher, ready to hit a home fucking run. "Now, why don't you and I have a little talk?"

Bryson advanced on her and Lauren countered his steps, easing back along her path. Faced with an enraged man, she was starting to rethink the whole plan. Who was she kidding? Plan?

She'd been told "he's doing it again" by the neighbor and got in her truck. No question on the "he" or what he was doing.

A movement behind Bryson caught her attention and she flicked her gaze to a huddled Anna. Her hand cupped her cheek, cradling her bruised face.

Fucker.

Bryson caught her inattention and shifted his weight to turn. Hell no, he couldn't focus on Anna again.

"Hey, asshole." She punctuated her yell with a well-placed slam of her bat against drywall. The end smashed through the wall and she yanked it free, leaving a four-inch hole. "What are you waiting for?"

"You bitch."

Lauren smiled, goading him, and shook her head. "Man, as the mayor, I figured you'd have a better vocabulary. A little less repetition."

He growled and rushed her, hatred edging every line of his face. Lauren raised the bat again and swung. Wood connected with his left bicep sending a jarring vibration along her arms that had her wincing in pain. Hitting flesh and bone wasn't like hitting a softball.

Unfortunately, the strike didn't slow his advance. He kept coming, his right arm cocked back, hand balled into a fist. She lifted the bat, intent on hitting him before he hit her.

Only… shit, he was moving too fast. She didn't have time to get into swinging position again. That fist came closer and closer, aimed at her face, and it was gonna hurt in the morning.

Lauren twisted sideways, readying herself to take the blow. She curled in on herself, presenting him with her shoulder. She psyched herself up for what was coming. Pain, pain, pain.

9

She grunted when he struck her, the weight and strength of the blow sending her sliding over the polished marble. A split-second after her mind registered the hit, it recognized the following agony.

Distantly, she realized the bat tumbled from her fingers, clattering to the ground and rolling away.

Another blow, knuckles digging into her side. The pain burrowed deep, racing into her muscles and bones.

Air rushed from her lungs, abandoning her, and she fought to breathe. The moment she was able to suck in a breath she wheezed out another taunt. As long as he remained focused on her, he wasn't hurting Anna.

"Hit like a fucking girl." She glanced at him over her left shoulder and saw him gearing up for another strike. "Only pussies hit women."

Fucking dick.

She spun to her right, away from the next blow. Bryson overshot his hit, taking a step to catch his weight, and Lauren attacked. She kicked, nailing him in the side of his knee, sending him crashing to the floor. He landed on all fours, gasping for breath, and she smiled. He was feeling the pain.

She drew in air, wrapping an arm across her waist to grip her side. She was, too.

While he was down, she'd give him another party favor to take to jail. Lauren pulled her leg back and then let the kick fly. She'd worn her boots for a reason. Steel toed. Hard ass leather. Thick sole. Her foot collided with his ribs and she imagined them cracking, breaking beneath her assault. Maybe she'd get lucky and pierce a lung.

She didn't want him to die though. Nope, prison would be the perfect hell for a man who abused women.

Bryson grunted, but it didn't seem painful enough to her. Nope. She reared her leg back, eager to hand more pain to the asshole. She

10

thought of Anna in the other room: black eye, busted lip, burned skin. The dick deserved whatever he got.

With that kick, he rolled to his side, curling into himself with a pained groan.

"How's it feel asshole?" She wanted to kick him again. Hell, screw that, where was her bat? "Feel like a big man when you hit a woman?" She lifted her leg. "You little dicked—"

"Police! Hands up."

Damn it.

Lauren lifted her hands, wincing at the loss of pressure on her ribs. Okay, they might be a little more than bruised. Maybe a lot more than cracked, too.

"On your knees."

She almost joked that she didn't know him well enough, but then she caught sight of Anna. Sweet Anna curled into a ball in the kitchen, tears streaming from her eyes, and stark fear filling her body. She swallowed her witty retort and lowered to her knees as ordered.

Beside her, Bryson moaned and pushed to his hands and knees.

"Hands up!" Dang, that order, that *voice*.

If she was anywhere other than kneeling on a hard-ass marble floor and trying to figure out whether to puke or pass out, that voice might make her shiver and heat up all those naughty places.

Instead, she swayed as she knelt and prayed the room would stop spinning. Pain did not-fun things to her head.

Bryson lifted his head and snarled. "Do you know who I am?"

An asshole?

"Mr. Davies, I know you're about to be cuffed until we straighten things out. On your knees, hands up." A growl filled the cop's words, sending a happy shiver to her pink bits.

God, if a cop about to arrest her got her hot, it'd been way too long since she'd gotten laid.

Finally Bryson did as ordered. Large warm hands encircled one wrist and then the other, wrenching them to her lower back. She sucked in a harsh breath at the pain zinging through her. She coughed and fought for air.

"Quit resisting." The words were garbled, the cop's mouth next to her ear.

"Not."

He pulled harder and she reacted, jerking back from the pain he caused. "Damn it."

A cuff wrapped around her wrist, tightening until she thought she'd lose her hand. Her muscles reacted on instinct, twitching and spasming.

"Stop." He yanked on her other arm a little harder, forcing her into position.

Agony pulsed through her, assaulting her from inside out, battering her with the pain from her injuries. She gasped and squeezed her eyes shut, fighting the tears that threatened. She wasn't about to turn into a sobbing girl.

Another set of booted feet echoed in the hallway, the owner moving at a brisk pace toward them. He dodged the cop holding her and came into view.

"Martin!"

He swung toward her. "Lauren?" He shook his head and sighed. "What'd you do—?"

12

"Anna's in the kitchen. She needs an ambulance."

The man holding her ignored her outburst and wrapped a hand around her bicep, yanking her to her feet. "C'mon. You have the right to remain silent…"

Lauren tuned out mister-not-so-sexy-anymore and focused on Martin. "Hurry."

When Martin spun away she released a relieved breath. Martin would take care of Anna.

She spared a glance for Bryson. He was in the same shape as her, hands cuffed behind his back and moving stiffer than normal. Good. She still hoped she had broken something.

The cop ushered her toward the front door and onto the porch. She stumbled on the steps, but his firm grip held her steady, keeping her upright when she would have fallen.

She hadn't spared him a glance, but she didn't need to. His voice was deep—sexy—and his cologne was all smoky with a hint of sweet. The man could look like a dog as long as he never stopped talking.

He led her to a nearby cruiser and helped her into the back.

That's when she got her first look at him.

Dayum. He was tall, gorgeous, and dead sexy. His shortly cropped brown hair matched the typical cop's haircut, but the rest of him was no typical cop. He wasn't wearing a uniform, instead he had a precinct shirt stretched across his broad shoulders, heavily muscled chest, and flat stomach. His brown eyes drew her to his face, with his chiseled features and angular lines. She imagined him to be strong, steadfast in his beliefs… immovable.

"Do you understand these rights as they have been explained to you?"

She tore her gaze from his lips and took him in as a whole. "What?"

Movement near the house grabbed her attention. Martin carried an unmoving bundle from the home, the slight package wrapped in a familiar quilt.

"Martin!" Lauren didn't miss the anger, the rage, filling the officer's face. "Anna?"

The hot cop, getting less hot by the second, stepped in front of her. "Ma'am, do you understand these rights as they have been explained to you?"

chapter two

The woman paced. No, not "the woman." Van glanced at the paperwork in his hands. Lauren Evans. Twenty-seven. Five-five. Hundred eighty-five pounds. Blonde hair, blue eyes.

The camera captured the station's holding cell and he saw *Lauren* pace. One arm across her stomach and pressed to her side, she walked from one end of the room to the other and back again. Never slowing, never increasing speed, she simply walked. Every other turn or two, there was a hitch in her step, a small stutter, and then she fell into the same rhythm.

They'd placed her in the holding cell while Bryson Davies was questioned, which left her alone.

His footsteps had faltered when he'd deposited her in the large space. His bear objected to leaving her there. Heavily. But she was alone, no one else with her while Davies was questioned.

He reasoned with his bear. She'd been hurt when left on her own. Wasn't it better if she was protected by the bars while the male who hurt her was elsewhere?

It grudgingly agreed and settled just outside the edge of his human consciousness. Its big body far enough back to let his other half do his job, but close enough to rush to her aid if needed. Fucking bear.

Lauren paused in her pacing and turned her head, gaze darting toward the room's door, which gave him another look at her fine features. Her plump lips, delicate eyebrows, little upturned nose.

He could stare at her forever.

Air in his lungs whooshed out in a rapid exhale and he sucked in a breath, coughing as it filled him.

Fuck no.

The click of a lock reached him followed by the door swinging wide to admit Martin. "Officer Abrams?"

Always with respect. His name was always preceded by his title.

Officer.

Enforcer.

Never only his last name like any other cop on the force.

I'm not any other cop, am I? Sometimes he wished he was.

"Yes?" He couldn't tear his gaze from the woman, from Lauren. He'd touched her, enjoyed her silken skin beneath his fingertips as he cuffed her and led her to the cruiser.

At the scene, he'd been intent on securing everyone so they could figure out what cluster fuck they'd walked into. Cuffing her was his priority.

But then…

Peaches and cream and sex on two legs.

Then it'd taken everything in him to get through the damn Miranda rights and keep his bear at bay at the same time.

The damn beast roared at him when he slapped the cuffs on her. The next time he'd need them would be to secure her to his bed. And hadn't that thought scared the fuck out of him. The bear had very specific ideas about Lauren Evans—handcuffed and naked.

Martin shuffled closer and the scent of the man's unease reached Van before his physical body. "Have you spoken with Lauren yet?"

The bear objected to Martin's familiarity, but Van mentally collared it and shoved it back into its cage. "No, I'm letting Miss Evans calm a little before questioning her."

He refused to admit that he enjoyed looking at her. That instead of asking her a few questions and letting her go, he wanted to watch her ass sway as she paced. He liked the long, loose blonde curls cascading down her back and the way her eyes flashed blue fire at him. Her curves were more than a handful and his cock *really* liked that.

"*Oh.*" Martin shook his head.

"What do you mean 'oh'?"

The officer rubbed the back of his neck, kneading the muscles. "Well, Lauren is… she…" He sighed. "Did someone at least tell her Anna's okay?" Martin's pain drifted to him on the cool air. "She's gonna have scars, but otherwise she's fine. If Lauren hadn't…" Martin's eyes shined a little brighter in the dim light. *Interesting.*

Martin had gone to the hospital with Anna Davies. The bear was intimately acquainted with the staff there. Martin had been attacked and left for dead by the same man who'd kidnapped Ty's son and injured the Itan's mate. Initially, he'd been assumed dead, but thankfully a clan member found him before he passed away on the side of the road. The thought of death had Van wondering what could have happened to Lauren had they arrived any later.

"Miss Davies will make a full recovery?"

Martin coughed and drew in a quick breath.

Damn interesting.

"She's good. She'll, uh, be staying with me until Lauren gets her head out of her ass."

A growl burst from his lips, the rolling sound filling the room for a split-second before he was able to cut it off. Martin took a giant step back, his gaze fixed on the floor while his head slightly tilted to the side. The man swallowed hard, Adam's apple bobbing along his neck, and the aromas of his unease smacked him.

Damn it. Why the hell was he getting so pissed?

"Sorry, Enforcer." His voice was low, placating.

Van shook his head. "No, I'm sorry. Long day I guess." He wasn't going to mention he'd only been awake for three hours. "What's going on with Miss Evans?"

"Well… it's just…"

"Spit it out, Martin." His bear wanted him in that room with her. Beside her. Touching her. Holding her.

"This is a human issue, sir. I'm happy to—"

Van gritted his teeth. He didn't want to hear that again, damn it. He wasn't that much of a prick, was he? "Spit. It. Out."

Martin's shoulders slumped. "You're not gonna like it, but remember human laws are different."

"Just tell me."

Martin sighed and gave him the information he needed.

Van listened with half an ear, his attention split between the bullshit the man fed him and the pacing woman filling the screen. The bear paced with her, growing more agitated the more he heard. The man's voice trembled, the wavering becoming more pronounced the longer he spoke. It was then he realized his hands weren't human any longer; fur coated his arms, and a deep growl lingered in his chest.

18

Van cracked his neck, rolling his head and shrugging his shoulders in an effort to throw off his beast's reaction to the news.

But it wasn't enough, wasn't what his animal needed to calm. For some fucked up reason, it wanted Lauren. It wanted to be near her, scent her, touch her, taste her…

He was so fucked.

"Enough, Martin. Give me the agreement." The bear wasn't quite so evident in his voice any longer.

The officer handed over the page. Short, sweet, and to the point.

Apologize and all is forgiven.

Van turned his attention to Lauren, to the black and white image of her curved body, and agitation filled his taut muscles.

This wasn't going to go well.

*

Lauren weaved between worry and anger. No, rage. Worry for Anna and rage at the asshole, Bryson. Well, a bit was left for the hot cop who arrested her. Except that was tempered by a good dose of OMG-he's-gorgeous.

Stupid libido.

Stupid dry spell.

She clutched her side a hair tighter, holding her ribs steady. The added pressure hurt, yet relieved the throbbing pain. As soon as she got out and hid Anna somewhere safe, she'd go to the urgent care clinic. They could give her something to take the edge off the pulsating ache. Not enough to knock her out, she needed to remain alert for Anna.

The asshole had done this too many times, had beaten Anna and then walked away free as a bird. Though, she accepted a good hunk was because Anna never pressed charges.

Anna had been hit by a lot of kitchen cabinets in the last two years.

But after the last time, she'd convinced the woman that if she wanted to give Bryson one last chance, it needed to be the last. If she didn't get out soon, he'd kill her. Each beating was always worse than the last and Lauren knew it was a matter of time.

She paused in her pacing and glared at the doorway, willing someone to come in and give her news, let her out, something.

It remained empty.

Dick cops. Dick laws. Dicks, dicks, dicks.

Though, that one guy was very, very nice to look at.

With a shake of her head she got back to moving. Walking kept her mind off the pain in her side and the pounding in her back.

The heavy thump of booted feet on thin carpet reached her and she stopped and turned toward the room's entrance. A second later, her hot arresting officer came into view.

Still tall. Still had muscles that looked carved from stone. Still had brown eyes that screamed sex and unbending strength. Still sexy as hell.

"When am I getting out of here?" She made her way to the bars, willing herself not to lean against them to keep upright.

Nothing good came from revealing weaknesses.

The cop didn't say anything, didn't even acknowledge she'd spoken. Instead, he went to the lone desk in the corner and snared the chair. Grabbing the back, hooking his fingers into the handle, he carried it toward her. He carefully lowered it to the ground at the opposite end of the cell near a bench bolted to the wall. Silent, he focused on her, a single eyebrow raised as he tipped his head toward the seat.

She glared at him, pinching her lips. Damn man, stupid cop. Thought he could just order people around… She wasn't about to address the fact that cops, by their position alone, were allowed to do that.

When he still didn't utter a sound, she huffed and stomped toward him. Well, stomped twice and then froze. She gasped as pain assaulted her. She braced herself against the bars, gripping one rod as she fought for breath.

"Shit, that was a mistake," she wheezed and waited for the agony to subside. She sucked in a breath and then forced it back out. "That was, too."

Breathing, moving, living was bad.

"Fuck," he spat the curse and rose from his chair, rushing toward the desk. He grumbled as he dug through drawers. A handful of garbled words reached her. Things like "human," "stupid," and "weak."

"Fuck you, I'm fine." She pushed herself vertical. She wasn't stupid, she wasn't weak. She was human, but she couldn't figure out how that became a curse. What the hell else would she be but human?

"You're not fine." He yanked on another drawer.

"You're right. But let's get this over with and then I can get checked out."

He paused long enough to glare at her. "You'll—"

"Get looked at after I'm released and take care of Anna." Crap, Anna. Here she was ogling the hot cop while her friend… "How is Anna? Is she okay? Where's the dickhead?"

"Miss Evans," he looked away from her, focusing on the wall.

Not good.

"Missus Davies is going to make a full recovery. I can't give you further details." He paused and took a slow breath. "We've spoken with both Mister and Missus Davies."

Lauren's stomach dropped. She knew that serious tone, she'd heard it often enough these last two years. "No, she's not going back to him. She—"

The cop shook his head. "No, she's not. Martin went with her to the hospital and indicated he'd take her home until you're released and able to care for her."

Okay. Not bad so far.

"So, when are you releasing me?" She clutched the bar. Pain pumped through her, but she needed to be there for Anna.

He still wouldn't look at her.

"Mister Davies is pressing charges."

She furrowed her brow. "For what? Who? His wife? The wife he beat to hell?"

"No." He shook his head. "You."

"Me?" she roared and then regretted the move. Fuck a duck that hurt.

"For assault." He looked to her. His brown eyes filled with anger. "Unless you sign a formal apology and confidentiality agreement. You'll never breathe a word about him or his marriage to Anna Davies."

"Apology?" she hissed the word, careful of her injuries. "For what? Saving Anna?" *Anna*. "What about Anna? Isn't she pressing charges against him? Why the hell isn't he in here with me?" At least she could kick the crap out of him in the cell. Okay, she'd get the crap kicked out of *her* again, but she could get in a good punch or two.

She saw it then, in his eyes, in his posture. It seemed like a wave of anger spread from him and consumed the room.

"No. She has to press charges. She promised. She *promised*." They were going to put him behind bars. Mayor of Grayslake or not, he wasn't going to do this to anyone else.

"In exchange for a quiet, uncontested divorce, she agreed to not say a word to anyone."

Pressure built behind her eyes, a precursor to tears, and she squeezed them shut. "He's not going to let her go. He says that now, but he'll kill her. One way or another, he will."

"I know." The word so quiet yet echoing with its intensity.

"Why isn't my word good enough? I'll testify."

His approach was slow, boots barely making a sound as he neared her. "Did you see him strike her?"

His scent, all musk and man, reached out to her and she found herself swaying toward the bars. "No."

"Between the two of you, who swung first?"

"Maybe I need a lawyer." She licked her lips, mouth suddenly dry.

"This is me and you. Van and Lauren. Not the cop and Miss Evans. Who swung first?"

Why the hell did she trust him? Why was she thinking of answering his question? Hell, she didn't know why, but it didn't matter.

"Me."

And she wouldn't ever apologize for it. In all honestly, she was sorry she hadn't had more time with the man. True, she ended up hurt but so had he.

23

"Which means you're on the hook for assault if he changes his mind." The shift of cloth, the rustling of his uniform indicated he eased even closer. "You can't watch over Anna if you're here, Lauren. It was a good thing you did, but now she needs her friend."

Lauren fought for calm. He was right. She knew he was, but that didn't make swallowing the bitter pill any easier.

"Fine. But I want something from him, too. He signs a similar document. As of today, right this second, I've never hit him, snarled at him, or done anything to him, his home, or possessions." She forced her eyes open and stared at the cop who both intrigued and scared the hell out of her. "As of right now, he's never even heard of Lauren Evans."

The cop—Van—grinned and the move changed him, transformed him from hard ass cop to sinfully sexy man. "What'd you do to him?"

"Nothing." She returned the half-smile. "But he hasn't had much luck with his cars. Especially after Anna had trouble with doors and kitchen cabinets."

Van reached past the bars and cupped her cheek, stroking her skin with his thumb.

For some reason, she liked it, liked this big man touching her so tenderly. She refused to look at why, refused to think about the reasons behind her instant trust.

"You're a fierce little hell cat, aren't you?" His voice rolled over her, stroking her with invisible hands. And those eyes, those dark brown eyes, were black now. Like midnight lived within him and peeked out from the shadows. Slowly he withdrew and she fought against the desire to follow his touch, keep their skin connected for as long as possible. "I'll speak with Davies and his attorney. Hopefully we'll have you out in a couple of hours."

Van ran his fingers over the back of her hands, his callused digits scraping her. The touch, the contrast between the tenderness of the gesture, warred with the fierce expression he wore.

"You'll get medical attention when you get out of here. I can take you—"

She shook her head. "No, I appreciate the offer, Officer Abrams, but I'll be fine."

"Your truck's at the Davies's house."

She shrugged. "And I have two feet. The clinic is down the street. I'll call Martin when I'm ready."

He pulled his hand away and gripped a bar. A low, animalistic growl surrounded her and cut off as quickly as it'd sounded. "I'll—"

"Van?" A deep baritone voice echoed in the room and she tore her gaze from the man before her.

A man larger than Van stood in the doorway. His uniform screamed "cop," but there was also this… powerful aura that flowed from him. Like a roaring storm, it bowled over her, sending her gently swaying and she tightened her grip to remain standing. While Van scared her with her own attraction to him, this man flat out scared her.

Van snarled and turned toward the newcomer. "What?"

"Excuse me?" The stranger raised a single brow.

Van stilled, his entire body freezing in place. "Apologies. What can I do for you?"

"We need to discuss the issue in Boyne Falls."

"Of course, Ita—" Van cleared his voice. "Of course, Ty."

Ty now raised both eyebrows to his hairline. "And do we need to discuss this?" He wiggled his finger back and forth, indicating her and Van.

"There's nothing to discuss." Van's voice was firm, and a tiny part of her cracked with his words.

25

She'd obviously read more into that tender touch than she should have. Better get that through her head now. Besides, she didn't have time for a man in her life, or even an unrequited crush. She had Anna to think about, not some gorgeous cop who made her knees weak.

Right. Maybe she'd believe that in a day or two.

Van turned back to her, his eyes brown once again. Weird. "I'll be back after I speak with Ty and then Davies."

Lauren shook her head. No, it was a bad idea to see him again. She needed to nip this little crush in the bud. "Just send someone with the agreement for me to sign. You're obviously busy."

"I'll—"

"Van!" Ty's voice sliced through them.

Black eyes stared at her. "Fuck."

"Just go." She stepped away from the wall of metal. "Thank you for your help, Officer Abrams."

It shouldn't have hurt when he turned and strode from the room.

It shouldn't have, but it did.

chapter **three**

It shouldn't have taken Van a full day to find Lauren, but it had.
He'd scoured half the town, going from one end to the other,
hunting her. She'd been released yesterday morning and the business
with Boyne Falls kept him occupied well into the night. Now, in the
light of a new day, his beast demanded he search for her.

The address on her license didn't match the address on her
registration, which didn't match the address she'd given when they'd
brought her in.

The woman was like a ghost. A dozen people had seen her, but no
one knew where she was. By the time he questioned the tenth
person, he'd recognized a nice little pattern. Then he'd come to an
annoying yet warming conclusion—the town was protecting one of
its own.

No, not like the bears, not like those in his clan, but the humans had
obviously adopted her as a treasured daughter, grandchild, or niece.
Young or old, no one gave him her exact location.

Equally annoyed and hungry, he stopped at the local diner and
snared a table while he let his problem roll through his head: Lauren
Evans. Specifically, the way his bear wanted Lauren Evans *now* and
not later.

At the moment, he kept telling himself he was following up on her injuries and to see how her friend Anna was doing. It didn't matter that Martin gave him the rundown that morning.

He spied several of the humans he'd questioned throughout the day sitting toward the back of the diner, talking low amongst themselves. The cop in him recognized their actions. They were exchanging information, all of 'em worried about Lauren, about why he was looking for her.

He had to hand it to them, they banded together like a clan to care for one another, not destroy. Something he never associated with humans. It made him think, made him wonder, made him question…

So focused on that group, trying to hear the whispered conversation, he nearly jumped out of his skin when a body fell onto the seat across from him.

Keen, his youngest brother and biggest pain in the ass, sprawled in the booth. "Hey." The boy—the man now— grinned at him. "How ya doin'?"

He glared at his brother. "Fine."

"Uh-huh." Keen snared a menu and opened it.

"What d'ya want?" He glared at the back of the menu, wishing it were Keen bearing the brunt of his expression.

"Well—" Keen cut himself off as the waitress approached.

They gave their orders, opting for meat and zero greens. The moment she was out of hearing range, Van asked his brother again.

"What do you want?" He was busy, damn it. He was on a hunt. He was stopping long enough to eat and then he'd continue his search for Lauren.

"There are rumblings about you in the socialsphere."

28

Van raised a brow and curled his lip. "The what?"

"The socialsphere." Keen placed the menu in its holder against the window. "You know, all of those social networks humans use."

"Social networks?" He scrunched his eyebrows.

"You're kidding, right?" His brother gave him a blank look. "You really don't...?" Keen shook his head. "Never mind. The point is, the 'town,'" his brother made air quotes, telling him without words that he was referring to humans, "is aware you're looking for Lauren. They've decided that until you explain yourself, you're going to be chasing your tail."

"They're obstructing—"

Keen shook his head. "You keep thinking of the world as us against them. Van, you need to—"

The waitress approached again and gently placed Keen's plate on the table. Van's? Not so much. She plopped it down, ignoring that his burger nearly went over the edge.

Van glared at the woman's retreating back.

"See? That right there?" Keen pointed at him with a fork. "That proves they don't like you." His younger brother leaned forward and lowered his voice. "You're our Enforcer, Van. You'll always have our respect. We know about structure, hierarchy. We're taught all that as we grow up." Keen stared at the table for a moment before continuing. "They're different. Because you can kick anyone but Ty's ass, you're the Enforcer. Their social structure is based on the person inside them. They love Lauren. They've watched her grow up, they've seen her go through hell, and they've seen the way she protects Anna." Keen sat up. "Unless you give them a reason to trust you, you're not getting anywhere."

Van absorbed Keen's words, rolling the concept through his mind. He took a moment and let his gaze wander the diner. He took in the distrustful stares, the whispers, the way attention danced to him and swiftly left.

29

Yeah, they were different. He was beginning to realize that different didn't mean bad.

In some ways they were the same. The whole town, all of the humans, banded together against a common enemy. Hadn't the bears and wolves done that for Ty and Mia's cub, Parker? But, in others, they were complete opposites. In their clan, Mayor Davies would have been exiled while in the human world, "agreements" were made and the man escaped punishment.

With a shake of his head, he grabbed half his burger and brought it to his mouth. "So, who do I have to talk to? What do I need to say?"

He took a bite and grimaced. Cooked well-done—almost shoe leather done. Ugh. He looked to Keen, specifically his burger, and noticed the bright pink of his meat. Rare as hell and probably delicious. When he glanced toward the kitchen, he spied the cook glaring at him.

He needed to do something.

"Start with Nellie behind the counter. That woman spends more time on social networks than anyone in the town, plus she owns the diner with her husband Edward. She talks to everyone in town when they come through for coffee. You win her over, you'll be fine." Keen took another big bite and Van did the same.

Keen's moan of pleasure was followed by Van's groan. Damn, he needed rare meat.

"'K, tell me more about their socialsphere."

Keen sighed. "Really?" He rolled his eyes and lowered his voice. "You know I'm working on WereWeb? A way for everyone to connect, share information, pics, and stuff?"

Van nodded. "It's a good idea. Letting us share status updates and crap. People should be doing that shit."

His brother looked at him with something akin to pity and sighed. "I'm not the first person to think of it. There's dozens of sites like that for humans. Probably hundreds."

Van paused in mid-bite. "Seriously?"

"You need to get over this hang up, man. You're missing out on so much."

Hang up. Nice way to label his distrust and near-hatred for humans. It was hard to let it go. Hard to release the anger and rage. There'd been so much blood, his and his uncle's. And the men… The *human* men had…

Van shook off the memory, swallowed back the bile in his throat, and brought the burger to his mouth.

"Yeah, yeah." Van sank his teeth into his *well-done* sandwich and let his gaze shift to the world beyond the diner. To the parking lot across the street. To the small, curvy blonde woman arguing with a man a hell of a lot taller and stronger than her.

"*Shit.*"

Lunch forgotten, Van jumped from the booth and bolted for the door, racing through the diner, anxious to get outside. His bear added speed and strength to his human body, allowing him to move faster than the average human male. He dodged customers and wove past waitresses. The pounding of his brother's booted feet told him he wasn't alone. Keen didn't ask questions, just raced after him.

That was the thing with brothers. They didn't need to know what the hell one of them was doing, just that one of them needed help.

Van burst through the door, sending it banging against the wall. He didn't slow when he hit the parking lot, didn't bother lessening his pace as he raced across the street. Distantly he heard Keen yell for him underscored by the blaring of car horns. He only had eyes for Lauren.

He kept his gaze on her as she pointed at Bryson Davies, as she raised to her tiptoes to get in his face, as she poked him with said finger.

Van couldn't hear the words past the roaring in his ears and the bellowing of his bear, but he could see. Specifically, when Davies raised his hand as if to strike Lauren.

He pushed a little harder, ran a little faster, and shoved his way between her and Bryson.

Without a hint of effort, he caught the man's fist in the palm of his hand, stopping the strike in its tracks. The man's eyes widened, the whites stark against the hazel irises. Van gripped the balled hand, tightening his hold in tiny increments until the male winced.

He sensed Keen's rapid approach, the heavy pounding of his run as the distance between them lessened. "Van?"

He was sure he should explain himself to his brother, but he couldn't tear his gaze from the human male. "Good morning, Mister Mayor."

*

Adrenaline filled Lauren, forcing her heart to race faster and faster. Bryson cornered her on the street, caught her while on the way back to Martin's home. Martin had wanted to drive her to the pharmacy since Mayor Asshole had her car towed from his house and impounded. But she wanted him to stay with Anna, watch over and protect her, if needed.

Now she realized she should have called a damned cab. The ache in her side reminded her she also should have filled the pain prescription yesterday after being released.

Of course, then she had to let her mouth get away from her as she spewed insults and told Bryson *exactly* what she thought of him. And poked him. Couldn't forget that.

When he raised his fist, she figured another trip to the urgent care clinic was in her immediate future. She stared at Bryson, took in the wild look in his eyes, the bright red hue of his skin, the sweat coating his brow, and the pure hatred covering his features.

Distantly, she saw his arm cock back, fingers balling. The muscles hidden by his button down shirt flexed and prepared to strike. Then it lowered, racing toward her face. She waited for the pain, the agony that'd fill her due to the powerful hit.

Then, it didn't come. Instead, she was pushed back as a massive body stepped between her and Bryson. She stumbled a step, hands flailing until a set of unfamiliar strong arms encircled her, saving her from sprawling on the ground.

"I've got you." The voice was warm, low, and comforting.

The next voice was decidedly... not.

"Good morning, Mister Mayor." The tone, the threat hidden beneath the words, sent a shiver down her spine.

"You're fine." The man holding her murmured, and she realized she was still held captive by his embrace.

Lauren wiggled and pushed away from him, stepping out of his arms and putting space between them. His hold felt... wrong. Made her skin itch and parts of her cringe. He hadn't done anything to make her feel that way, but she didn't want to be cradled in his arms. No, she wanted Van—

She cut off that direction of thought.

"Officer Abrams, I'm glad you're here." Bryson sounded so smug, so full of himself. Abusive prick. "I'd like you to arrest Miss Evans for assault."

"What?" She practically screamed the word. "Are you fucking kidding me?"

She stomped toward the mayor only to have her path blocked by Van. He stepped to his left, giving her his broad back. So she stepped right and was met with the stranger's back. While not quite as broad as Van, he was still big enough to keep her from her target.

Then she noticed the similarities between them. The curl of dark brown hair, the shape of their bodies, and even the curve of their asses...

Okay, she wasn't staring at asses. Especially not Vans. And she wasn't going to fantasize about nibbling it either.

"Assault? I find it hard to believe Miss Evans would assault anyone." Van's low rumble vibrated through her.

"Really? After yesterday when...?" Bryson sputtered.

Lauren shifted enough to see Van's face, to catch sight of his reaction to the mayor's response.

"Yesterday? Well," Van rubbed his jaw, palms scraping along his cheeks. "Well, from what I recall, Lauren didn't do much of anything yesterday except sign an agreement that nothing happened and you two don't know each other." Van shook his head and she heard the good old boy tone once again. "At least, that's what I recall. I tend to forget things, though." He glanced at her and winked before turning his attention to the man she didn't recognize. "That's what I told you yesterday though, Keen. Right?"

"Yup."

Bryson's face glowed red. "I want her arrested. You saw her assault me."

"Did I?"

"Abrams..." The mayor's voice was low, threatening. "I'll have your badge for this. I want her arrested for assault."

"Uh-huh." Van shoved his hands in his pockets, his whole body seeming relaxed. But she saw his fists balled beneath the fabric. No, he wasn't relaxed at all. "I didn't see anything, Mister Mayor. Not a thing. Keen? You see anything?"

"Nope." Keen shook his head.

"Well, there ya go. Sorry, Mister Mayor." Van shrugged, but there was no way he was sorry. She saw it in the tension that lingered in his shoulders and the way he leaned forward just a tiny bit. He was ready to pounce.

Bryson glared, first at Van, then Keen, and finally at her. A loud bang, the diner door swinging open roughly once again, reached them and the mayor's attention shifted to the diner across the street. He pointed at the gathered crowd. "They saw her. One of them saw her!"

"You think?" Van shrugged, still feigning nonchalance. He jerked his fists free and cupped them around his mouth. "Did any of y'all see Lauren assault the mayor?" he yelled across the expanse and as one, the customers crowding the lot shook their heads. Smiling, her savior turned back to Bryson. "Well, there ya go."

The mayor's face grew even darker, pure hatred directed at her and her alone. She saw the promise of retribution in his gaze and she fought to stay strong, not let him see that inside, she shook like a leaf.

Without another word, Bryson spun on his five hundred dollar heels and stomped to his waiting luxury car. The man spent thousands supporting his "lifestyle" while Anna lived with worn clothes. Oh, in public he dressed her friend in fine clothes, but everything else was threadbare.

The three stood together, watching the mayor slide behind the wheel and tear into traffic.

Finally, Keen spoke. "You should pull him over for reckless driving."

Van snorted and shook his head. "I'm in enough trouble with Ty." The man froze and then slowly turned toward her. "Speaking of trouble, what were you doing? Taking on a man like Davies. You know what he's capable of."

Yes, she did. How many times had she patched up Anna? She knew exactly what Bryson Davies could do.

"I was walking to the pharmacy." Mention of her destination reminded her of the pain wracking her body. Today was worse. She hadn't expected the added ache but should have. She'd warned Anna over and over that the second day always hurt more. Funny how she didn't remember that when it came to herself. "He just pulled over and started yelling."

Calling her a bitch and a two dollar whore. Ordering her to turn over his wife. Telling her she wasn't any better than her penniless parents and Anna shouldn't be around her kind of trash.

The first bit pissed her off and the last bit had her reminding him she and Anna grew up in the same trailer park. If she had to decide between trash and his high class prison, she'd stake her claim on a dumpster while she put down a deposit on a double-wide.

"And you didn't encourage him?"

She took a page from Keen's book. "Nope."

"Or poke him?" Van raised an eyebrow, drawing her attention to his eyes. They changed color with his mood. Brown when he was calm or amused. Midnight black when he was angry.

"He had something on his shirt."

Keen laughed and Van just sighed. "What am I gonna do with you?"

"Take me to the pharmacy and then the impound lot?" She smiled wide, hoping he didn't sense the pain she concealed or how much she wanted him to say yes.

Van shook his head. "The pharmacy and home. Why do you need to go to the lot?"

"Bryson not only had my truck towed, but impounded."

"Asshole," Keen growled. His growl, his anger, frightened her. She found herself easing toward Van, sidling up to his much larger body.

Van glared at the other man, and Keen's growl shut off as quickly as it started.

"I'll give you a ride. Keen will grab your pickup."

"I will?" Keen scrunched his forehead.

"You will. Take someone from home if you need to."

"Van…" Lauren tried to put in a word.

He didn't let her finish, kept talking to Keen. "Actually, bring Walker. Stop by his shop and get him to check under the hood and make sure it's in good shape. Tell him I'm asking in an official capacity."

Lauren huffed. "I hardly need—"

Keen's demeanor changed, transformed from one of supposed relaxation to alert and tense with the flip of a switch. "Yes, sir."

"Van…"

"Where are you staying?" Again the man spoke over her.

"At Martin's with Anna. It seemed…" She gulped, trying not to let the additional worry overtake her mind. "It seemed safer to stay with him."

Van didn't say anything at first, simply stared at her for a moment, capturing her gaze with his. "We'll talk about it in the car."

*

Except… fuck Van sideways, they couldn't talk about it in the car. Mainly because they didn't make it two feet before he got a call from Ty, probably about the shit in Boyne Falls.

37

He stared at the screen and then looked back to Keen. "Take her to the pharmacy and then home. Then you can take care of her truck with Walker."

"Van…" Her voice was thin, tentative. Minutes ago, she'd been ripping into the mayor and now she was out of strength. He noticed the paleness of her face, the pinched quality to her lips, and the heavy scent of pain in the air. It scorched his nose and enraged the bear. They'd sat around arguing with the mayor while she hurt.

"For me, Lauren. Let him take care of you, for me." Her shoulders slumped and she swayed ever so slightly. "Shit."

The phone in his hand kept ringing, his brother's name flashing across the screen. He was faced with a choice, Lauren or Ty. Heart or duty. Fuck. Lauren had nothing to do with his heart.

Right, he'd keep telling himself that.

"Keen, catch her."

His brother's wide eyes met his and then he was on the move, sweeping her gently into his embrace. Van's bear went crazy, roaring that their brother bear touched her. The animal was possessive as hell when it came to little Lauren Evans.

Lauren squawked, but didn't fight Keen, instead she clung to his shoulders.

Didn't that piss off the animal even more?

The ringing of his phone paused, only to pick up once again. Shit, Ty wasn't giving up. He stared at the screen, thumb hovering over the flashing green button. "Take care of her, Keen." Screw it. He strode forward until her scent surrounded him. He bent and brushed a gentle kiss across her forehead. It was odd behavior for him, this need to touch her and be close to her surprised him, but he couldn't suppress the bear's desire for Lauren. "Take care of yourself for me."

Before he could say or do something else gloriously stupid, he turned his back on them, intent on getting to his cruiser in the diner parking lot. He jogged across the road, cars slowing to allow him to pass and he waved in thanks, earning him a smile and a wave in return.

Weird. Most… didn't do that to him. Ty, Keen, even Isaac, but not… him.

Huh.

Nearing his car, he didn't notice the few humans gathered nearby until he was almost on top of them.

Still, his cell phone rang. Fucking Ty.

"Um, can I help y'all?" Two men and two women stood near the front end, Nellie among them.

"We just wanted to thank you for that out there." Nellie gestured across the street.

"Doing my job, Ma'am."

She shook her head. "No, you did more for our little Lauren." She looked at the other three and then back at him. "We wanted to thank you for looking after her."

"Ma'am…" He wasn't going to tell her it was his pleasure. That the idea of someone like Bryson Davies touching her made his blood boil. That the fact his brother even now walked away with her cradled in his arms enraged him.

Instead of heeding his tone or recognizing his frustration, she simply stepped forward, her path taking her past him. She paused long enough to pat his chest, her weathered hand sliding to stroke his bicep before gently squeezing. "Hush. You look big and mean, don't you? But you're like my husband's dog, Bear. All bark and no bite." She focused on him, her eyes seeming to bore into him. "Or is it roar?"

With a small smile, she moved on, the rest of her little group trailing in her wake. The other woman rubbed his arm much like Nellie while the men shook his hand and pounded his back.

39

He watched them go, watched the merry band of old folks make their way back to the diner and inside its packed interior. A chill raced down his spine. She knew. Somehow she knew that non-humans lived in the small town.

Van's phone rang once again, the noise cutting into his worried thoughts. He'd talk things over with Keen and then Ty. Later.

For now, he pressed the flashing icon and placed the phone against his ear. "Abrams."

He winced at the roar that filled his ear. It was still going as he unlocked his car and continued when he settled behind the wheel and started the cruiser.

Damn, his brother had some lung capacity.

Finally, Ty quieted, but his brother's heavy breathing was audible. "Is this because of the mayor or the wolves?"

"Both." Ty huffed and the audible squeak of his brother's office chair reached him.

Well, at least he was a little calmer.

"I haven't spoken with the wolves since last night and I stopped the mayor from physically assaulting Lauren Evans."

"He tells a different story," Ty countered.

Van shrugged. "Probably one that paints him as the victim. However, there's not a single witness, myself included. I saw nothing besides the mayor raising his hand to her."

A low, frustrated growl came across the line. "Fine. Consider yourself duly chastised." He snorted, but Ty ignored him and moved on. "Now, what the hell is wrong with the wolves?"

That had him sighing. He hated all this political bullshit, this posturing and growling that came with cooperating with other species.

Fuck it, maybe he was a speciest pig like his brother told him weeks ago.

Then again… Van stared at the diner, at the *human* customers who waved at him with wide smiles when they caught him looking.

And image, a flash of a memory, flickered and suddenly he was staring at a familiar *human* male. One with evil in his eyes and a blade in his hand.

"Van!" Ty's shout grabbed his attention once again, tearing him from the past. "What the hell is going on in Boyne?"

"Well," he dug into his pocket and tugged his keys free. The moment the door swung closed, securing him within the relative privacy of his cruiser, he finished his thought. "The wolf Beta is a dick."

chapter four

Lauren couldn't tear her attention from Martin's front windows. No, it wasn't the windows that held her focus, it was what lay beyond. The porch, the driveway, the road. All of them empty when she wanted them filled with a certain annoying, commanding male.

And that kiss. No, she couldn't call it a kiss, could she? It was a brush of his lips, gone before she registered he'd leaned into her. And yet…

"Whatcha doin'?" A deep voice, similar to Van's, but not quite right, startled the hell out of her.

Lauren jumped with a squeak and then spun on Keen, glaring at the large man. "Damn it, Keen."

That earned her one of those "who me" looks. Yeah, him.

He managed that innocent expression for all of a second before breaking out his grin. She shook her head, smiling along with him.

"Don't sneak up on me."

"I don't know what you're talking about."

"Uh-huh." She picked up one of the napkins she was about to fold and threw it at him.

It was coming up on dinner time and she, Keen, and Anna were eating at Martin's. It'd been a long time since she'd done something so normal. For years she'd settled for the living room coffee table or even the kitchen counter. To gather with friends? She shook her head. Weird.

The dark green napkin nailed Keen in the chest and he staggered back. "Oh, I'm hit. Save me." He gasped and coughed. "Tell my girlfriend I love her…"

Lauren snorted. "Which one?"

That had him pausing and straightening. "Good point."

Another little boy grin and she saw the potential man hidden beneath Keen's boyish good looks. Then again, there wasn't much "boyish" about Keen Abrams even if he was only a hint over twenty. He'd taken his job seriously, ushering her to the pharmacy and calling them from the parking lot. He then ordered—*ordered*—the tech to come out to the car to get her prescription. Then he demanded the man deliver it to the vehicle when it was ready.

She tried explaining that their little pharmacy didn't have backward drive-thru service. To which, he replied: "For you they do."

Weird, but appreciated since she hadn't wanted to get out of the car. Hell, she hadn't wanted to go from the car to Martin's house, either.

Again he refused to let her do anything other than what Van ordered.

She was *this close* to telling Keen where he could shove his orders. Then she remembered Bryson's face, his threats, his fist aimed for her face and the way Van caught it before it struck her. There was also the fact the men had stood shoulder to shoulder to protect her from the bastard.

So she slowly made her way from the car to the house and when he asked her to sit on the couch, she sat. When he held out a glass of water and a pill, she popped that sucker in her mouth and swallowed. Now the prescription strength Tylenol had worked its way through her system, and she was able to move without wincing every other step.

The clang of pots and pans from the kitchen filled the house. Martin was working his magic with food while Anna rested in one of the chairs at the kitchen table. There was something between those two. Friendship with the obvious desire for more. At least, on Martin's part. She wasn't sure about Anna's.

A flare of light shone through the window and Lauren whipped her head around, staring into the darkness beyond the glass. She waited for one beat, and then two, before realizing it was nothing more than a passing car.

Not Van.

A napkin struck *her* in the face and just as quickly as she'd stared out the window, she turned a glare on Keen.

"What? If you're doing what I think you're doing, I can tell you he'll call me when he's on his way." The boy-man shrugged.

"I don't know what you're talking about." She sniffed. She wasn't about to admit the truth.

"Uh-huh." He didn't sound convinced, but she didn't care.

"He didn't say he was stopping by anyway." She folded the napkin in her hand and placed it on the tabletop, settling a set of silverware on top before moving to the next place setting.

"Oh, he didn't order me to take care of you just to leave you to my tender mercies. He'll be here."

Lauren kept her gaze focused on her task, refusing to let Keen see her hope. Something about Van drew her in, called to her in a way no man ever had. "He asked you to deliver me and organize getting my truck. That's it."

Keen chuckled. "Nah, he was in full-on protective bea—" He coughed. "I mean, protective papa bear mode."

Oh. Right.

When she thought about it that way, she saw his actions in a different light. He'd protected her like he would any other woman. He was a cop, right? And that kiss… Well, she'd needed comfort, hadn't she?

Shaking her head, she snapped the last napkin into shape and slammed the silverware on top, jostling the entire table.

"Everything okay in there?" Martin called to them.

"Yes," she raised her voice. "Sorry, Martin. Just…" Throwing a temper tantrum. "Slipped."

She sensed Keen approaching, but ignored him. "Lauren, that's not what I meant."

She shook her head. "No, you're right. He was being a big, bad protective papa bear, just doing his job." She stepped away, putting distance between them. He reminded her too much of Van, and now that she realized Van's motivation, it was the last thing she wanted. "Call him. Tell him I'm fine. You can eat dinner with us and then go visit one of your girlfriends in the neighborhood." She forced a teasing grin to her lips as part of her heart cracked. "You've got to have one nearby, don't you?"

There was no reason for her to be so attached to Van Abrams. He was a cop doing what he'd do for anybody. He'd obviously recognized the evil in Bryson Davies and was protecting her. Well, she didn't need him or his brother. She had herself.

She'd keep telling herself that lie and hoped she believed it someday.

"Lauren…"

Lauren shook her head and eased past him. She patted him on the chest, trying to assure him of her uncaring attitude. "Call him, tell him not to waste his time. We're fine and we've got Martin to act as our papa bear."

46

"You don't understand." Keen's cell rang and the man growled—growled—at the phone. "Damn it." He pressed a button and held it to his ear to answer. "This is Keen."

"If that's him, tell him not to waste his time." Lauren didn't wait for a response, didn't pause to listen in on the man's conversation. She needed to get a hold of herself. In the last forty-eight hours, she'd built a tiny, happy fantasy in her head and now she realized it was just that—a fantasy.

She hadn't had time for dreams while growing up. What made her think she should have them now?

*

"...waste his time." Van recognized Lauren's voice, the tones reaching through the phone and caressing him. It soothed his beast with the tinkling syllables while it also enraged the animal with the words.

Waste his time? Never. She'd never be a waste.

"I'm on my way. I'm leaving Boyne Falls. Gimme fifteen minutes," he barked into the phone, not letting his brother talk.

"She said..."

"I heard her and I'll talk with her when I get there." The bear urged him to go faster. He was a cop after all. Couldn't he bend the speed limit law a little? Van was tempted, but he turned the beast down.

"What's going on, Van? With you and Lauren?" His brother's voice was a low whisper. Audible to him, but not to the humans in Martin's home.

"Fucked if I know." Van shook his head. "Fucked if I know."

The only certainty was he needed to be near her. He'd tolerated Ty's roars and the half-assed negotiations with the wolves because of her. Challenging the asshole Beta, Morgan, would have delayed his

47

reunion with Lauren, so he'd kept his mouth shut. The dick could complain all he wanted, but if engaging in a pissing contest meant it'd take him longer to get to her, he'd refrain from entering.

He had more important things to do than dealing with an angry mayor and an angrier pack of wolves.

Not waiting for his brother's reply—because what could he say?—Van wrapped up the call. "Fifteen minutes."

He navigated the streets with ease, the familiar route to Grayslake engrained in him after years of living in the area. The travel was almost instinctual which gave him a chance to think over the day's events.

The mayor was a pissed off asshole, but Ty had managed to smooth things over with the promise Van would engage in an anger management course. Not that he would, but the mayor didn't have to know that. Supposedly, Van "attacked" the mayor and his "delinquent" brother assisted in the assault.

But Ty knew the truth and Van's Itan respected him and had his back, so nothing more would come of the incident. Though, Ty did mention he'd keep an eye and ears on the situation.

The thing with the wolves… Damn, that was fucked. Ty and Reid, the wolf Alpha, were trying. It was the rest of them who were resisting. Van was man enough to admit his part in the tension between their groups. Not that he'd say that to anyone other than Ty.

But it boiled down to Ty and Reid having a "more active" hand in the evacuation plans. Ty shared Van's opinion—slowly ease the elderly and injured from the lands. Reid shared Morgan's—get them the hell out of town, even if they had to be dragged out.

The only difference between Reid and Morgan were their methods. Oh, Morgan played the "yes boy" in public very well, but Van saw the glint of evil in the wolf's eyes. Morgan wouldn't have trouble slitting a few hyena throats if needed.

Something to talk to Ty about.

Van spied Martin's house and pulled into the driveway. Lauren was inside. He saw her through the front window, the drawn curtains allowing him to watch her smile at his brother.

He'd talk to Ty about Morgan… tomorrow. He had shit to do tonight.

He cut the engine on his SUV and climbed from the vehicle, letting the door swing closed. Two sets of midnight eyes met his through the window.

Good. Keen and Martin needed to keep their bears within reach inside themselves. Sure, Mayor Davies was a prick, but he was a powerful prick. Van had done his research, knew the number of times Anna Davies had encountered an aggressive "door." He also knew how many times the man got away with it.

Van's bear pushed forward, recognizing they, too, needed to be prepared for an attack. Davies had gone after Lauren on a public street. What'd stop him from sending someone in now?

Nothing. Nothing but him, Keen, and Martin.

The women noticed the men at the table were focused on him and their gazes strayed to the window. The tension in Anna immediately eased, but Lauren's seemed to gain steam. Her face flushed red, her hand shaking as she placed her fork on the plate. Apparently, he got to her, too. At least he wasn't the only one affected by this thing between them.

Tearing his gaze from her, he moved to the porch. He took the steps two at a time and stomped onto the wooden surface, shaking any residual dirt free of the soles. His momma didn't raise a rude slob.

The locks on the door flicked and it swung open to reveal an uncomfortable looking Keen. "I may, or may not, have screwed shit up."

Van groaned and let his head drop back. "Will anyone be injured or killed because of what you did?"

"Besides me? No."

He looked to Keen. "Then lemme see Lauren and feed the bear. Then we can talk."

His brother winced. "Well… you see… about Lauren…"

chapter five

Lauren hid in Martin's spare bedroom. Cowardly? Absolutely. But it was better than staring at Van and wishing there was something more between them than obligation and hero worship.

Worship. She groaned. She wanted to worship something.

Nope. Not happening.

Yesterday had been too busy and hectic that neither woman had nothing more than the clothes on their backs. Earlier in the day, Martin took Anna to her home to pack a few things. Lauren had the same plan in mind when she'd first left Martin's, but Keen hadn't given her that option. Or rather, Van gave specific instructions and Keen was sticking to them.

She grabbed Anna's PJs from the bed. Thankfully, her friend's clothes fit her. Well, fit-ish. The top would be tight across the chest and a little snug on her ass, but it was better than the clothes on her back.

Night clothes in hand, she walked down the hall to the bathroom. The house was mostly quiet. The low rumble of Van's and Keen's voices reached her, but she knew Keen would be leaving soon. During dinner, Van stated he would be guarding the house overnight and Keen would be back in the morning.

She ignored the small shiver of pleasure that raced down her spine at the idea of Van being so close. Ig-nored.

Lauren stepped into the small bathroom, noting the counter was barely big enough for the sink and the single toilet to the left. The shower was a combo-shower deal—tub on the bottom with a showerhead.

She quickly stripped, keeping her gaze from the mirror as she peeled off her clothes. She knew the location of the bruises, she didn't need to see them in color to know they existed.

Her dirty top and shorts were left on the ground while she tossed her panties and bra into the sink. She'd wash and rinse them after her shower. She didn't mind handing her shirt and shorts to Martin to be run through his machine, but she drew the line at a near stranger fondling her underwear.

Fondling…

Damn it, she couldn't get distracted by Van and ideas of fondling.

Shaking her head, she focused on showering, getting clean and washing away the hellacious day. The water heated and she stepped beneath the spray, enjoying the warm liquid rushing over her muscles, easing some of her pain.

She dropped her head forward, stretching her neck, and worked out a kink or two in the process. A tip to the left, then right, had the joints cracking and she moaned at the release of pressure. The sound echoed off the walls, slowly dying, buried by the ping of water against the tiles.

A heavy vibration traveled through her feet, the rapid thud of someone running immediately following the noises.

What the…?

Lauren brushed the shower curtain aside and reached for the towel hanging from the rack. The men's awareness and anticipation of trouble had her nerves on edge. The last thing she wanted to do was take a shower if there was a looming threat.

Hand on the fluffy, white towel, the door burst open, panel slamming and banging against the wall. Lauren screamed, dropping the drying cloth, and yanking the curtain across her body. Okay, it was stupid to use the flimsy piece of plastic and fabric as a shield, but she had to hide behind something.

"What's wrong?" Van stood framed in the doorway, his chest heaving, looking larger than before. His clothes stretched taut over his body, outlining each muscle. Damn.

"Nothing."

Keen's head appeared over Van's shoulder and she squeaked, holding the curtain a little tighter.

Van looked over his shoulder and growled at his brother, shoving the man from the doorway. "Stop looking."

"You're looking," Keen fired back and another growl filled the area.

Van stepped into the bathroom—*into the bathroom*—and slammed the door behind him. She heard other voices, Anna's worried tone followed by muffled, placating words from Keen.

Good, she didn't want anyone worrying. Then again, she was panicking because a very agitated, very large Van Abrams was currently in the very tiny, very cramped bathroom with her.

And she was naked.

Her body reacted to that fact, nipples pebbling, and an unfulfilled ache settled between her thighs. *No, bad body, bad.*

Except… except he was sex personified.

"I-I said nothing was wrong."

Van raised a single brow and leaned against the closed door, arms folded across his massive chest. "I heard you the first time. But you moaned." A grin teased his lips. He inhaled deep, nostrils flaring, and then his grin turned into something purely sexual. What the hell? "If you weren't groaning in pain, why'd you make that sweet sound?"

Sweet sound?

Lauren gulped and she let her gaze wander before answering. His body pushed his clothes to the edge of tearing. Every muscle seemed larger, more defined. She took in his bulging biceps and flat stomach as well as his rather large, rather impressive, package.

And then it twitched.

She snapped her eyes closed. "I cracked my neck. My muscles are tight and—"

"I can take care of that for you, baby."

She forced her lids apart and jumped in surprise. He'd moved from negligently leaning against the door to less than six inches from her. He crowded her, his mere presence overwhelming.

And the heat… Sensual promise, want, and need lived in his gaze. He really was walking, talking hotness. His body was built to arouse a woman and she was sure he knew it.

The warmth between her thighs grew and increased in heat. Her pussy clenched, practically begging for Van. It was screaming a big 'ole "yes, please!" and she was sad to disappoint that part of her.

"I'm… I'm fine." He reached for her, his massive hand heading toward her face like when she was locked up. Instead of letting him touch her, she jerked back. No sense in teasing herself with something he wasn't offering.

Protective papa bear, right? Right.

Desire fled his gaze and her heart twinged. Had she hurt him? Well, she didn't want to let herself get hurt.

She licked her lips and offered an explanation. "Look, I know this situation has you wanting to play papa bear. Keen explained it to me. So," she shrugged, "I get it. I'm just… a damsel in distress."

His gaze darkened, brown eyes changing to black. Already she could read him, recognized the frustration and hint of anger in his expression. "Papa bear? Damsel in…"

He took a deep breath and let it out slowly. His nostrils flared, irises darkening further. The snap of string filled some of the silence and she wondered if he'd popped a stich in his shirt or jeans.

"Keen said this?"

Lauren nodded.

Van eased closer and his scent surrounded her, the hint of man and sweat reaching her. The ache grew, filling her with desperate desire. She wanted him, wanted him inside her while his lips tracing her curves. All of them. And thank goodness she had so many that it'd take a while.

His chest brushed hers, the curtain the only thing separating their bodies, and she swallowed her whimper. The added pressure had her nipples hardening further, begging to be touched, stroked, and pinched.

"Baby," he leaned into her, mouth hovering out of reach. "Daddy stuff isn't my kink, but you can call me 'papa' if it means getting you in my bed. Feel free to indulge yourself."

"Daddy… Indulge…" she sputtered and shook her head. "That's not… Bed…"

Van darted forward, his teeth nipping her lower lip, and she shivered with that sting of pain. "I gotta tell you, though. The last thing I feel about you is paternal."

A thick muscular arm wrapped around her waist, stroking her bare skin. The touch sent her arousal skyrocketing, soaring higher. Her pussy clenched, growing slick with her need and want. She released the curtain and placed her damp palm on his chest, noting the way his muscle flexed beneath her hand.

"Van, wha—?"

Her question was silenced by his mouth, his lips fusing to hers. His tongue slipped into her. He lapped at her, tasting her, and she reveled in the beginnings of their kiss, she let him direct the heat, the intensity of the meeting. And then she took control. She twined her tongue with his, tangling as she sought out his flavors.

Heat blossomed, growing and burning as they remain connected.

Her pussy throbbed, clit twitching with the desire to be stroked, petted, and kissed. Yes, she wanted his mouth between her thighs, tasting and caressing her until she came.

Lauren moaned against his mouth, pressing harder, sliding deep into him. The dark flavors inherent to him exploded across her tongue, luring her need to rise to new heights.

The hand against her back moved, stroked the upper curve of her ass, and slipped lower. Van squeezed the globe, hand kneading her, touching and arousing, making her need so much more.

She sucked on his tongue, showing him what she could do with her mouth if they ventured that far. She'd suckle him, lick and taste and…

A harsh cough from outside the bathroom broke into her desire-filled world, reminding her where she was and who she was with.

Van Abrams. Cop. Protector. *Papa Bear.*

But… *"The last thing I feel about you is paternal."*

Well, the last thing she wanted to be was a notch on a belt or a duty.

Lauren pulled her lips away from his and snatched her hand back, snaring the curtain and holding it tight. She shifted her body, leaning back, hoping he got the hint.

Unfortunately, he did not. Nope, he let her mouth remain free, but that arm lingered like a steel band across her back. Those eyes, those midnight eyes locked on her.

"What?"

The scruff on his cheeks looked longer than before. That, or the lighting was different, making it look like he had a lot more than an afternoon's shadow.

"Uh, the Ita—" She recognized Martin's voice. "Mia's on the phone for you, Van."

The body pressed so intimately against hers tensed and stilled for a moment. He tightened his hold the tiniest bit, and then released her. "I'm coming. Gimme a minute."

Lauren squirmed, intent on getting away. She didn't like the heat in his gaze, didn't like the desire flaring in his eyes. She pretended not to like the long, thick hardness pressing against her hip, too. Except… notch or duty, he couldn't feign his arousal, his need for her. No other half-naked women were in the bathroom which meant his hard-on was all for curvy, not-so-little Lauren Evans.

"We're gonna finish this." His deep voice rumbled through her.

"There's nothing to finish. I need to focus on Anna and the mayor and—"

Van nipped her lower lip, silencing her with that small bite. "Let Martin focus on Anna."

"She's my best friend."

"And I'm pretty sure she's his mate," he countered. "No one will protect her more fiercely than him."

Mate?

"You mean her boyfriend? Martin's a nice enough guy, but Anna's still married. She doesn't need to get mixed up—"

Another kiss, this one deeper, dominating and aggressive. He took control from the first touch of their tongues. He growled and snarled against her lips, seeming to consume her. She responded to his authority, arousal shooting high and she rocked her hips against his, enjoying his low moan. Her body screamed for his possession, to have him sinking into her over and over again as she came around his cock.

Just as the kiss threatened to overwhelm her, it ended, Van wrenching his lips from hers. He pressed his face against her neck, nuzzling her, burying himself in her wet hair. His lungs heaved, their heavy pants joining the patter of water against the smooth tiles in the shower.

Van set his teeth against her skin, biting down hard enough to send a sliver of pain tinged pleasure through her. He held her flesh, for one second and then two before releasing her. He laved the ache and soothed it with his tongue.

Lauren nudged him away, pushing until a little more space separated them. He was overwhelming her with his closeness. "You've got a call to answer. And you need to tell Martin to leave Anna be. She's healing and will be going through a divorce soon. Bryson is a dick..."

"Who has his sights set on the two of you," Van finished. "Martin will take care of Anna. No one will get to her. It's you I'm worried about." And he was, she saw it in his expression.

"Why? I mean, I've pissed him off, but—"

"But he has friends. Friends that aren't bea— That I don't know about. You beat him and helped his wife escape. I'd rather be safe than sorry. He attacked you on the *street*, Lauren." He didn't touch her after that statement, but she sensed his desire to reach for her, place his hands on her body. Part of her wanted the same thing, wanted to enjoy his touch. But she also knew that'd be a mistake. "I can't let anything happen to you."

A pounding on the bathroom door ended their conversation. He stared at her, his gaze boring into her, and then turned toward the door. He grabbed the knob and pulled it open. Keen lingered outside the door and she tightened her flimsy shield, ensuring she wasn't exposed.

As Van stepped across the threshold, he turned back to her, desire banked, but still simmering in his expression. "This isn't done, Lauren."

Oh.

Well, then.

She should have taken it as a warning, a threatening precursor for the future. Instead, it made her hot.

Stupid dry spell.

*

Van's cock was so hard he could pound nails with the damned thing. His uniform pants were tight, strangling his dick. Hell, every piece of fabric on him was tight. The bear had come out to play, nudged him, and managed to increase his bulk. The damn animal didn't think about things like buying new clothes.

"What's wrong?" He snarled at his brother as he followed him through the house.

"Mia was worried about you."

He furrowed his brow. Mia was his brother's mate. The woman was a few weeks pregnant and his brother doted on her. "But, why?"

"I dunno," Keen shrugged. "Something about the jerk in Boyne Falls. I told her you were off doing some huma—"

59

Van didn't hesitate, without conscious thought, he wrapped his hand around his brother's throat. He backed Keen up until he collided with the wall. Then he lifted, raising his brother so his feet barely touched the ground.

"Excuse me?"

Keen scratched and pulled on Van's arm, but Van wasn't moving. How dare he refer to Lauren as "some human?" Didn't he understand…?

"Van." A lyrical voice drifted to him, sliding into him, and the bear rumbled in approval. "Van, stop that," the voice snapped at him. Well, the bear didn't like that. "Let him go." Then the voice growled at him and the beast was back to rumbling.

Even if the voice yelled at him, it was strong—stood up to him. It was good for the Enforcer's mate to be strong. The Enforcer's mate—

Van released Keen, snatching his hand back as if his brother burned him, and he looked for the voice's source. It didn't take him long to find it. Didn't take him long to spy a wet-haired goddess glaring at him from the entrance to the living room.

Mate?

The bear rumbled in approval.

Shit.

Keen sucked in air, bent at the waist as he fought for breath. Which left him distracted by Lauren, her damp hair, and the way Anna's clothes clung to her moist body. The shirt was just tight enough to be nearing obscene. It cradled her plump breasts, and her nipples were hard and pressing against the thin fabric. The tiny shorts outlined the dip of her waist and flare of her hips. He wanted to grip them as he slid into her, buried himself in her slick pussy.

The bear *really* liked those ideas.

Beside him, his brother eased up until he stood and leaned against the wall for support. "So," he sucked in more air. "I guess things have changed."

Van couldn't have torn his gaze from the delectable Lauren if he'd tried. "Yeah."

"Interesting," Keen murmured, and Van looked to his youngest brother staring at his mate with appreciation in his gaze.

Hell no.

Van reached for Keen again, stretching out his arm, curling his fingers in preparation of strangling the man. His mother gave birth to four boys, she wouldn't miss one, right?

The tinny voice of Mia came through the discarded home phone, and Van realized he couldn't kill Keen. Not when he needed the male to keep an eye on Lauren while he spoke on the phone. The animal rumbled in protest so he amended his thought. They couldn't kill him… yet.

Once Bryson Davies ceased being a threat, it was on. Until then, he needed Keen. Because Bryson Davies, Mayor of Grayslake, Georgia was as mean as a snake and it was only a matter of time before he struck.

61

chapter six

Three hours later and Lauren still couldn't get Van out of her head. That look, that fierce expression... it made her wonder what it'd be like to have that passion unleashed on her.

A shudder overtook her, a spark of arousal slinking into her veins. Nope, that was the wrong direction for her thoughts to take.

Papa bear. She had to remember that. He only wanted to take care of her and...

The last thing I feel about you is paternal.

The memory had her arousal doing a little more than slinking. It brought forward the feel of his lips on hers and then the rough way he wrapped his arm around her and jerked her against him. She recalled how she'd grown hot for him, her pussy aching with need while her clit twitched and begged to be stroked.

And now she was an aroused jumble once again. She was back to hot, needy, and craving Van Abrams. Except instead of being pelted by warm water in the shower, she now had a bed nearby and fantasies spinning through her mind.

Lauren stood in the middle of the room, filled with indecision. She looked toward the bed, the full sized mattress. Then she focused on the bedroom's door. She could flick the lock. It wouldn't hold up against Van if he fought to get in, but she could engage it and then try very, very hard to be quiet…

There was no better remedy for pain than pleasure right? A quick "O" and the aches would be a distant memory.

She tiptoed to the door and twisted the small button, wincing when it snicked into place. Somehow Van had super hearing and the last thing she wanted was to alert him to her "activities." Getting caught in the shower was bad enough.

A warm ache formed between her thighs and a slow, gentle rolling need blanketed her. Excitement filled her, along with a hint of naughtiness combined with craving.

The object of her lust—how lame did that sound?—lay on the couch down the hallway, the massive man squeezed onto a five-foot long piece of furniture.

There was an additional empty guestroom in Martin's home since Anna was sleeping in Martin's room. Anna wanted to be close to Martin to feel safe, but she reminded the male a time or two that there would be no hanky-panky until her divorce was final.

So, there was a nice empty bed, but Van wanted to be in the common area in case of trouble. Or if someone tried to gain entrance through the front or back doors.

Lauren slipped beneath the sheets and settled against the mattress with a soft sigh as it welcomed her. Without waiting another moment, she slipped one hand beneath her tight top, lifting it as she reached for her left breast. She cupped her flesh, weighing it in her hand, stroking her skin with teasing brushes before focusing on her nipple. The nubbin was already hard and aching, just begging to be pinched and petted.

She grasped the bit of flesh and pinched lightly, imagining his large, callused fingers doing the same. He'd pluck and squeeze, listen as she cried out for more and more. Then he'd lick her, his warm mouth kissing her there, gently sucking her nipple.

Each suckle would send another jolt of pleasure through her, each pull on the hardened nub going straight to her clit.

Her clit…

Lauren brought her other hand into play, sliding her palm over her body, over the curve of her belly, and she toyed with the waist of the tiny shorts. She imagined him, dipping beneath the elastic, tormenting her with a barely-there touch. His fingers would burrow under the fabric an inch or two only to pull away again and again.

"Stop teasing," she whispered into the darkened room. "Please."

Van would smile at her, mischievous glint in his eyes while his expression promised wicked, wicked things. That's when he'd give her what she wanted, slide his hand beneath the elastic, and over her bare skin.

"No panties?" he'd murmur while he played with her cropped curls.

She'd bite her lip and shake her head, silently willing him to continue.

Lauren did as she imagined, caressing the top of her slit, rubbing the tiny patch of skin. Just that small touch alone had her pussy clenching, tightening, and sending a tiny shiver through her.

"Need you," she whispered into the empty room.

"You'll have me," he'd answer.

Because he'd want her as much as she craved him.

Those fingers slid between her sex lips then, separating her pussy and delving into her wetness. The first touch had her gasping. The second, the one that brushed her clit, drew out a moan.

Each brush of the bundle of nerves traveled through her body, zinging through her from head to toe. It electrified her, sent her arousal flying higher.

"Feel good, baby?" His voice was a deep growl.

In real life, Lauren nodded. "More."

Fantasy Van chuckled and gave her what she craved. He circled her clit in tiny rotations, focusing on the nubbin. Then he turned his attention to her breast, suckling her once again. He pulled, tormenting her with his attentions. Her cunt spasmed, screaming to be stuffed full of him. Yes, that was what she wanted.

Her fantasy altered to her desires, Van's fingers abandoning her clit and circling her heat. 'Round and 'round he traced her hole, her cream easing his way.

"In me. Please." She needed to be filled, to have her desires sated.

Once again, her Van didn't disappoint. Two fingers shoved into her cunt, spreading her wide. He didn't stretch her like she imagined his cock would, but he still touched those delicious places inside her. He pumped in and out, fucking her with his hand.

Lauren rode the caresses, rocking in time with each plunge, gasping and moaning as the heel of his hand rubbed her needy clit.

"Yes, yes, yes." She was conscious of the need to whisper, to not alert the house to her dirty fantasies. "Fuck me harder." She lifted her hips up, pretending he fucked her, plunged his fingers in and out of her sopping wet pussy. "More."

She pinched her nipple harder, tugging on the nubbin. She imagined him nibbling and softly biting the small bit of flesh. Yes, he'd be rough, but careful with her.

The wet squelching sounds of her fingers moving in and out of her cunt joined with her heavy panting. Her body knew what it fought for. She wanted to come all over Van, claw him, and scream as she found her peak.

Fuck, it was gonna be soon.

"Please. Close." She sped up her attentions, fucking herself harder and harder, the heel of her hand rubbing her clit in the perfect way…

Her pleasure grew, forming an ever expanding ball within her, the need increasing with every breath. She didn't stop fingering herself, didn't stop imagining Van toying with her pussy and bringing her to her peak. The ecstasy filled her, crept into every nook and cranny, growing as it promised more and more.

Any second now, any moment, she'd pop the bubble and send it careening down her spine.

"Please…" she whimpered and moaned, her body searching for something else, anything else. One more push…

"Please…" She allowed herself to say it aloud, to voice his name once and one time only. "Please, Van."

That was enough to solidify her fantasy and thrust her over the edge. Lauren's orgasm burst past the dam and exploded within her. The pure, unadulterated pleasure careened through her. It coated every nerve ending and forced spasm after bliss-fueled spasm to overtake her. She bit her lip against the sob that threatened to explode from her chest, the ecstasy almost too much for her to bear.

The molten sensation of release seemed unending, thrumming through her with no end in sight. Oh god, he'd keep fucking her, too. Plunging his fingers in and out of her until…

"No more. Please…" she whimpered, but her fantasy Van wouldn't quit, wouldn't give in.

"One more, baby. Come for me one more time."

"Can't…"

But he didn't listen, he picked up a punishing pace, fucking her in earnest, pounding her cunt.

Laurent panted and moaned, writhing on the sheets. She needed to come again, to let her orgasm assault her once again.

She abandoned her breast and lowered her hand, rubbing her clit with her left while her right continued to plunge in and out of her cunt.

"Oh fuck, oh god, oh fuck…" She whispered the litany over and over.

Her pussy was soaking wet, her body slick and prepared for him.

"Give it to me, baby."

And she did. Back arched, eyes wide, and air frozen in her lungs, Lauren came apart. She exploded into a million pieces, shattering beneath the force of her release. It overwhelmed her, destroyed her senses to anything but the pleasure pummeling her body and filling every nook and cranny inside her.

She rode the wave of ecstasy, riding on the rush of sensations, and reveling in what he could do to her body. She panted and heaved, gasping for breath while the ripples continued to lap at her nerves.

In gradual increments, she slowed her ministrations, easing the rapid pump of fingers and the fast rub of her clit. She allowed herself to be brought back from the abyss until she floated on the aftershocks. Her heartbeat reduced, easing toward normal as her panting slowed.

Finally, her hands stilled, no longer tormenting her pussy, and she slipped them from beneath her shorts. Fingers sticky with her juices and cunt wet from her multiple orgasms, the dark side of sex, masturbation, reared its ugly head.

Ew. Sticky.

A low, deep yet muffled sound reached her. A groan?

No. No. No. He couldn't have heard her. Did she scream his name when she came?

No. Yes. Maybe?

Damn it.

She wiggled to the edge of the bed and rolled free of the mattress, careful to keep her hands from touching anything. She did not want to explain the need for cleaning supplies to Martin in the morning.

Lauren tiptoed to the door and listened, ear pressed against the wood panel as she sought an indication of another's presence. She found nothing but quiet.

Using her wrists, and her miraculously clean pinkies, she managed to get the door unlocked and opened. She poked her head into the hallway and glanced in both directions, hunting for any hint of life.

She found nothing.

Thank. God.

She tiptoed to the bathroom and took care of all the messy repercussions of super-fun-alone-times, and then retraced her steps to silently slip back into her room. She pushed the door closed, careful to make the action as quiet as possible.

Then she leaned against it. Safe and sound and no one the wiser.

chapter **seven**

Lauren crept through Martin's home, tiptoeing down the hallway, toward the front door. She was careful, quiet, while she moved. She held her sneakers in one hand and purse over her shoulder as she hunted her car keys. Regardless of the tiny—super über tiny, in her opinion—threat Bryson represented, she needed to work. No one else was gonna pay her rent.

So, okay, it was probably a little more toward "stupid" on the idea-o'-the-morning spectrum, but she didn't have a choice.

Her travels led past the kitchen and… *there*… her keys sat on the counter, happy as they pleased. Perfect. Ever so carefully, she placed her hand atop the mass of metal and gently lifted them. They softly clinked together and she winced while she waited to see if anyone would react.

When an alarm didn't sound and no massive man came barreling down the hall, she breathed a sigh of relief. Part one of her plan was a wrap and now she could move on to phase two.

Lauren gulped. That involved getting past Van and out the front door. A sensation of wrongness slithered into her. Okay, she really, really knew it was a bad idea, but then the image of her landlord with his greasy hair and disgusting leers entered her mind. A shudder raced down her spine at the thought of having him on her doorstep looking for the rent check.

Okay, go, team Lauren Needs To Work.

She paused and carefully slid her feet into her shoes before continuing. The soles didn't make a sound on the soft carpet. She halted when she came to the archway that exposed the living room. Van lay scrunched on the couch, his massive frame folded onto the piece of furniture.

Memories of the kiss they shared floated to the front of her mind. The feel of his lips, the press of his body against hers, the flare of possessiveness in his eyes...

Lauren wanted to stay, wanted to crawl atop him and beg for a few of those kisses and maybe more.

Of course, it'd be a mistake. Her focus needed to be Anna and her happy-ish life. She didn't have space in her world for Van Abrams and, honestly, he didn't have time for her. Whenever she turned around, he was answering another call, dealing with another crisis.

Nah, he was hot, but she didn't want that hot mess.

Silently, she tiptoed past him and on to the front door. The solid wood panel loomed before her, taunting her with its presence. She glanced at the hooks on the wall, particularly the line of keys occupying each one. When Martin invited her to stay—okay, she refused to leave—he'd pointed at a set she could use.

Again she was conscious of the noise created by her moves. She lifted the key and turned to the door. Three locks total, all with the same key. As quietly as possible, she flicked one after the other until they were all disengaged.

Thank god there wasn't a security system. Martin intended to have one installed later in the day, but for now, she could escape without waking the house with random beeps from a keypad.

Lauren opened the door and slipped out, tugging it quietly closed behind her. Relocking the doors caused three low *snicks*, but again, no response from inside.

Whew.

Now she had to worry about driving away undetected. Already the morning sun peered over the horizon, lighting the front yard. It also brought early traffic. Hopefully enough to mask her departure.

Her feet crunched over the gravel, shifting the pale rocks as she walked.

At her truck, she slid the key into the lock and turned it, granting herself entry. She tugged on the handle and—

"Going somewhere?" The voice was deep, sleep roughened, and sexy as all get out. Also familiar.

Didn't stop her from screaming. Lauren jumped, yelling and spinning around to face Van. Her heart rate sped, adrenaline flooding her at the surprise.

"What the hell are you doing?" Her eyes were open wide with the shock. "Don't sneak up on me like that!"

He loomed over her, crowding her against the pickup, forcing her to lean back. Except she had no place to go. Nope, he surrounded her, his large body so close she felt both threatened and aroused. His heat engulfed her, caressing her with his warmth, and stoking her desire.

Damn it, she couldn't go to work with wet panties. Well, at least, not that kind of wet. She didn't have time to swing home and change. Thank god she had an extra uniform at work.

"I wouldn't have surprised you if you hadn't been sneaking out of the house." His voice was a low, deep rumble, and he stepped closer, his hips brushing hers. The bulge at the juncture of his thighs grew, a semi-hardness thickening and firming. "Where are you going, baby?"

That wasn't the first time he'd used that endearment. Baby. He'd called her "baby" and then he spoke with "Mia." Well, he could go back to her then. He was all kissing her and then running off to talk on the phone and… She mentally sighed. He did give the best fantasy orgasms though. Now she mentally slapped herself because

73

she shouldn't be thinking about fantasy orgasms after he'd scared her and she was mad, damn it.

"Work," she snapped. "Some of us have to work for a living."

Van grinned. "You don't think keeping after you, protecting you, is work?"

Lauren narrowed her eyes. "You…"

Hell, she didn't know what else she wanted to say. Asshole? Jerk? Fine as hell man?

No, definitely not that last one.

"Look, I need to go. So, run on back into the house and…" She glanced at the home and a thought struck her. "You were passed out and I just locked the doors. How'd you get from there," she furrowed her brow and pointed at the front door, "to here so fast? And I didn't hear you?"

Van shrugged. "Quiet, I guess. I can be real quiet when need be." His eyes heated and he seemed to stare into her, plucking thoughts from her mind. "Like in the middle of the night when everyone is sleeping."

Oh, god, no. She was going to pretend he didn't say that last part because she most certainly didn't hear a groan last night and it definitely wasn't his. Lauren swallowed, her mouth suddenly dry.

"Uh-huh." She shook her head, pretending his insinuation never hit the air. "It doesn't matter." She huffed and got back on track. "Me, work. You, go do whatever it is you do that doesn't involve me. It was fun, love you madly, yada yada, buh-bye."

Lauren turned from him and her hip brushed his hardness. She tried to ignore the low hiss that escaped his lips and the moan when he leaned forward and his hard dick settled against her ass.

"Lauren, I need you to stay here. Stay safe. I told you last night, Davies is dangerous. Men like Davies don't like to lose and you got his wife away from him."

She didn't acknowledge that his words might have a tiny bit of truth to them. Or the fact that his rumbling voice got her hot. Looked like she *would* be going to work with wet panties.

Van pressed his face to the side of her neck, nuzzling her, his morning scruff teasing her sensitive skin. He breathed deep, as if drawing her scent into his lungs. He rocked his hips against her, fabric-covered dick caressing her, and she pressed her ass into him. It was a mistake to encourage him, a mistake to toy with him, but it was so damn delicious.

He groaned and something sharp and firm scraped her neck. "Did you just bite me?"

He repeated the caress, teeth capturing her flesh and nipping before releasing. He lapped the semi-wound, tongue soothing the ache. "Depends. Do you like it?"

Lauren swallowed hard. She wanted to say no. She wanted to ask him what woman would get off on any kind of pain. But... she didn't want to be a liar, either. So, she kept her mouth shut and wiggled against him, tilting her head to the side, giving him more room.

Van chuckled, all cocky and full of himself, but he did give her a repeat performance. All the while he breathed her into him. She understood the action since she felt the same. His flavors were so deep, dark. Intoxicating.

Her pussy wept, growing moister by the second and all the man did was nibble on her. No hands stroking, pleasuring her. Nope. A tongue and teeth. She was so freakin' weird. And turned on. Couldn't forget turned on.

He drew in another breath, his chest expanding and brushing her back. Except this time, he held his breath and froze, unmoving against her.

75

"Fuck," he spat the word and pushed away from the truck, leaving her cold and alone against the vehicle.

"What? Van?" Confusion filled her and she furrowed her brow. One minute they were almost-kinda making out and then he was gone. She followed him, easing away from the hunk of metal.

Van paced around her car, breathing deep, and holding each for a few seconds before releasing it from his lungs. He repeated the move, taking a few steps, and pausing as he slowly circled her vehicle. Step, step, inhale, hold it, release and move on.

"Uh, Van?" He held up his hand, but didn't look at her, so she kept her mouth shut.

What the hell?

He made a full lap and then moved back to her front right tire, pausing a moment before squatting and out of her sight.

Well, then. Way to kill a happy buzz.

She went to him. He'd obviously finished his heavy breathing-slash-steam train impression.

Van's gaze was locked on the ground, the gravel surrounding her vehicle.

"Van? You're kinda freakin' me out." Okay, no "kinda" in there. This was a full-on freak out.

He brushed at the small rocks with his fingers, shifting gravel with his touch. He picked up a few and brought them to his nose. Weirder and weirder. Finally, he ducked farther and looked under the car.

He reached beneath her vehicle and snared a handful of rocks before rolling to his feet beside her. She peered at the bits of gravel he'd collected, noting the dark brown something-or-other coating them.

"What's that?" She wrinkled her nose at the oily scent.

Van let most of the rocks fall to the ground, retaining one of the largest and rolling it between his fingers. "Brake fluid. Normally I'd tell you that you should have had the lines flushed and fluid replaced years ago."

Lauren frowned.

"But the question today is—why is your brake fluid coating the ground?"

She looked at the piece of stone in his hand and then her gaze wandered to the handful on the ground. All of them were coated in the dark brown liquid. "Um, it's an old truck?"

She wanted that to be the reason her brake fluid stained Martin's gravel. Like, really, really. Because if it wasn't a simple mechanical failure, it meant the stuff had been released on purpose. It wasn't a huge stretch to figure out who'd like Lauren to drive her truck sans brakes.

Van wiped one hand on his wrinkled pants, a piece of gravel still clutched in the other. "Yeah, I'm not thinking that's the answer. C'mon back inside. You're not working today and I've got a few calls to make before I head out."

He reached around her hand, pressed his large, mostly-clean palm to her lower back, nudging her toward the house. "I have to call in sick, but you get to work? I have bills to pay, damn it."

She really tried to dig her heels in, keep him from shoving her toward the door, but he was bigger and stronger and hotter and… A heated blush stole over her cheeks. Anyway.

"You get a choice. Not working and living, or working and dying. Because those brake lines didn't cut themselves."

*

Van's bear fumed, paced, and released the occasional deafening roar.

77

Her brake lines had been cut. He hadn't seen the severed lines, hadn't taken the time to crawl under and feel for them, but the amount of liquid spoke for itself.

Lauren resisted a tiny bit, but she finally shuffled along with him. He ignored the sharp pinches to his bare feet and kept their pace brisk across the rocky driveway. He hadn't bothered with finding shoes when he'd heard those low snicks of the locks. At first the bear roared at the possibility of an intruder. Then it'd simply roared when it caught her scent and followed her path.

Stupid woman leaving on her own when they were dealing with an asshole like Bryson Davies.

He stomped up the porch steps and then snared the front door, holding it open for her. She shot him a glare, but he ignored it. She'd be even more pissed a little later.

The moment they were both in the home, Van shoved the door closed and yelled for the other bear in the house. "Martin!"

No sound came from deep within the house and Van sighed. He hated waking other bears. Bears in general got too cozy at night, a throwback to the animal's desire to hibernate. Getting to sleep was easy, waking up… not so much. He was actually surprised his beast woke when Lauren snuck out. Then again, the animal was looking at her as a potential mate. It made sense it'd wanna keep track of what belonged to him.

Van lowered his voice. "Can you make some coffee, baby? It's gonna be a long morning."

Lauren glared, and jerked away from him, stomping toward the kitchen. She tried to keep her grumblings low, but his hearing was quite a bit better than a human's. "Stupid man… hotness… coffee… where does he get off… sexy jerk…"

She thought he was hot. Good to know, since he planned on showing her just how hot *he* could make *her*. After listening to her come last night, whispering his name along with her breathy

78

whimpers. Yeah, he couldn't wait to get close to Lauren Evans. Naked.

It'd taken everything in him not to burst through her bedroom door and give her exactly what she begged for. He ached to strip her down and lap up every drop of her juices. The scent called to him last night and it'd teased him well into the early hours of the morning.

Yeah, him and Lauren naked sounded like a very, very good idea.

"Yo, Martin!" He moved further into the house. He'd gotten the grand tour, but wasn't sure where exactly he was going.

He poked his head into the first bedroom and recognized Lauren's scent filling the space. More importantly, the delicious hints of her arousal and musk. His cock filled and pushed against his pants. Damn. They really needed to ensure Lauren's safety so he could strip her down and taste every inch of her lush body. Soon.

The next doorway led to the small bathroom where he'd spent a few moments up close and personal with her. He kept moving. The next door revealed the other guestroom which left him with one last place to check. Shit. He didn't want to intrude on a bear with his mate, but it couldn't be helped. Plans had to be made and relocation was necessary all around.

Van cracked his neck, snapping it side to side. He rolled his shoulders and shook out his hands, body loose and relaxed before he faced a snarling beast.

He knocked on the door, a quick rap of his knuckles on the wood and got… nothing. Fuck. He wrapped his left hand around the knob and twisted it, slowly easing the panel into the room. He kept tapping, hoping he wasn't surprising Martin too bad.

The last thing they needed was an enraged werebear shifting with two ignorant humans in the house.

"Martin?" He peeked around the edge of the door and spotted a small, tangled lump in the middle of the bed. He let his gaze travel further and locked eyes with an enraged shifter wrapped in a blanket and laying back on a nearby chair. It looked like the bear had spent the night there. "*Shit.*"

At least he'd kept his skin on.

Martin growled and flashed his fangs while his normally blue eyes darkened to black.

"Remain calm, Martin." He released the knob and held his hands out to his friend and subordinate. "We have a situation." Martin curled his lips, baring his teeth. "Damn it, Martin. We got shit to do." A rumbling growl vibrated through the room. "Fuck. Things are getting deadly. We need—"

"Martin?" The lyrical voice was husky with sleep. The mass on the bed shifted and then a brown-haired head popped into view. "What's wrong?"

Like a switch, the bear's growl ceased and he transformed into a man filled with love and patience. It'd taken three words to shift the male from "ready to blow" to "sweet as pie."

"Nothing, sweet. Van just needs to talk for a second. I'll be right back." The bad ass cop rose and leaned across the bed. He dropped a soft kiss to Anna's forehead before turning back to Van. "Let's go."

Martin pushed past him and strode into the hallway and Anna waved to him as he turned to follow the male. He returned the gesture, earning him *another* growl from Martin.

Shit. Bears and their mates. Was he gonna turn into this kind of overbearing, possessive, protective asshole?

Van took a moment and thought over the events of the last day… He wasn't gonna turn into that guy, he *was* that guy.

He was so fucked.

"What's wrong and why'd you have to wake Anna to tell me?" Martin spun on him in the hallway, stalling their progress to the kitchen.

Van held up his right hand, fingers still clutching the piece of gravel, the surface sticky with the aged brake fluid. "Lauren's truck had a visitor last night."

Martin inhaled. "Shit."

"Yup." He nodded. "I'm going to go have a chat with our mayor while you relocate the women."

"Where?" Martin scrunched his brow.

Van knew the bear wouldn't like his idea any more than he really did. Not that he didn't want Lauren close… He just didn't want *anyone else* close to her. But, he couldn't let his own feelings override good sense. The perfect location was a hundred yards from his brother's place where bears always wandered the grounds. The only drawback was… bears always wandered the grounds.

"My place."

chapter eight

Snooping was bad. And Lauren knew that. She'd grown up being told not to pick and poke at other people's belongings. But… but Van wasn't home. He'd dropped off her and Anna with instructions to stay inside and safe. His brother owned all of the land, no one could get close, and blah, blah…

Now that she'd had time to think, there was no way her brake lines had been cut. She was sure that as soon as they got old Betsy to a mechanic, they'd find that Lauren was a shitty truck owner. Nothing more, nothing less.

In the meantime, she was stuck in an unfamiliar house alone. Mostly alone. Anna had crashed the moment her head hit the pillow. Martin urged her best friend to down another pill, and *boom*, out like a light.

So, alone. In the big old house. With lots of little things to magically nudge aside.

So far, she hadn't found anything worth finding. Damn it.

Her first impression of the home had been one of breathtaking awe. It was just… glorious. From its clean lines to the rich wood used on the exterior to the exposed beams in the ceiling. It was a combination of rustic charm with modern influences. Wood accents were sprinkled throughout the space, delicate swirls and the occasional scene of bears, both adult and cubs.

Truly, it was a place she could happily call home.

Not that she would, but she could. It'd definitely be a more welcome home than her ratty apartment and all of the ratty apartments and trailers that came before.

Lauren ran her fingers along the polished mantelpiece, tips sliding over the smooth wood. She'd asked about the fireplace's frame, stroking one of the carvings of a small cub. That's when he had revealed he'd done the work himself, every delicate decoration created with his hands.

She pet a realistic leaf, the ridges ticking her fingertips. He'd leaned over the hunk of wood for hours to create the masterpiece that graced the living room. His hands had touched, stroked, and sanded the hardness beneath her palm.

Her big, bad cop had an artistic streak a mile wide.

Then again, he wasn't hers, was he?

Nope. Regardless of her midnight fantasy, he didn't belong to her.

With a shake of her head, she moved on, exploring the place. Four bedrooms, three bathrooms. Big enough for a family, he'd said. Of course, as the words tumbled from his lips, his gaze focused on her.

Lauren shuddered at the memory. Heat filled his eyes, the irises darkening, and she'd felt the look all the way to her toes. Even now her nipples pebbled and her pussy heated. The man was sex on two legs and he knew it. Well, she knew it, too.

She padded through the living room and toward the back of the home. If she went through the front door, she'd see Ty's home. But out back, she was met with a breathtaking sight.

The sun shone high above the hills, but it was the hills themselves that called to her. They were rolling swaths of green tipped with tall trees and decorated with bushes of varying shades. In the distance, a hint of the lake peeked at her. Grayslake.

She'd never been there. While most kids and teens spent summers on the lake, Lauren spent summers working.

Now, it was so close. Could she…?

She pressed her fingertips to the glass, tracing the lake's shore. Sun glinted off the smooth water, the calm surface begging someone to run and splash through its contents.

Unable to resist the call, she placed her hand on the door handle, fingering the satin finished lever. A flick of the small button-shaped lock, she pushed down, releasing the door from the frame. The glass panel swung wide, freeing her.

The fresh air swept over her, urging her to leave the house and explore. It seemed crisper here, cleaner. She let the door swing closed behind her. The grass and trees beckoned and she followed, padding across the solid wood porch toward the steps.

Lauren ran her hand along the smooth railing as she descended the handful of stairs to the ground below. The grass crunched beneath her feet, the softness welcoming her with that first step.

The wind ruffled her hair and she smiled, dragging a few wayward strands and tucking them behind her ear. She took another few steps, enjoying the outdoors.

She had all of Bryson's asshole drama in the back of her mind, but it couldn't overshadow the excitement of being outside, being close to Grayslake, and able to enjoy the day. Tomorrow she'd go back to her crappy job and struggling to keep her crappy apartment.

Tomorrow.

A woman's yell reached her, the sound slicing through the quiet. The voice was unfamiliar to her, but Van warned her a lot of friends and family visited his brother's house each day. Considering how close that house happened to be, she figured it belonged to a visitor.

Well, she wasn't going to worry about it now. Not when—

Lauren fell with a squawk, her feet flipping from beneath her and sending her crashing to the ground. She toppled to her back, grunting when she finally collided with the firm surface.

"Parker, no!"

Warm fur brushed her bare legs, the body wiggling against her, and obviously excited about managing to knock her on her ass. A cold nose nuzzled her knee and snuffled along her thigh, getting closer to…

"No," she pushed at the snout nearing her no-no place. The narrow, rather long snout. A greyhound? No, too furry. She raised her head to look, but the pain of her fall was getting to her. It grew with every passing second. She brought her free hand to the back of her head and didn't find any wetness, but… damn.

"Crap on a cracker. *Parker*."

Parker. Funny name for a dog.

The pup kept pushing at her hand, easing back, and trying to avoid her capture. Well, she had more motivation to keep him away from the goods.

Groaning, she eased up onto one elbow, propping herself so she could get a good look at Parker and his owner. Except… Lauren gulped… except what was supposed to be a dog—because people owned *dogs* in the country—was *not* a dog. No, it was so anti-dog it wasn't funny. It was the antithesis of dog in all of dogland.

She fought to keep her heart rate steady. She couldn't show it fear, couldn't antagonize the beast. They could smell fear, right? Totally. She read that somewhere. Or saw it on TV. Who cared? She sure as hell didn't. Her only concern was getting away from the non-dog, freakin' *bear* cub. Bear. With big teeth. Sure, he was small for a bear, but that didn't change the fact *he was a bear*. Maybe a baby bear. The maybe-baby-bear grinned at her, exposing two rows of death-inducing teeth. Oh, god, it was gonna eat her.

Lauren snatched her hand back, unwilling to lose her fingers because she was trying to save her pink bits from a snuffling. Getting her hands beneath her, she used them to tug her back and clear of the animal's body.

A woman came careening around the corner of the house, jogging when she finally spied them. "Parker Abrams, so help me!"

The small bear swung his gaze to the woman and Lauren took her chance. She scrambled backward, struggling to get to the safety of the house.

Fucking Van hadn't fucking mentioned fucking anything about fucking fuckity-fuck bears!

Her right hand touched the stairs, a low *thump* sounding when her palm struck wood. Oh shit, that got the bear's attention back on her. She was gonna die. She was a bear snack or a bear meal with all of her fat and jiggly bits. God, it could live a week on her ass alone.

The cub pounced on her, heavy body landing on her chest, and licking her with that slobbery pink tongue.

It started with her face. Maybe it could crush her skull and then eat the rest of her. Yes, that'd work.

"Parker, no TV for a week, young man." The woman was close now. No, not close, she stood right next to them. She was short, shorter than Lauren anticipated considering her yelled threats. Her small hands reached for the cub, sinking into his fur, and then the weight was gone. "I told you, we don't jump on strangers. How many times do we have to have this conversation?" The bear whimpered and whined and Mia released the cub. Thankfully, it remained in place and didn't make an attempt to come at Lauren again. "And don't think we aren't talking to your pop about this."

The lady had the audacity to wag her finger at the cub as if it understood her. Then again, considering the animal whimpered and dropped its eyes, she figured it did. Like a child, he ran one of his front paws through the grass and digging his toes into the soft surface while whining a little more.

"Back to the house. Now." The woman pointed up the hill and it slunk toward the corner of the house. "And Gigi better not tell me you asked for cookies, young man!" A low whine, but the woman snapped her fingers and the bear trotted out of view.

Ballsy bitch.

The woman brushed her hands together and then wiped them on her jeans before turning back toward Lauren. "Sorry about that. Parker gets excited when he meets new people." She moved closer, extending a hand. "I'm Mia, you must be Van's Lauren."

She wasn't Van's anything. Unfortunately-ish. She still wasn't sure if she should jump his bones or run away.

"Uh… Yes?" She reached up and shook Mia's hand, allowing the other woman to help her stand. She pushed to her feet, ignoring the twinges of pain that came with the new injuries. She hadn't even healed from Bryson's tender care and now she added more.

"How are you finding our little tucked away place?"

Okay then, no explanation as to why she had a *pet bear*. Then again, Lauren was just a visitor.

Lauren looked toward the lake, to the area that'd drawn her from Van's home in the first place. "It's gorgeous."

Mia followed her line of sight and a blush stole over her cheeks. "Yes," she shook her head. "We have a lot of beautiful spots here. When all of this mess is over, you should have Van take you to the lake."

"Uh…" A sting finally made itself known and she looked down at her hands, noting the scraped knuckles and blood welling. "Shit."

"Language. *Shoot* and you're bleeding. Van is gonna kick my fanny." Mia grabbed her wrist and tugged her toward the stairs. "Let's get this bandaged up and then we can sit and chat a little."

"It's fine, really."

Mia waved her free hand. "We're family." She grabbed the door handle and tugged it open. "And I'll make sure Parker comes by to apologize later."

"Apologize?" Lauren shook her head. "How's a bear going to apologize? And why are you keeping a bear as a pet?" Screw it, she'd approach the furry elephant in the room.

"Well... you see..."

Lauren's attention was snared by movement near the tree line. "And wolves, too? Are you guys running a freakin' zoo?"

* * *

Van's bear paced inside him, snarling as it stomped from one side of his mind to the other. His animal had been on edge since he'd discovered the stained rocks. There'd been no hint of the perpetrator's scent, but it wasn't a stretch to believe the mayor had decided Lauren didn't need to be alive any longer.

Asshole.

He couldn't sit still. Like his animal, he paced the waiting area at the mayor's office. The woman behind the massive desk at one end of the room paid them no attention as she worked at her computer and answered calls. After they gave their names, they'd ceased to exist for her.

Damn it, he was antsy, anxious to confront Davies and then send the dick to hell. Fast or slow, he didn't care. The man had threatened his—friend, woman, mate?—and he'd pay. Actually, slow seemed the best way. He'd tie the mayor down and run his claws along the male's skin. He'd be dead by the time Van was done, so exposing his inner-bear should be fine.

Yes, he'd cut and scrape and...

"Van," his brother murmured.

89

He ceased pacing and turned to Ty. "What?"

He nearly snarled the word, but kept his beast in check. Barely.

"You need to remain calm. I allowed you to come along but," Ty approached and flicked Van's hand. Van's furry, claw-tipped hand. "But you have to chill the hell out."

He took a deep breath and asked his beast to retreat. They both wanted to gut Davies, but they couldn't expose weres to everyone in the process. Slowly the fur receded and black nails lightened to their human hue.

"Sorry."

"Uh-huh." Ty folded his arms across his chest. "What's really going on?"

"Nothing." Nothing but the fact that he kept replaying Lauren's death in his mind.

She would have pulled out of the driveway and noticed the brakes were a little soft, but would have brushed it aside. The truck was old as hell and she'd get the mechanic to look at it later.

It wouldn't be until she drove over the top of the next steep hill that trouble would invade. Because when she rolled to the bottom and slowed to go around the curve, the brakes would fail. Her two ton truck would crumble the metal barrier easily and then it'd tumble to the valley below. The damned thing was old, so that meant aged seatbelts and no airbags.

By the time she got to the bottom, she'd be dead and Davies would be one happy asshole. At least until Van gutted him.

Yes, his bear was on board with that plan to gut the mayor even though Lauren was safe and sound in his home on Ty's lands. A satisfied purr came from the bear. His den. That's exactly where the animal wanted her. Forever.

Van's human mind still kept trying to wrap around the idea. A *human* woman, in his home and by his side, forever. It had trouble reconciling his disgust and general hatred of humans with his desire for Lauren.

The phone on the secretary's desk buzzed, drawing their attention, and she spoke into the receiver briefly before replacing it on the cradle. "Through that door." She gestured to the opposite side of the room. "Mayor Davies will see you now."

A growl built in Van's chest and then a sharp thump to the middle of his forehead cut it off.

"Keep it under wraps or go back to the station," Ty hissed at him.

Van glared at his older brother and rubbed the spot. "Damn it, Ty."

He pushed past Ty, but he halted Van's progress with a rough yank on his arm. His brother leaned in close. "You will keep your shit together, Enforcer."

Van's heart stopped for a second and then picked up double-time. He swallowed hard, demanding the bear listen. "Yes, Itan." He held his breath as the beast inside him grumbled and finally settled. "I'll stay calm."

"Good." Ty released him and moved to the door, opening it and leaving it wide so Van could follow in his wake.

Until Ty asserted his dominance over Van, he hadn't realized how close he lingered to the edge of losing control.

He followed his Itan, because Ty truly acted as the Itan now, regardless of the circumstances.

Davies sat behind his desk, the scent of smug satisfaction filled the space. That flavor was tempered with the lingering rage permeating every surface. It wasn't a new aroma, it wasn't what he projected right that second, but it was recent.

It was probably from when he realized his attempt on Lauren's life failed.

"To what do I owe the pleasure, Sheriff?" Davies rose from his chair and extended his hand toward Ty.

The Itan had no way to deny the gesture, but Van did. When Bryson reached for him, he remained motionless. The uncomfortable situation spread longer and longer until the mayor finally gave up and shot him a glare before retaking his seat.

"Have a seat," Bryson gestured to the two chairs before his desk.

Have a seat? How about I feed you the fucking seat, asshole?

Well, that's what Van wanted to say. Instead, he followed his Itan's lead and settled into one of the leather chairs.

"Did my assistant offer you any beverages? Water, coffee? I have—"

Okay, his beast was obviously not one to stand for chit-chat when its mate was threatened. "Why don't we start with why you tried to kill Lauren Evans and move on from there?"

It was as if the whole room held its breath. Silence reigned and no one moved. He sensed his Itan's rage and Van knew he'd be in for a big ass-kicking, but he wanted answers. He also wanted the mayor to know *he* knew.

Davies's scent changed, the anger rekindling while a sliver of fear joined the aroma. Oh yes, he was very pissed he'd failed and now he wondered how they'd discovered the truth. Well, that was what the mayor's scents told him. On the outside, the man's smile held firm with no hint of guilt. In actuality, he feigned surprise rather well.

"Lauren? Kill her?" Bryson's eyes were opened wide. "Murder is still illegal, Officer. Besides, I'd never think of harming anyone."

"Not even your wife, mayor?" Ty cut in before Van could release a ball of curse-filled threats.

The mayor's expression remained innocent. "Sheriff, you know my wife is rather clumsy." He opened a desk drawer and withdrew a familiar sheet of paper. "As it says in this affidavit, Anna had quite a few spills this last year." He placed it on the clean desktop and slid it toward Ty. "Here's a copy for yourself." Smug satisfaction filled the air.

Fucking asshole needed to die for what he did to Anna. The bear inside him snarled, agreeing with the idea. Again they wanted to go to bat for a human.

"You're right, Mayor. I'd forgotten about that agreement." Ty left the page on the desk.

Van nearly snorted. Forget something signed and filed so recently? Not likely.

"Good, good." The mayor leaned back in his chair. "Now, why don't you explain why you're here and flinging wild accusations? I'm a public official. I take disparaging remarks against my character seriously."

Did he take a claw to the belly seriously? That's what Van wanted to know. He wondered how loud and hard he could make Davies cry.

"Miss Evans's truck had its brake lines severed. Had she driven the vehicle, she more than likely would have perished in an accident." Ty's voice was all business.

Perished. Nice way to say murdered. Van's skin prickled, a hint of his bear pushing past his mental barriers.

"Well, that's horrible. What makes you think I was involved? I have to admit, as an upstanding pillar of this community, I don't understand how suspicion could have been cast upon me."

Because you're an abusive asshole?

Van leaned forward in his seat. "Lauren intervened in the middle of Anna's most recent 'accident' at your home." He made air quotes with his fingers when he said accident. "You then accosted her on the street. At this time, you're the only suspect."

"I object to your implication." The mayor pushed to his feet and Van did the same. His beast rode him hard, pushing and shoving, demanding they put the evil man down. That was how shifters were treated. Evil and insane? Then you're gone. Forever.

"I object to you—"

"Object all you want. It doesn't change the facts." Van's phone vibrated in his pocket, buzzing against his keys, but he ignored it. It took everything in him to not rip out the man's throat. He'd never been this violent before, but it was Lauren…

"I—" the mayor tried again.

"Enough!" Ty cut through them and silence reigned. Well, except for the ringing of his phone once again. Ty pointed at him. "Silence." Van seethed, but bit his tongue. He was letting his emotions, his need for Lauren's safety, cloud his judgment. "Mister Mayor—"

Van's phone buzzed again, earning a glare from Ty.

"Mister Mayor, there are certain facts associated with the events of the last forty-eight hours, which cast… suspicions… in your direction." Davies opened his mouth to respond, but Ty held up a hand, forestalling his response. "It would be helpful if you could provide an accounting of your whereabouts last—"

This time, Ty's phone rang, the jingle slicing through his speech. His brother breathed deep, his chest widening the tiniest bit as his biceps thickened. At least Van wasn't the only one annoyed with Davies and cell phones.

"Where were you last night, Mayor?" Ty cut through the nicey-nice bullshit.

"I don't have to account for my whereabouts to you over someone like Lauren Evans," the man blustered.

Ty pushed to his feet and placed his fists on the desktop. "Yes, you do."

"I'm the mayor—"

Van's cell phone made itself known again while Ty's phone rang for the second time. Shit. Someone wanted them.

Ignoring the stare-off in front of him, he dug into his pocket and yanked his phone free. Crap, it was his own house. He pressed the button to answer the call. "This is Van."

"Oh, thank god." Mia's relief was evident in her tone. "You need to come home." A crash sounded, something glass shattering. "Right now. Now would be really good."

This time it was a yell, loud and long and filled with fear, and… Lauren's.

chapter nine

"Wolves?" Mia seemed surprised by the question, but Lauren sensed the lie lingering beneath the surface. "What wolves?"

She gestured toward the tree line. "Over there. Gray. Big as hell."

"Language. *Heck*." Mia corrected her. "And no, no wolves or bears or hyenas… nothing." Mia tugged her into the house. "No animals here."

"Except your bear." She stated the obvious while also fishing for a little more of that story.

"Huh? My bear?" She smiled. "Oh, you mean Parker. Well," she nibbled her lower lip. "He's special." Mia licked her lips, a nervous tension overcoming her. "We do have a few special animals here and there." She waved her hands. "Anyway, we were going to get you patched up. Yes." She jerked her head in a sharp nod. "Yes, we were."

Lauren allowed herself to be dragged into the house and toward the bedrooms. They passed the one given to Anna and then the one assigned to her. They kept going until they came to the room at the end. Mia marched in as if she owned the place. Or, as if she was a frequent visitor. Something inside Lauren twisted at the idea that Mia came and went through Van's room.

"And here we are." Mia tugged her into the master bathroom and then released her.

Lauren stopped and gasped. Holy cow, the room was gorgeous. The shower was large with glass walls and more showerheads than she could ever count. A massive Jacuzzi tub occupied the space beneath a huge window that looked over the open area behind the house. At this angle even more of the lake was visible, its soothing waters calling to her.

"Isn't that gorgeous?" Mia's question interrupted her thoughts and then the woman was beside her, the two of them staring out the window. "It's actually got a film on it that gives a mirror-like finish to people outside while it's only a hint of tint in here. That way you can use the tub without flashing your rear end all over the place." She bumped Lauren's shoulder. "A good thing with all the men around here. One of the guards got a glimpse of me and Ty went all bear fur and—" Mia coughed. "Anyway, let's get you patched up."

She allowed herself to be led to the counter, a long, granite slab with modern sinks and beautiful knobs. All of it, from the tile on the floor to the toilet to the sinks… it was her dream bathroom come to life.

Lauren studied the room, spying the pattern built into the shower wall, while Mia prodded and cleaned her wound. The first few brushes to remove the dirt weren't so bad, but then she busted out the alcohol.

"Holy shit!" Lauren gritted her teeth, trying to bear the pain from the scrapes.

"Language." Mia bent over her hand and she spared a glance. "Almost there."

Hell no she wasn't "almost there."

"What the fuck?" She couldn't hold the curse back. Not when the woman practically dumped the alcohol on her hand. Okay, really, it was just a soaked cotton ball, but damn.

"Freck or frog leg. We try to keep the cursing down around Parker."

"Parker?" Another dab. "He's a frog leg bear. What the— Woman! Get your frecking hands—"

Lauren didn't do well with pain.

"Don't yell at my mim!" A young boy's voice cut into Lauren's tirade and she just got going, too.

"No yelling, Parker."

Parker? The woman had a kid and a bear with the same name? Where the hell did Van leave her?

"What the—" This time it was like she dug her nails into the scrape and she glared at Mia. "Ow! Quit that."

A low growl bounced off the walls and she turned toward the source of the sound. A small, wide-eyed and definitely angry child stood in the room's doorway.

"Parker." Mia placed the red-hued cotton ball on the counter. "No." The growl didn't stop. "Parker, no!"

Lauren watched, horrified, as the next events unfolded. Sure, there was a mad little kid and then there was… She didn't have words to describe it. He was a boy and then he had fur and dark black eyes and fingers that were paws and clothes were tearing and then…

"Oh, fuck. Oh shit, oh fuck, oh shit, oh fuck."

The boy-bear growled, baring his small, sharp as hell teeth at her. Panic assaulted her, sending her heart racing, slamming against her ribcage, and fighting to burst through her chest. It wanted to run and hide and… holy fuck the kid turned into a bear. She couldn't wrap her head around that fact. One second—kid. Next second—furry thing with sharp ass teeth.

And fuck her, it ran toward her.

Parker took one step and then another, coming nearer. Mia stepped between her and the tiny ball of death.

"Parker, no. We talked about this."

They'd talked about it? *Talked* about it? As in the woman knew her kid going batshit was a possibility?

The kid darted around Mia and Lauren spun away, hunting for a place to hide. Her head whipped side to side as she sought a safe haven and found nothing. A big assed bathroom and Van couldn't have bothered to install a damned linen closet?

The only area with a door was the glass shower. Perfect. She darted for the enclosure, wrenching the door wide, and then tugging it closed behind her. It wouldn't stop a fifty pound bear, but it'd at least slow it until animal control could tranquilize the thing.

"Mia get help!" she yelled to the other woman who simply stood by while yelling at Parker.

"Darn it all, Parker. Your pop is gonna be angry at you."

"Angry at him? *Angry?* Are you fucking kidding me here, Mia?"

The woman spared her a glance. "Language." She looked to Parker once again. "Parker, you're being bad. No cookies from Gigi if you don't stop right this second."

The kid did *not* care. The cub threw himself against the glass, banging and shaking the entire enclosure. "The kid doesn't care about cookies, Mia. Get this science experiment gone wrong away from me."

The boy-bear snarled and jumped at the door again.

"Crap on a cracker." Mia disappeared, she bolted out the door, and Lauren heard the rapid thump of her feet striking the ground as she fled.

"Are you fucking kidding me?" The cub paced in front of the shower, snarling now and again as he passed the glass door. "Look, kid. Whatever I did, I'm sorry. Please don't eat me, okay?" He flashed a fang at her. "Fuck. Me."

She usually tried to keep her language clean around little ears, but she figured she could be forgiven when the kid in question was trying to *eat* her.

The pound of feet on carpet overrode Parker's snarls and Mia slid back into view, a phone clutched in her hand. "Do you see this Parker Abrams, I'm calling your pop right this second."

Lauren pressed harder against the tiled wall at her back, trying her best to get as far away from the bear as possible. She must have made some sort of sound, or—she'd admit it—whined, because suddenly the kid threw his body against the door again. The glass cracked, a single line bisecting the large sheet.

"Oh shit, oh fuck, oh shit, oh fuck…"

"Language." Mia pressed the phone to her ear spoke, but Lauren couldn't hear a word.

Not when the cub threw himself at the door again. Or when the thing shattered against the newest strike. Or when she screamed.

A ball of fur flew toward her, his front legs outstretched, mouth open wide. Distantly, she recognized Mia's answering yell as well as the woman racing forward.

"Keen!" Mia screamed for one of the other Abrams brothers. What the hell was he gonna do if he wasn't *here?*

Another movement near the door caught her attention and a person was on the move. Okay, maybe Keen was nearby.

He soared through the space. One blink and he went from twenty feet away to in front of her. He wrapped one arm around the cub's middle while he shoved his forearm between Parker's teeth, giving the kid something to gnaw on.

101

Fuck, the bear was biting down on Keen's arm, sinking his small bear teeth into the man's flesh and blood was everywhere and…

Keen's eyes met hers. Dark, dangerous, black eyes. Eyes that looked a lot like Parker's.

"Oh, shit."

The man wrestled the cub from the room, fighting with it as they finally left the destroyed space. Mia lingered near the sinks, a phone pressed to her ear while she gave Lauren a wide-eyed stare.

A splash of red caught her eye. No, several splashes. The trail of blood from Keen's wound stained the pale tiles, reminding her of what'd occurred.

"I'm gonna be sick. Or pass out." Lauren's stomach churned, making its unhappiness known. "Maybe both."

Her vision narrowed, the edges dimming, and the full weight of the last few minutes crashed in on her. A boy, who was a bear, and Keen, who had boy-bear's eyes.

Here. In real life.

She looked to Mia. "I'm passing out first."

Lauren felt her consciousness flee, the darkness closing in on her.

"You should get here. Fast."

Lauren wondered who Mia was speaking to. Van? Ty? Martin?

That reminded her about Anna. Lauren hoped the bear didn't eat her. That would really suck.

* * *

Van didn't wait for the SUV to stop. Ty had barely tapped the brakes before he burst from the vehicle and raced across the grass. He hit the front porch at a dead run, only slowing to open the door rather than tearing it off its hinges.

The moment he entered his home, he scented blood. The coppery stench overwhelmed him, slamming into him like a bat. Oh, god. Had Parker bitten her? Another bear could live through a werebear bite, but if he got a hold of a human... They took so long to heal.

He drew in another deep breath and sighed in relief. No, it wasn't Lauren or even Anna. It seemed like his brother Keen took the brunt of the boy's attack.

Van took a moment to look at the space. There were a few blood stains on the wood, dried droplets. But one thing snared and capture his attention—Keen held a quietly sobbing Parker on his lap. The boy was covered in a blanket, his clothes probably shredded during his shift. Keen's right arm was a mass of bright pink lines, showing how deep and hard Parker had gone after Lauren.

A shudder overtook him, the feeling of worry and outright fear assaulted him in one overwhelming wave. That could have been Lauren. If Keen hadn't been there...

"Lauren?" He didn't disguise his anxiety.

"Your room." Yelling came from that direction. "With guns from what I hear. Or she's bluffing."

Van grimaced. "She's not bluffing."

After the trouble with Mia and Parker, he'd added a few firearms to his collection. He hadn't gotten around to asking Keen to install them throughout the house yet, but it'd been in his plans.

The rapid pounding of Ty's feet on wood announced his brother's approach. "Parker? Mia?"

Keen quickly supplied the answers. "Here and back by Van's bedroom. Lauren's having difficulty with things and, uh, has a few guns."

103

Ty grumbled and growled, fur pushing through his pores and the bones in his face snapping and reforming. The overwhelming urge to drop to his knees and prove his submission nearly did Van in. The bear was torn between placating his Itan and going to his mate.

Thankfully, Keen was quick to defuse the situation. "She thinks she's protecting Mia while protecting herself from Mia. The point is, Mia is probably safe, but you are not. At all."

Okay, that wasn't exactly a diffusion.

"Ty, I'll get her." Van fought to remain standing, demanding his bear reject their Itan's dominance this one time.

Ty snarled, baring his half-shifted fangs at him. "Mine."

"I'll send Mia out. Gimme a sec to talk to Lauren." He didn't want Ty getting anywhere near his human.

The Itan growled, but a low whimper from Parker silenced that in an instant. The man's half-shift was upon him, but it didn't advance. It froze in place and never budged while Ty moved through the room and scooped Parker into his arms.

Ty nuzzled the boy and Parker clung to him. "Send Mia out and decide what we're going to do about Lauren." The Itan looked at him, his gaze weighing heavily on Van's shoulders. "She's human and she's not mated to one of us."

The rest of the law didn't need to be voiced.

So she must mate or be eliminated.

Nice word for murder.

Brushing aside his Itan's veiled order, Van moved to the hallway, quietly padding down the length and toward the bedrooms.

The whispers hit him first, the low, frantic mumblings from Lauren softly answered by Anna and Mia's frustrated murmurings.

"Get. Over. Here. I can't protect you if you're across the hall."

Anna, in the room to his right, sighed. She sat in the doorway, her purpled face the only thing destroying the peaceful look. "What are you protecting me from?"

"The *bears*. They're people and then they're bears and they bite people. Rawr, rawr. Get. Over. Here." Lauren hissed that last bit.

"Lauren, hon, they're not dangerous."

Yes, listen to your friend.

"And how would you know anything about them, oh best friend of mine? The one person who I share everything with. The person who knows my soul. How do you know they're not dangerous?" If Anna didn't get Lauren's sarcasm, Van definitely scented the emotion.

"Well... you see... Martin is..."

"Are you fucking kidding me?" Lauren wasn't even trying to whisper. "He's a bear, too? How fucking many of them *are there?*"

The yelled question was answered by a roar from Ty at the other end of the house. That was answered by Lauren racking the slide on one of his handguns. Nice.

"Lauren, honey..." That was Mia.

"Are you one too? One of them?" The panicked tone in Lauren's words worried him.

"Lauren?" He kept his voice low, soothing. At least, he hoped. When he heard her scrambling and dropping the gun quickly followed by the snap of his bedroom door's lock, he realized she wasn't soothed in the slightest. "Lauren, I know you're scared and upset, baby."

Anna looked up at him with wide eyes and raised eyebrows as if to say "you think, dumbass."

Yeah, well, he was working with what he had.

105

"Lauren, why don't you send Mia on out. Her mate," he coughed. "Her husband is worried about her."

"Why?" The word was muffled by the closed door. "I'm not the fucking bear in this house."

Mia's whispered language immediately followed Lauren's curse.

"Really? Faced with shapeshifting bears and you're gonna 'language' me?" She fell quiet for a moment. "Wait! You're fucking the fucking bear."

Suddenly his bedroom door opened and Mia was shoved unceremoniously into the hallway, then the door was slammed shut once again. The Itana stumbled for a moment, catching herself on the wall, and then straightened while tugging her top into place.

Mia hissed at the now closed door. "Language."

Van wasn't gonna laugh. Really. "This way, Itana. Ty's waiting for you and I think the two of you need to talk about Parker." He stared at the door. "She's okay?"

Annoyance immediately left Mia's face. "She's fine. A couple of scratches from the broken glass. Otherwise, she's just scared."

He nodded and stepped aside as she passed. "Thanks, Mia."

"I could-I could talk to her?" Anna's quiet voice drifted to him.

"Thanks, Anna, but I'll take care of this. Why don't you go out to the living room? I'm sure Martin will be here soon." Van had no doubt that since the situation was under control, Ty put in a call to the other man.

"Anna? Are you leaving me?" Lauren's voice was filled with panic. "Don't go to the bears! It's like Poltergeist all over again. Don't go into the fur-lined light!"

Anna licked her lips, wincing when her tongue glanced her wound.

"Go ahead, hon." Van stepped forward, his body blocking Anna as she tiptoed down the hall and toward the living room. The last thing he wanted was an errant shot hitting the small woman. He stopped near his bedroom door and pressed his back against the wall opposite Lauren. He eased himself down, sliding along the firm surface until he sat on the ground. "All right, baby. Let's do this."

The door cracked a tiny bit and one, glaring eye was revealed. "I'm not your baby and we're not doing anything."

With that, she disappeared from sight once again, the panel swinging closed with a low *thunk*.

"I'm sure you've got questions, huh? I could answer them…" He used a cajoling tone, trying to appeal to a human's innate inquisitive nature. Then again, bears were a little similar when it came to hunting answers.

"No."

"Nothing? Like maybe how we shift?"

"No. I know how you do that. You go *poof* furry and then try to take a chunk out of Lauren. Thank you, but no."

Van grinned. "Baby, I'd like to shift and nibble on you, but that's about it. Wanna know where I'd start?" He extended his legs and crossed them at the ankle. "Now, first, I'd taste those lips. Damn baby, you're so fucking sweet."

Lauren groaned, then growled at him. Too bad she wasn't a werebear. It'd be so damn sexy to have her snarl around his cock.

Speaking of… Thinking of tasting her had his dick hardening within his uniform pants. Coming at her with sexual innuendo would be hell on his prick, but it was better than trying to soothe her fear.

"Do you know where I'd go next?"

"Nowhere because we're not having this conversation. You're gonna take your sometimes furry butt and leave me alone."

"Well, now, you're in my bedroom. How about this? We can be alone together." Another growl and he went rock hard. "Baby, you need to stop or you'll have my cock in your mouth so fast—"

The door whipped open and she glared at him. "There will be no whatchacallits in my mouth or tasting or," she waved his gun around and he stilled, waiting to see if she'd fuck up and pull the trigger. He really didn't feel like getting shot today. "Or anything else." She stomped her foot and dropped her arm to her side. "At all."

"Uh-huh." He let his gaze flick to her hand and he breathed a sigh of relief. Her finger wasn't on the trigger but resting along the side of the barrel. "But I got ya out of the room, didn't I?" He grinned, flashing a wide smile that brought his dimple into play. He didn't try for it often, it made him feel like a kid, but he needed every advantage he could get.

Lauren glared at him some more. "You, are dangerous."

"To your pussy or your health?" He couldn't help nudging her a little. "Did I mention what your moans do to me? The other night… damn, baby."

"Oh!" She turned away and he realized she was ready to slam the door once again.

Without hesitation, he jumped from the ground and pounced, grabbing the wooden panel before she could shove it closed and lock him out. "Now, baby, don't be like that."

She whirled on him, trying for another one of those fierce looks, but he saw beyond her growly exterior. He noted the beginning of tears in her eyes and the way the armed hand trembled. She was pale, color absent from her face, and her breath came in shallow, rapid pants. She was scared as hell and trying not to show it.

"Lauren, come into the living room with me. Let's sit. Talk. Nothing's gonna happen to you, I promise."

Her eyes filled even more. "No, Parker, he…"

A single tear trailed down her cheek.

Shit. He took a chance and reached for her, placing his hand on her shoulder and easing her forward. She resisted at first, refusing to move as he directed, and then she followed his silent command.

Van pulled her into his embrace, enfolding her in his arms as he snuggled her close. He trailed one hand down her arm and wrapped his fingers around the pistol. She released it without complaint.

"It's not loaded," she mumbled into his chest.

He raised an eyebrow, but she couldn't see his expression. "You racked the slide."

She shook her head, rubbing her cheek against him. While she was doing it to say "no," he enjoyed the fact that she rubbed her scent on his body. "No, dropped the mag and emptied the chamber."

Van grinned. "So you held off Keen and kept Anna and Mia captive with an empty gun?"

"Uh-huh."

He grabbed the gun by the grip and tossed it onto the bed, watching it bounce innocuously on the soft surface. He wondered how Lauren would bounce on his mattress.

And… that thought had his cock inflating once again.

Lauren wiggled against him and froze. "You get off on scaring women?" She fought his hold, giving a token protest, and he held her firm.

"No, I get off on holding you. You know I'm attracted to you. In fact, you're gorgeous when you're angry. In the future, I might annoy you just to see your face all flushed." Okay, he was a liar, but he needed to needle her; get her attitude away from scared and over to annoyed.

She huffed. "So, you're a bear?"

"Uh-huh."

"Is there anyone here who isn't a bear?" Her voice was so tiny, a hint of that fear still lingering.

"Anna and Mia. Well, Mia is half werebear, but she can't shift."

"Are they going to attack me? Like Parker?" She shuddered and Van stroked her back, rubbing along her spine in an attempt to soothe her.

"No. Parker is only four. He's got a lot to learn. Plus, he had a rough time of it recently and he's very attached to Mia. If he thinks she's threatened, he attacks. Usually it's another bear, but you're…"

"Human."

"Yes." He swallowed the terror still lingering inside himself. "If he'd gotten a hold of you, Lauren." He leaned down and buried his face against her neck, inhaling her sweet scent and allowing it to calm him. "You'd be scarred. Severely injured."

"Van…" A fear fueled tremor filled her.

"In the last two months he's lost his parents, his uncle attempted to kill him, and that same man nearly killed Mia and Ty. He has issues we're all dealing with. No one else in the clan is like that, Lauren. Ty is a good Itan. Mia is a better Itana, but don't tell her I said so. Our inner-circle is strong."

"Itan? Itana? Inner-circle?" she murmured against him, her smooth cheek rubbing his roughened neck.

"Uh-huh." He couldn't resist the allure of having her so close. He scraped a fang along her throat, restraining his smile when she

110

shivered. "Ty and Mia are in charge, our Itan and Itana. They lead the clan and their word is law."

"What if you didn't like their word?"

That was something he'd never imagined. "It's ingrained in them to do what's best for the clan. But if there was a problem, if they ordered someone to break clan law, then we could go to the Southeast Itan."

"And inner-circle?"

"I'm the Enforcer, I'm essentially the clan cop. Keen is our Keeper, or Keeper of the Knowledge. He knows every law and uses that to help Ty when it comes to doling out justice and determining a sentence. He also handles security both physical and electronic. Isaac recently left, but he was our Healer."

Lauren breathed him in, her breasts pressing against his chest and he couldn't wait to suck her nipples deep into his mouth. Her pretty sounds from last evening surged forward in his memories.

"Wow."

Van didn't have an answer to that, so he remained silent, enjoying her in his arms while she worked through everything she'd been told. He knew it was a lot of information. He couldn't imagine coming to terms with the existence of werebears. All his life he'd known there was another race. This was being dumped on Lauren all at once.

"What happens now?" Her voice was so low, he almost missed her question.

"Now… now you decide how you'd like to move forward." He wanted to squirm like a little kid, but remained still. "Clan law states that the only humans allowed to know about us are those mated to bears."

Lauren stiffened in his arms. "What if they're not?"

Van winced. "The threat is dealt with."

111

Her panic surrounded him, bludgeoning him with the acrid scent of her fear. She fought his hold, struggling against him, but like before, he refused to let her free.

"Just listen, Lauren. Wait. Just listen."

"You're gonna… Dealt with… And I…"

He kept hold of her shoulders, but eased her away from his body. "Listen to me." He jostled her slightly, attempting to get her attention. Fuck Ty and fuck the clan laws and just… *fuck*. "Lauren, it doesn't matter. You have a mate. There's nothing to deal with. You'll always have someone at your side, protecting you, cherishing you."

Please don't ask me who. Please don't ask me who. Please don't ask me—

"Who?"

Fuck him sideways.

Van gulped, knowing he couldn't lie to her. "Me."

chapter ten

Me.

Me. Me.

Me. Me. Me.

The single word swirled through her mind, attacking from all sides. Was it an attack, though? Really? Because deep down, in the places she'd long ago locked away, she wanted it to be true. She wanted to belong to someone irrevocably. Hers forever and ever, amen. No take backs. Hers.

Van was gone now. He'd left her in his room, snuggled with one of his blankets in the window seat. It, too, looked out on the lake. He said every room was planned to have the best view possible. He'd done that job well. It was a different view, an alternate angle, but no less gorgeous.

She tapped the glass, tracing the trees with her finger as she stared at nothing in particular. Her mind whirled with all the new knowledge.

Mates.

Fated mates.

Cubs.

Forever.

Destined.

Dealt with.

She'd made him spell out that aspect and it was as bad as she imagined. Full humans who knew of werebears were silenced through death unless they were mated to a bear. There were suspicions, of course. Humans could make up whatever nonsense they wanted. But if they *knew* then the law applied.

Lauren really, really knew now.

Which brought her back to mates and fated mates. And the difference.

She gulped, swallowing past the knot in her throat. He'd said she was his fated mate. His and his alone. Destined to be together.

She wasn't so sure. At least, not yet.

Which was why Van left her snug in his room while he went to his brother's house. He had to speak to the Itan as the clan's Enforcer with the Keeper at his side. Politics, posturing, and a little begging, he'd said.

She cursed herself for resisting. Damned herself for not jumping into his arms and screaming, "Yes, please!" That's what Anna had essentially done, right?

No, the difference was Anna refused to mate until she was officially divorced. She didn't want to tie herself to Martin unless she was legally free to do so. They wouldn't sleep together, would engage in "carnal relations" until Bryson no longer had his hooks in her.

That was the distinction between their situations. Anna said yes, soon. Lauren said no, but maybe yes… eventually.

She ached to say yes now. He was gorgeous. Hands down, he was the sexiest man she'd ever seen. But he was also protective as hell.

Fierce when it came to someone terrorizing her. She idly wondered if that level of ferocity was limited to her or if it applied to everyone. She thought back to the darkness of his eyes. Back to the hint of scruff she'd attributed to not shaving. In reality, his "bear" was threatening to come out and play.

Then there was the way her body seemed to call for his.

Could he be…? Should she …?

Shaking her head, she pushed the worry aside for now. She'd know more when Van got back from his meeting. There was no sense in rolling it through her mind over and over again, until she had facts. Hopefully, they'd have a little time to get to know one another before she had to open herself to him that way.

Lauren focused on the distance once again, watching the trees sway with the wind, dancing for her. Movement amongst them drew her attention and her heart rate picked up. He'd told her not to be surprised about bears in the area as it was common for clan members to hang around. The clan grounds were the one place they freely moved in their shifted forms.

She strained to see if a bear lingered in the forest. Except… except it was that wolf she'd seen earlier. Wasn't it? The animal stared at the house, his gaze seeming to focus on her. It didn't scan its surroundings. Nope, it only had eyes for her.

Weird. Were there werewolves? Probably, now that she thought about it. If there were bears, there was nothing that said shapeshifters were limited to one species. She'd have to ask Van when he returned.

The wolf darted from view, disappearing into the forest. At the same time, the front door of the house opened, the sound of it granting someone entrance reaching her with ease in the quiet house.

The heavy cadence of Van's stomps told her he'd returned. A hint of fear assaulted her. Even if Van told her not to worry, she couldn't help herself. There was a chance she'd be "dealt with."

He drew closer with each passing second, growing nearer and nearer until he was framed in the doorway. His hair was mussed, strands sticking up in different directions. His cheeks were even darker, the beginnings of a beard coating his face.

She rubbed her own cheeks. "Your bear?"

He gave her a half-smile. "We yell a lot. Get hot." He stepped into the room and slowly approached her. "How are you?"

"Fine." She gave voice to the question spinning through her mind. "What's going on?"

He eased onto the other end of the window seat and she finally had a good look at him. He appeared to have aged fifty years in the last hour. Worry lines were deeply carved into his face and she grimaced, knowing it was her fault.

"Well, we only have a couple of options at this point." He sighed and ran his hand over his face. "One: Ty 'deals with' you."

Lauren immediately shook her head as trembles overtook her body. "I don't wanna… I don't…"

Van pounced, grabbing her and cuddling her against his body, forcing her to sit sideways across his lap. She didn't fight the hold, instead burrowing further into his arms. "Hush. I told him that wasn't happening. I'd run with you before I let that happen."

"What else is there?"

"You can mate a bear."

A bear. Not him, but *a bear.* "Who?"

"That's where your choice comes in. You can allow yourself to be courted. There are plenty of clan members who would happily take you to mate, Lauren. Plenty of good, honest men who would treat you well." A growl filled each word and she knew he wasn't thrilled with that option.

116

"Or?"

"Or you agree to be mine. We're fated mates, whether you accept that right now or not. If you agree, it doesn't mean we consummate our mating this second. We have time. Not a lot, but time to get to know one another before taking that step. Like others, you'd be courted. The difference is I wouldn't be competing with anyone for your heart." He tightened his hold. "It'd only be me trying to get into your bed."

Lauren smiled against him. "You'll get into my bed quicker than my heart."

He shrugged. "I'll take what I can get at this point. Does that mean…?"

"I don't want anyone else to court me. You. Only you."

He relaxed against her, and she realized he questioned whether she'd choose him or not. How could he have doubted? The man was a catch and a half, even if he was a bear.

"Good. That's good." He gently squeezed her. "So, what are you doing for dinner?"

"You." She grinned and pressed her face against his chest, hiding her smile. A sudden hardness dug into her ass and she realized how much the single word affected him.

"You can't say things like that. The bear is thrilled you're giving us a chance." He rubbed her hip and smacked it lightly. "No poking the bear."

She chuckled outright. "You're all roar and no bite and you know it."

He heaved a heavy sigh. "When it comes to you, you're right. Seriously though, Ty invited us over for dinner and Parker wants to apologize."

She stiffened at the mention of the boy's name, memories of his small teeth digging into Keen's arm assaulting her with vivid clarity. "I don't... I can't..."

"Hush. It's okay. Dinner's not for a couple of hours. Think about it. Anna's there now with Martin. Talk to her. You'll see he's a four year old boy who had a temper tantrum."

Lauren snorted. "A human kid's temper tantrums don't scar people for life."

He didn't have a response. Simply stayed quiet.

She didn't want to talk about this, stress over this when they had so much other crap to deal with. She stroked the hair on his jaw, noting the fine strands and it brought another question to mind. A safe question that didn't involve sharp teeth and vulnerable flesh. "Hey, Van, are there werewolves too? I mean, here on clan lands?" He stilled for a moment and she tilted her head back to look at him. "Or is it just bears?"

"There are wolves in Redby, why?"

She shrugged. "I saw a wolf in the woods. I wondered..."

He squeezed her for a moment and she watched his eyes darken to fully black. She now knew that meant his bear was near the surface. "Show me where." He stared at her with those eerie, deadly orbs. "Now."

*

Van followed the gentle sway of Lauren's ass as she strode over the grass and toward the tree line. Other guards were on their way, all of them in skin since she hadn't been around full grown bears yet. A few grumbled about wearing clothes because they spent most of their time in fur, but he demanded they obey.

It didn't take long for them to get to the place she'd pointed out. She paused ten feet out as he'd asked. He didn't want her scent marring any of those left by this wolf she'd spied.

Rage burned in his gut, churning and swirling inside him. He had to work with the wolves. Fine. But that didn't give them permission to waltz onto their land unannounced and without permission. Ty was just as angry, just as enraged over the trespass. They both assumed it was someone from Redby.

Van slid alongside his Lauren. His Lauren. She belonged to him. True, he had a lot of wooing to get through, but she was giving him a chance and that was all he needed. He'd win her over and snatch her heart when she wasn't looking.

He stroked her back as he passed her. "Thank you, baby. Stay right here."

"Okay." She remained in her spot as he approached the area. He sensed his fellow bears closing in on their location and he glanced back at his mate.

She spied them, too. He'd left her directly behind him, but she eased further away from his position and the approaching males as the clan members grew closer. He'd have to work with her on her fear.

One thing at a time.

First was the intruder.

Van drew in the air, pulling it deep into his lungs. He caught the scent of other bears, clan members that belonged in the area. But beneath that… He drew in another lungful, tasting the scents with his tongue.

"Enforcer?" Ash's deep voice intruded on his thoughts.

"There's something here." Van turned his gaze to the ground, hunting for any tracks that'd identify their visitor. Nothing. "Just not sure what. Something's masking the wolf's identity."

Ash grunted. The man was one of the loudest to object showing up in skin. "You could get a better scent if…"

"Yeah, yeah." He waved away the guard's words.

"If what?" Lauren's lyrical voice washed over him.

"Nothing, baby. Do you wanna go back to the house?" He turned to her, taking in her twisted, twined fingers and the way she seemed to have folded in on herself.

"No," she shook her head rapidly. "But what does he mean?"

He sighed and glared at the guard, ignoring his smug look. "If I shift, I'll get a better hold on the scent. I can get a lot with my human nose, but the bear is better at sorting through everything." Wide panicked eyes met his while her chest rose and fell in rapid succession. "It's fine, baby. Stay put for a minute and then we'll go back to the house."

She was quiet for a moment, wide eyes centered on him, and then she squared her shoulders while she set her jaw and gave him a determined expression. "Is it just you? Shifting?"

He stared at her, hunting her face and trying his best to discern her expression. Oh, a hell of a lot of fear circled her, but he recognized her resolve. "Yes, just me, baby."

"O-okay then. You can… Should I…? I don't know…"

Van gave her a small smile. "I need to strip and then I'll shift. You can watch or turn your back, baby. Whatever makes you comfortable."

He wanted her to watch though, wanted to show her his strength. The bear snarled at him for giving her a choice, but it recognized Van made the right decision in providing her with options.

Lauren licked her lips, pink tongue darting out to lick the plump flesh. Damn, he wanted to follow the action with his tongue, chase it into her mouth and swallow her flavors. Fuck. That thought had his cock twitching in his jeans. He hoped like hell she decided to hold on to her modesty and turn around. The last thing he wanted to do was strip and have her get a look at his dick when he couldn't do anything with it.

He glanced at Ash and noted the man's smirk. The asshole knew Van's condition. Dick.

"I'll…" She spun, not finishing her sentence.

Van rolled his eyes and got to stripping, tearing off his shirt while slipping off his shoes. Jeans and boxers were next. The moment he was nude, he let the shift wash over him, let the bear come out to play and take over.

Arms lengthened, legs thickened, hands became paws while his skull reshaped and mouth transformed into a snout. Dark brown fur sprouted from his pores and within seconds he went from a two-hundred-plus human to a several hundred pound bear.

Van chuffed and snuffled, his bear urging her to turn and face him.

Slowly, Lauren did as he quietly asked, taking her time as she turned toward him. A low gasp was the first indication that she caught sight of his shifted form. The moment she had that first glimpse, she spun around fully. Mouth agape, she stared at him, wide-eyed. She didn't utter another sound, simply stood still, her gaze locked on his bear.

Was she disgusted? Awed? Scared?

Van drew in a deep breath, tasting the scents on the air, hunting through the aromas for hers. The bear caught them with ease, identifying tendrils of fear and an overpowering sense of curiosity and wonder. No, she definitely wasn't scared stiff.

"Van?" She took a step closer and Ash held out his hand, closing the distance between him and Lauren.

Hell no, the bear didn't like that. He swung his head toward the unmated male, curling his lip, and exposing a fang. He didn't utter a sound, afraid of frightening his mate, but he wanted to get his point across.

Ash immediately stilled and held up his hands. "No need to get mad. I don't want her contaminating the scene, Enforcer."

Van glared at the other bear and relaxed. The man had a point, but he didn't need to touch Lauren to get it across.

Chuffing, he returned his attention to Lauren and padded toward her, his paws sinking into the soft earth. He approached slowly, unwilling to frighten her with his presence. He knew his size had to be intimidating, especially considering the scare she'd had earlier in the day. When a mere four feet separated them, he paused, gauging her reaction. Still, she was filled with wonderment and excitement.

He moved closer still, slowly easing forward. The moment he was within touching distance, her hands were on him, fingers sliding over his muzzle and stroking his ears. He nuzzled her palms, earning a giggle when his cold nose rubbed her digits.

"Oh god. Van?"

He nodded, showing her that he remained cognizant when in shifted form. He wasn't a mindless beast when his bear had control.

"Gorgeous." She released the word with a soft sigh.

Van lowered to his haunches, sitting on the ground and doing his best to remain a passive participant in the encounter.

Lauren took his quiet acquiescence as the invitation he'd intended. She eased to his side, fingers digging into his thick fur, stroking and petting him as no other had before. "Wow. Just, wow."

She continued circling him, palms exploring his animal's body, handling him and caressing him with her gentle touches. Any hint of fear she'd harbored washed away with her joy.

She ended her circle at his head once again, fingers toying with his right ear. "You're beautiful."

Ash released a choked laugh and Lauren defended him before he could release his snarl. "Do you want him to hand you your ass?

How about me? I may not be able to take you in a fight, but it doesn't take claws to hold a gun, dick head."

If he'd been a human, his cock would have gone hard at her threat. Yes, she was the perfect mate to an Enforcer, the clan's protector.

Van chuffed and nuzzled her, rubbing her side with his snout and trying to get her attention.

She turned on him with a frown. "What? He's a jerk."

He poked her stomach with his nose and then looked behind him before returning his attention to her. He had a job to do. One that involved finding out who'd trespassed on their territory. Then he'd know if there was anyone he needed to kill.

She nodded. "I understand. You need to see who it was. Then we can talk more about this." She stroked his ear again. The woman seemed to have a fascination with that part of him.

He kinda wished she'd fall in love with a place south of the border.

With an animalistic sigh, he turned and headed toward the spot. With any luck, the trespasser was Morgan and he could challenge the wolf, fight to the death, and then that annoyance would be gone. Wouldn't that be awesome?

Van breathed deep, sorting through the scents and huffed. No such luck. He still didn't recognize the scent.

chapter **eleven**

Lauren leaned against Van's porch railing, watching the sun set lazily. In the distance, Parker played in Ty's yard, the small boy shifting from human to cub and back again in an instant. Ty—*the Itan*— retained his human shape as he played with the four year old.

Watching them, seeing the way they played, laughed, and giggled, reminded her that deep inside, Parker was just a boy. A dangerous boy, but she couldn't deny he was sweeter than words.

Especially after they returned from snooping around the woods and Mia dragged Parker to Van's house by the ear and demanded he apologize. He'd snuffled and whined, but eventually said he was sorry and he promised he wouldn't ever try to eat her again.

That little episode ended with confirmation of dinnertime and Mia assuring Parker that cookies *were not* in his immediate future.

She grinned at the memory of his crestfallen face and the beginnings of tears in his eyes. Just a boy.

Chuckling, she leaned against one of the support posts. She relaxed as she waited for Van to finish his shower. Shifting took a lot out of him and he'd needed a snack and shower to feel like himself again. Then they'd walk to Ty's and she'd be introduced to some of the other clan members. As long as she wasn't "dealt with," this place would be her home soon. She needed to meet and mingle with the other residents, the other bears.

She really didn't want to do that.

Then again, she didn't want to be "dealt with" either.

Nope, all she *wanted* to do was sit around Van's gorgeous home and get to know him, find out what made him tick, and figure out if she could come to love him someday.

She wasn't going to address that she was at least one-third in love with him already. He was sweet when he wasn't being bossy, and sexy as hell, and he turned into a fuzzy *bear* for goodness sakes. How was that not awesome?

A man came strolling around the corner of the house, his strides eating up the ground as he approached her. A smile was plastered across his lips, but it didn't quite reach his eyes. A shiver raced down her spine and she measured the distance between her and the door. There was something there, something that made her stomach tie into a knot.

The closer he drew, the better she could see him and she recognized him as one of the men who'd been near the forest with her and Van.

"Hey there. Lauren, right?" His stride was slow and easy, but she felt like prey.

"Yes. I didn't get your name, though." She stepped away from the rail. Fight or flight pushed at her. At the moment, fight had taken a vacation, and flight was all about stepping up to the plate.

His smile widened and she noticed that the irises that were once blue were now nearing black. Oh, so not good.

"Charles. My friends call me Charlie." He placed one booted foot on the bottom porch step.

She took another stride toward the door. She'd left it unlocked, figuring she was stepping outside for a mere moment. She needed distance to keep her from jumping into the shower with Van.

"Why don't you call me Charlie?" He climbed another step.

Lauren glanced behind her, counting the feet between her and the door. Her heart raced, pumping adrenaline through her body. He hadn't done anything overt to her, but she didn't trust him. Didn't trust his easy smile and sweet-as-pie approach.

"Maybe," she licked her lips, internally shuddering as his gaze traced the action. She took another step back. Another glance toward the door revealed she was within four feet of her destination. Good. This guy creeped her the fuck out.

She turned back to Charles and jumped, releasing a scream. He stood inches from her, his massive frame occupying her vision and surrounding her with his presence. His broad chest filled her gaze, a hint of his skin revealed by the shirt. His bear's fur pushed through his pores and a wave of fear overpowered her.

She stumbled back a step, fighting to put distance between them. She didn't want another male close to her. She didn't want another bear touching her or breathing her freakin' air for that matter.

"Hey there." His voice was deep, barely more than a growl. She let her gaze flick to his face and caught the leer plastered across his features.

"Hi-hi." She couldn't suppress her stutter. "I'm gonna-I'm gonna-I'm…" She swallowed the next round of repeated words. She was so fucked.

Charles brought his hand up, palm nearing her face, and she froze, unable to move. "You're so pretty." His voice came out with a gravely rumble. Van told her it was from the bear. That when it was close to the edge, it pushed some of its characteristics on the man. "And you know about us."

She really wished she'd stayed ignorant if it meant not being approached by some weird bear.

"Um…"

His fingers neared her cheek, then his goal changed to her neck, his hand lowering ever so slightly. "I bet you're soft."

Inches separated their bodies while his digits hovered barely a centimeter from her skin. She couldn't move, couldn't force her body into motion. Damn it.

Then it didn't matter. Not one bit. Van's massive body nudged her back and he stood between her and Charles, his broad shoulders filling her vision and cutting her off from the other bear. She hadn't heard his approach, hadn't even heard the front door open, but he was there to protect her.

A growl rolled through her, Van's deep tenor embracing her as he threatened the other male. "You've got balls, Charlie."

"She's not claimed," the bear countered.

"She's as good as mine and you know it, the clan knows it."

Charles growled and she heard the familiar snap of bone indicating the man was not a happy bear.

Crap. Crap. Crap.

"You really wanna do that?" Van's voice still held the growl of his bear, but it was also calm and quiet. Too quiet. "Think about who's standing in front of you."

Another snap. "I'm the stronger bear, Enforcer."

Van cracked his neck, his body loose and fur free. "Really?" His shoulders broadened, widening while his biceps thickened. "You wanna test that?" He flexed his hands and those fingertips were deadly claws. "If you keep going, I'll take you down and it won't be pretty."

Take him down…

"She's unclaimed. Every male has the right—"

"She's mine," Van roared and the floor shook with the lingering vibrations.

"I'll win and then—"

No. No way.

"Stop it," she grabbed the back of Van's shirt and tugged. "Make him stop. I don't want to be his." Panic assaulted her. They'd fight over her? Hadn't she made her choice? "I told you, Van. I don't…" She fought for breath, demanded her body draw air into her lungs.

Without turning, he reached back and hauled her forward until she was plastered to his back. She took comfort in the touch, reassurance in the feel of his body against hers. She wrapped her arms around his waist, holding him close.

"She made her choice, Charlie. Don't make me do something we'll both regret." She heard the reluctance in Van's voice. He didn't really want to fight the other bear, but he would if pushed.

"She's not claimed. Any—" Charles pushed that same argument forward, slapping her in the face with the truth.

She'd selected Van, hadn't she? She'd essentially proclaimed her choice for one and all. She just hadn't followed through with the rest of the process. It wasn't like she was going to back out now. Agreeing to be wooed simply delayed the inevitable.

Maybe she didn't need the full course of woo-age. She licked her lips, mind tumbling through the possibilities. No, she didn't *really* need weeks of dates. Maybe one really, really good one so she wasn't so panicked at the idea of baring herself to him fully.

Lauren fisted Van's shirt while she buried her face against his back. He didn't deserve to get into a bloody fight because she was afraid of the truth. "I'm his. I belong to Van."

Silence reigned and she thought Charles got the clue.

"She's still unclaimed and knows about us. That means—"

Apparently not.

Taking a deep breath, she released Van and looked around her large shifter. She glared at Charles, ignoring his half-shifted face and the abundance of fur that coated his features. She'd freak out about his appearance later.

"I. Belong. To. Van. Period." He didn't show any acknowledgement of her words. "Do you understand? I'm his. He's mine."

"The law—"

This time she bared her little human teeth at him. It was probably funny as hell when she considered she wasn't a danger to him at all. "Does it say that the minute you say the words 'we're mates' you have to fuck and claim your woman? Do not pass go, do not grab a condom?"

Charles reared back, his eyes going wide. "She…"

"Has a mind of her own and has stated her choice." Ty's voice overrode the other bear and his presence had an instant effect on Charles.

The man went from cocky dickhead to deflated man in a blink, the fur receding and his face reshaping to adopt his human form. One minute he was a half-beast and the next he was as human as could be.

Lauren turned to Ty, to the man who could halt a tense situation in its tracks.

"Charles? We'll talk in the morning." The Itan—because he was the embodiment of power at that moment—dismissed the other bear.

Charles strode down the porch steps without a word and passed Ty, tilting his head to the side. It was a sign of respect, submission, Van had called it.

It was instinctual in bears, the desire to submit to those stronger. She wondered if she'd ever feel the same.

The moment the other bear disappeared from sight, his path taking him around the side of the house, Ty looked back to them. "I saw him come up. Thought you might need a little help."

Van eased her forward and wrapped his arm around her shoulders. "Thanks. I could have taken him, though."

Ty shrugged. "My way involves less blood. Plus, we're down a Healer. Don't want to bury a bear because he's an idiot."

"Van's not—"

The Itan laughed and shook his head. "Sometimes, yes, but today I'm talking about Charles. A human woman who knows and accepts bears is a big draw to some. He wouldn't have to bother with revealing his nature. Plus the law requires…" He shrugged. "It's a good deal for a desperate man."

Van stilled, his body going stiff against her. "How desperate?"

"Yeah, how desperate?" she echoed Van. How on guard would she have to be? Would he ra…?

Ty shook his head. "Not like that. He'd have *encouraged* you to spend time with him. Not…" The Itan rubbed his cheek. "It'd be good if you two figure things out between yourselves. Sooner rather than later." He sighed. "Or I don't know how many times I'll be here repeating myself." Ty looked to them. "Maybe it'd be best if she lived in the clan house while you two settle things?"

"No." They spoke in unison, their denials instant.

Lauren knew Van wanted her near, he'd said as much through words and deed. And she… she dug deep into her soul, crept into the hidden recesses where she'd tucked away her feelings, and urged them toward the light. She'd given up on love a long time ago. Who needed love when it didn't put food on the table?

But here, safe in Van's arms, she wondered if love was an emotion she should tug out of hiding and dust off. Put it on and see how it fit.

Van's gaze weighed heavily on her, blanketing her with hope and need. She ignored his stare and kept her attention on Ty, on his curious expression.

"No, I'd prefer to stay here."

"Until you—"

She cut the Itan off. "It'll be resolved. Soon."

Van stiffened, a new tension thrumming through his body with her statement. His fingers dug into her flesh, the digits squeezing her tight.

"Really?" Ty raised a single brow.

"As soon as you leave."

Van's brother gave her an appraising look, one that weighed her and judged her sincerity. Finally, he nodded. "All right. I'll tell Mia we'll see you at breakfast."

Lauren licked her lips, a hint of panic starting to set in. Okay, saying the words in her head, and even out loud, was a lot easier than hearing what she'd committed to. Oh, shit.

Did she want this? Fuck of a time to change her mind or worry about it now.

She shook her head at Ty. "No, tomorrow at dinner."

The Itan grinned, a snapshot of what he was like as a boy peeking past the leader's exterior. "All right." He nodded. "Tomorrow at dinner."

*

Tomorrow at dinner.

Tomorrow at dinner.

Van heard the words, the syllables clanging through his mind, but their meaning hadn't quite set in yet.

Tomorrow at dinner.

Which meant…

Holy shit.

Ty left them, his ground-eating stride taking him back to his own home. Which left him shocked to his soles with Lauren in his arms.

Tomorrow at dinner.

"Van?" Her voice was quiet, softer than he'd ever heard and unsure as hell.

He tightened his hold on her, wrapping his other arm around her waist while he buried his face in her hair. He drew in her scents, absorbed every nuance and sorted through them.

Trepidation. Worry. Excitement. He took a deep breath. And arousal.

"Lauren." He released her name on a husky sigh. "My Lauren."

Her trembling hands stroked his arms, sliding over lightly furred skin and he realized his bear hadn't yet retreated. He couldn't overwhelm her with shifter-hued sex yet.

Then another question popped into his mind. "Lauren, you need to tell me what you want. Before we go into the house, I need to know what will happen once we close the door."

She pressed a cheek to his chest and he felt the heat from her skin as she blushed. "Whatever happens when bears, you know, claim their mate."

He forced his grip to remain comfortable to her human body. "Normally, a couple…" Fucks? Makes love? Bumps uglies? "They have sex and while they come, they bite each other to solidify their mating. It's painful, which is why they do it when they're overcome with pleasure. Most say that the bite makes the pleasure that much better."

Lauren's breathing picked up, her lungs working faster than before. Damn it, he should have said that some other way. He didn't know how, but now she was… He scented the air once again. She was… aroused. Hotter and wetter than before. He bet if he slid his hand between her thighs, they'd be coated in her sweet cream.

Then again, being excited wasn't permission to do anything.

"Lauren? What are you thinking?" He had to know. He couldn't move forward unless he knew she wasn't about to hunt down one of his guns and use it on him.

"Do we…? Is that the only way…?"

Oh, he could think of so many ways to take her, make love to her. Not all of them involved his cock in her pussy. Those were just the best ones. Others included her coming on his tongue or his fingers or a toy or…

"I can bite you," he reached up and brushed her hair aside, exposing her shoulder. "Right here," he circled a patch of skin. "Without doing much more than we're doing now. It'll hurt though. My bear's teeth will sink deep. It wants to make sure you're fully claimed, that you're ours."

"What else?"

Van nipped her earlobe and then licked away the hurt. He brushed his lips over the shell of her ear. "If you're not ready for my cock, I can lick your pussy, suck on your clit until you're coming, and then claim you." Lauren shuddered. "I can slip my fingers into your cunt. You can ride my hand while I sink my teeth into your shoulder." He skimmed her neck with his teeth. "The claiming is one of the most erotic, beautiful things a couple can share. It can be fast and fierce or sweet and gentle." More of her cream soaked her panties, the air filling with the musky, salty scent of her arousal. "Which do you want, Lauren? Is that even what you want? Tell me. I'll give you whatever you desire. Just say the words."

He needed her to voice her wants, but he also needed them before he took another step or allowed himself to touch her further. Fifty years from now, he didn't want to listen to some "when we mated..." speech. He mentally shook his head. No, that wasn't the truth. The truth was he always wanted her to trust him and this was a first step in that direction. There, he'd bared his pussy-assed soul already.

"I don't know if I can." She trembled, but he didn't taste the sour tang of fear on his tongue. "We just met and," she huffed and pulled her head from him, propping her chin on his chest so they could gaze at one another. He'd been right, her face blazed a bright red from her blush. "I don't know how far I can go. I don't know what I can do with you. It takes a lot of trust to let you inside me that way and we just met each other. But I do want to belong to you. If—" She paused and sucked in a breath, releasing her next words in a rush. "If you still want me."

Van's bear growled, snarling at their mate's unease and questioning their desires. The animal pushed him into motion, urged him to take action, and he listened. With a low rumble, he bent down and grabbed Lauren below her ass. He manhandled her as he desired, spreading her legs while easing forward and placing her on the porch rail. He eased his way between her thighs.

She squeaked and squawked, but he sensed no fear or fight in her. Simply surprise.

Pressed against her heat, the warmth of her pussy bathing him, his cock snapped from half-hard to rock solid. He pushed firmly against her, rocking his fabric-clad dick along her cleft.

"Does that feel like I don't want you, Lauren?" He flexed his hips. "I want you, baby. More than anything, I want you."

"Van," she whispered.

Then her mouth was on his, lips soft and supple while she slid her tongue into him. His bear reacted in an instant, roaring in approval, reveling in her aggression.

She wrapped her arms around his neck, pulling him closer and he did the same, encircling her with his arms while pressing their bodies together. Not an inch separated them, her lush breasts against his chest, her hard nipples teasing him. The seductive flavors of her arousal permeated the air, covering him with her desire.

He wanted to sate her need, her craving.

He let his touch shift to her ass, cupping what he could and kneading the areas he reached. The globes were full and soft, begging to be nibbled and maybe someday… spanked. He'd love to see her butt flushed red for him.

His cock pulsed in his jeans, a shudder of need racing down his spine, and he fought back the urge to come. Damn. He needed to leave those thoughts for after he'd taken the edge off with an orgasm.

Lauren tightened her legs, squeezing him while digging her heels into his ass.

Fuck. Maybe ten orgasms.

Van caught the hem of her shirt and dug his hands beneath the fabric. He needed skin, needed to touch her without a barrier. He wrenched at the garment and finally… ah, his fingers slipped over her silken flesh. He stroked and petted her as their kiss continued. He refused to give up his prize.

He let his touch wander along her spine, tracing the delicate line until he got to her bra. Damn it. He didn't want any barriers. He allowed one finger to shift and transform into a sharpened claw. It took one slice and then the back of that bit of fabric fell away.

Lauren pulled away from him, sucking in a harsh breath. "Van." She shuddered, panting against his lips, imbuing him with her scent. "We-we should go inside."

He wanted to say, "Fuck yeah." Instead, he simply said, "Yes."

No sense in scaring her with his intensity before they were tied together for eternity.

chapter twelve

Lauren trembled from head to toe, her legs shaking. She allowed Van to help her down from the railing, didn't protest as he led her through his home. They passed the familiar walls, decorations she'd traced with her fingers not long ago, and the places that held new, frightening memories.

And yet, with Van at her side, it meant nothing. No matter what, he wouldn't let anything scare her or allow anyone to hurt her. He was hers, lock, stock, and big scary teeth.

Even knowing about his inner-bear, she wasn't afraid of him. He'd already proven he held control over the animal, that it wouldn't hurt her when it came out. It'd taken her petting pretty well.

He was also ready to fight for her, going claw to claw with another bear to keep her, keep her safe.

So, he got a little furry now and again. So, what?

Van led her into his bedroom. He released her hand and reached around her to softly close the door. Her gaze drifted over the massive, wood-framed bed and other furniture that matched. She ignored the discarded clothes and carelessly dropped towel. Considering the state of the room when she'd last seen it, she figured he must have thrown everything aside to hurry to her. Her attention swayed to the open bathroom door, hints of the gleaming tile visible.

Okay, maybe the "so what" was a tad premature.

Overwhelmed, she wobbled a little. "Van?"

He pressed his front to her back, wrapping his arms around her waist, and she took the comfort he offered. "Right here. I've got you. You're safe."

Oh. Right. That's what she was feeling. The tight chest, thundering heart, blood racing through her veins. Panic. A panic attack. Air heaved in and out of her lungs. The oxygen was there, but her body didn't want to absorb it.

"We shouldn't do this," Van murmured against her hair before dropping a soft kiss to her head. "You're still—"

Lauren shook her head. She wasn't a child. She just needed… "I'm fine." She turned in his arms, stared into his midnight eyes. It seemed his bear hung out close to the surface more and more. "Show me that you can love me. Take away the fear. I know it's irrational—"

"Baby, there's nothing irrational about being afraid of a predator. Nothing. In a fight between a human and a bear, even a cub, the human isn't the one winning. You should never look down on yourself for having a good dose of fear when it comes to us."

She weighed each word, saw the sincerity in his gaze, and nodded. She'd felt so stupid for freaking out over a child. A kid, she was scared of a kid. With super sharp teeth.

"Claim me," she whispered, begging.

His skin darkened while a new heat burned in his gaze. "Mine."

Van backed her up, forcing her to retreat and shuffled across the room until her legs collided with the bed. Even then, he nudged her, sending her flopping onto the soft surface.

"Mine." He bared his teeth, his canines a hint longer and sharper than before.

140

A shiver snaked down her spine. Of fear? Desire? Terror? Need?

God, all of the above.

He licked his lips and she recalled his taste, the warmth, sweetness and heat that came from his mouth. She took him in with her eyes, letting her attention drift over his muscular body. Starting at his shoulders, she slowly meandered until she got to the bulge between his thighs.

Would his cock be as delicious?

She ached to find out.

"Lauren?"

A blush stole over her cheeks at being caught staring and she returned her attention to his face. "Huh?"

"Are you sure?" Questions lurked in his gaze, inquiries that stretched beyond. "Are you sure you want to do this?"

Are you sure you want me?

Are you sure about belonging to a bear?

Are you sure…?

"Yes." She nodded to punctuate her agreement. She moved her hands to the button of her shorts, toying with the button for a moment before un-snapping it. She lowered the zipper, easing it down and then spreading the two flaps. "I'm sure."

His eyes were pure black, nothing of the human half of Van visible in his gaze. He was all bear. He fisted his hands, uncurling and curling them, while his body remained still as stone.

"Van?" She hooked her fingers in the waist of her shorts and nudged them lower. Not a lot, but enough to expose another inch of skin. She could go this far. She could bare part of herself to him.

She wasn't sure if she was ready for his penis in her vagina.

Oh god, she mentally rolled her eyes. Had that thought really drifted through her mind? Lame.

Lame or not, it didn't remove the hint of fear at exposing herself that way. Hands, mouths, they were intimate, but him being inside her was so much *more*.

"Lauren." He drew in a ragged breath. "I need you. Crave you."

She got her hands beneath her and wiggled toward the center of the bed. Sitting there, she reached down and grasped the hem of her top. She whipped it over her head, her destroyed bra going along with it. "Then claim me."

Breasts bare to the room, the cool air caused her nipples to pebble and harden in preparation of his lips.

"Damn, baby." He whipped his thin, worn shirt off as well, exposing his body to her gaze. Muscle after muscle drew her attention, the rippling strength holding her captive. She counted his abs, gaze sliding farther south with each rise and fall of his muscles.

Carved lines at his hips disappeared beneath his jeans. That had her wondering what else lurked underneath the fabric. The bulge at the juncture of his thighs was large, hinting at the size of his cock, but that didn't tell her if he was cut or uncut. Whether he was long and thick or long and thin. Fuck it, she didn't care.

She wanted….

Crap, she had to decide what she wanted. A taste? A touch? More? Less?

He toyed with the button of his jeans, fingers flicking the small bit of metal. "Baby?"

She tore her gaze from his groin and back to his face. Trepidation, worry, and desire warred for dominance, but she focused on his need. "You'll stop? If I say…?"

"If you even hint at saying the word 'no,' I'll stop. It'll always be at your pace, baby."

She recognized the sincerity in his gaze and nodded. "Strip for me."

She didn't recognize the hoarse voice from her throat. Didn't recognize the low timber and sex filled syllables.

"Anything." And then he was bare, fully nude and exposed to her gaze.

Note to self: long, thick, and cut.

Those lines at his hips traveled south and framed his cock, presenting it to her on a metaphorical platter. Yum.

Van stroked his shaft, fingers wrapping around the base, sliding over his skin to the tip. He repeated the caress, a gentle glide up and then down. When he neared the head, he gathered the droplets of pre-cum and used the moisture to ease his path.

What would he taste like?

The question had a shudder of want traveling through her. He'd be hot and tinged with a hint of salty, musky male. His other hand came into play, the palm cupping his balls and gently squeezing.

She whimpered and shifted, her pussy silently begging for his touch. More of her cream escaped, slickening her lower lips and soaking her panties. She was so wet for him, so hot and desperate for him.

Her mouth watered at the idea of tasting him, of running her tongue over every inch of his body and discovering every rise and fall of muscle.

"Lauren, you can't do things like that?"

"Like what?" She couldn't tear her eyes away from the seductive picture before her, of the way he stroked his cock and squeezed his shaft.

"Like that. Makes me think you want more than a quick orgasm and a bite." Another droplet of pre-cum joined the others.

Damn.

"A slow orgasm? With lots of touching? Just no…"

Van released his cock and leaned over the bed, placing one knee and then another on the soft mattress as he crawled toward her. "Anything, everything, nothing. It's all on you, baby."

She liked reaffirmation. Enjoyed the power she held.

"I want to touch you." She'd never been so brave, so ballsy, and stated exactly what she desired.

His skin rippled, a hint of fur appearing on his arms and then just as quickly disappearing. "How?"

"C'mere." She eased over and patted the space beside her.

He was there in an instant, his lean body spread alongside her. Lauren didn't wait for an invitation. He'd said "anything" so she hoped he meant it.

She reached out and stroked his chest, running her fingers over his warm skin. A wave of his bear's fur followed her touch and immediately receded. Like the bear wanted to kiss her fingertips, but knew it was time for their human bodies to come together. She liked that idea—the bear knew how important this time was to them all.

She stroked his pecs, fingers nearing his nipples, and the nubs hardened with her approach. This was it, her first "sexual" touch of his body and nerves assaulted her.

If she did *this*, would he expect *that?* She froze, drifting into the abyss of "what ifs."

"Baby?" His warm hand covered hers and she shifted her attention to his face. "Whatever you want, however you want. Something or nothing. I want you to touch me any way you want, get comfortable with my body. And I won't touch any part of you without your permission." He settled against the mattress, his hands folded beneath his head. "I'm yours."

Lauren stared at him, weighing his words combined with his passive position and decided to take him at face value. He hadn't done anything to earn her fear. Well, other than being a bear shifter.

She began her travels once again, stroking his chest until she neared his nipple. The small nub hardened further as she circled it with her finger, drawing a tiny shudder from Van. She smiled, happy she'd drawn that reaction from him. Yes, she aroused him.

Speaking of arousal…

Lauren traced the ridges of his abdomen. With every inch down his body, her heart rate picked up, the muscle pounding out an unsteady rhythm. She counted the carved layers of muscle. One, two, three… Most men she knew had a "six pack," but Van had eight that eventually led to a smooth expanse of hardened flesh above his cock.

Her gaze went with her touch, eyes following her path and finally settling on her destination.

His cock was thick and long, hard and firm as it rose from the shortly cropped hair at his groin. She teased the beginnings of the light fuzz, fingers toying with the short strands while she pondered her next move. She spared a glance for his face and noted the restrained desire in his features. His entire body was tense as if he were on edge, waiting to be released from his self-imposed prison.

"Whatever you want, baby." The words were filled with his bear's growl, but she understood him nonetheless.

Refocusing on her task, she eased closer to him, pressing her curved body along his side. She wanted the added intimacy, the additional nearness as she touched him. Laying her head on his chest, she grew comfortable in her position.

Breasts against his chest and waist snug against his, she let her touch wander once again. She sifted her fingers through the short strands and finally stroked the base of his cock. She teased a single inch of his flesh, rubbing back and forth.

Van's breathing increased to shallow pants, his chest heaving with every breath. Enjoying her power over him, she pushed further. She wrapped her hand around his girth, encircling him with her fingers, and then carefully stroked his shaft. She eased from the base, along his length, and finally paused at the tip before retracing her path.

"Baby." He growled the words past clenched teeth. His body was a study in tension-filled lines. "Lauren."

She sensed the need in him and it furthered her own. With each tug on his cock, her pussy clenched. With his slow slide down, it released more of her cream. Her body was prepared for him, slick and ready to have him deep inside her.

But not yet. Soon.

Van spread his legs and soon his hips joined the rhythm of her caresses. He thrust into the circle of her hand, increasing the force and tempo of her playing.

He pushed harder and her clit twitched, he moved faster and her nipples hardened. Her body was a ball of need and want, and all due to Van.

Luscious, gorgeous Van.

She continued jacking him, enjoying the silken flesh as it slid through her fingers.

She wanted him. Over her. In her. Filling her. Stretching her.

And yet… yet some part of her said no. Said she should wait. Just a little longer. She didn't know his favorite color or his birthday or—

"Baby, I'm gonna come if you don't stop." She hardly recognized the syllables as words, but finally deciphered his message.

Slowing her attentions, she eased back to a gentle touch, fingers barely gliding over his skin. She let her hand drift to the base of his shaft, to the hint of curls there. She toyed with the strands, listening as Van's heart rate slowed and panting breaths eased.

Of course, she had to ruin his gentle calm.

"Van?" She turned her head and propped her chin on his chest. His hands were tucked out of sight. Though she was sure she saw a hint of fur on his forearms.

Midnight black eyes focused on her, his gaze intent, filled with sexual heat. "Hmm?"

"Will you…?" She let the question trail off and she licked her lips, unsure of what she was asking while entirely sure at the same time. Screw it. "Will you touch me, too? Like I," she swallowed past the nerves rising in her throat. Only the flare of heat in her gaze had her continuing. "Like I touched you?"

His eyes burned her, the need and desire written across his features scorching her with their intensity. He eased to his side and then nudged her, urging her to her back. "Where am I touching you, Lauren?"

A blush burned her cheeks. Why was this so damned hard?

Because I have fucked exactly two guys in my life. That's why.

She brought a hand to her bare breast and brushed her skin, noting the heat of her flesh. "Here."

"Here?" He followed her path, his own fingers ghosting over her warm skin. He circled the nipple on her right breast, toying with the sensitive bit of flesh. He plucked the hardened nub, gently squeezing it between thumb and forefinger. "Right here?"

147

"Y—" she cleared her throat. "Yes."

"Anywhere else?" His touch drifted to her left breast, treating her nipple to the same attentions.

Each rub and pluck went straight to her pussy, causing her need and want to rise higher. She craved him, craved his touch, his possession.

Now.

Lauren brought her hand to the button of her shorts and toyed with the piece of metal. She flicked the bit and then grasped the zipper pull. She tugged the tiniest bit, lowering it just an inch. "Here?"

"Show me." His voice was deep and husky, a hint of his natural eye color shining through. "Show me, baby."

She licked her lips, arousal warring with unease at exposing herself so thoroughly. Then again, Van bared his body for her. What should she feel embarrassed about?

Grabbing every ounce of courage, she tightened her hold on the zipper and eased it lower. The purr echoed in the room, pinging through her mind. The cool air bathed her lower stomach, rifled through her curls and crept down to the damp lips of her pussy.

"Here."

His hand followed her arm, skimming her skin as he traced a path from her shoulder to her wrist. He cupped her cloth-covered heat, pressing firmly against the juncture of her thighs. "Right here?"

"Yes." Today. Now. Forever.

"Show me."

"Van," she whined.

"I won't touch your skin until you show me exactly where, baby," he responded, the rumble coming from deep within his chest.

And that's when she saw the request for what it was. Baring herself to him wasn't a punishment, but a way to tease them both, making sure she was comfortable.

Giving in, she grabbed the waist of her shorts and wiggled. Van removed his touch so she could raise her ass. She eased them down until they rested near her knees. From there it was a quick kick and she was nude. Bare and open and completely at Van's mercy.

Pushing past her nerves, she reached for him. She wrapped her fingers around his wrist and guided his hand toward where she wanted him most. He didn't object or tug free of her hold. No, he allowed her to direct his movements.

His gaze became darker, the lines of his face tightening with sexual tension as his hand neared her pussy. Finally... finally, his fingers brushed her heat, his touch searing her with the first tentative press.

"Here. I want you here." She spread her thighs further to show him exactly how much she desired him. "Touch me."

He took a deep breath, body shuddering. "Lauren."

Van eased even closer, their skin touching as much as possible while he stroked her pussy. The first touch was tentative, his fingers exploring her outer lips. Then he gave her more.

One digit traced the seam of her sex lips, teasing her with the barely there touch. Up and down, he tormented her, taunting her with the caress. She rocked her hips, searching out a deeper stroke. Instead of giving her what she desired, he smiled and chuckled.

The jerk.

"Van..."

"You're so wet, baby. Wet and hot for me." His finger delved further, grazing her clit and stroking the small nubbin of pleasure. His digit slipped easily through her cream, petting her inner sex lips until the tip of his fingers nudged her opening. "Someday soon, I'm gonna be right here. I'll slide deep, fill you. You want that someday, baby?"

Lauren nodded and reached for him, needing an additional touch to ground her, to remind her she was safe and happy in Van's arms. She clutched his shoulders and rolled to her side while bringing her right leg up and across her body until she was able to hook it over his hip. Now they were face to face, so close it would simply take a small adjustment and flex of his hips and he'd be inside her.

But he didn't do any of that. No, he continued his teasing, smiling at their new position and how open she was to him.

His fingers continued their torment, sliding through her abundant cream and stoking her pleasure.

"In me. Fingers in me. Please." She whimpered and moaned, gasping when he gave her what she desired.

"Like that?"

Lauren nodded, unable to say anything past the pleasure bubbling inside her. Instead of speaking, she reached for his pulsing cock, ready to give him the same amount of pleasure he gave.

She wiggled her hand between their bodies and wrapped her fingers around his shaft, squeezing just below the tip.

"Baby," Van groaned and then he retaliated, rubbing a tiny circle over her pulsating clit.

A bolt of pleasure shot straight through her, dancing on her nerves and sending a wave of bliss down her spine.

"Van!" She couldn't withhold the shout, couldn't keep it inside herself.

"That's it. Let me do this for you."

Lauren rocked her hips in time with his attentions, rolling with every flick and rub of his fingers. Then she did the same to his cock, pretending they were consummating their mating, their future. She stroked his dick, pumping him with a steady, unhurried, sexually charged rhythm.

Part of her wanted to tear their hands away and allow him to slide inside her. They were so close already, practically making love, yet something held her back.

Then… Oh god, she was sure she'd died and gone to heaven.

*

Fuck, her tiny hand did wonders for Van's cock. She stroked him, jerky and untutored, but his dick didn't give a damn. She had her hands on him, fondling and petting him and any fucking minute he'd come.

Van was dead. Died and gone to heaven and it came in one Lauren-shaped package.

Fuck. Fuck. Fuck.

He needed to get her off first.

"You want me in your pussy, Lauren?" He loved this, asking and telling at the same time. He let his hand venture down once again until he was able to tease her opening. Based on the new rush of her juices coating his hand, he figured she enjoyed it, too. "Right here?"

She squeezed his shaft, the next tug rough and hard and fuck his balls felt that one. He was ready to be covered in her cream as he thrust in and out of her cunt. And he would… when she was ready.

"Please." Her face was all flushed pink, arousal filling her and the musky scent of her cream called him.

His mouth watered, teeth lengthening, and pressing against his lower lip as the need to mark her rode him hard. The bear craved the connection, the solidification of their mating. One bite and she'd be theirs.

151

Taking her plea as permission, he slipped two fingers into her sheath, sliding his digits along her silken walls. She immediately arched into his thrust, rocking against him.

"That's it, baby." He picked up a steady rhythm, working to grind the heel of his hand against her clit.

And thank fuck, she picked up the same pace. She jerked and tugged on his cock in time with his hand, pumping his dick.

If he closed his eyes, he could almost imagine himself inside her, claiming her and filling her.

Then again, he didn't want to close his eyes, not when he could watch Lauren come apart in his arms. The woman he craved, the woman he desired, the woman he lo—

Lauren gasped and moaned deep, her pussy clenching around his invasion. "Oh god, there."

He noticed the subtle change, tiniest hint of a different texture within her pussy. *Her G-spot.*

Now that he'd found it, he'd always rub that special place and make her scream.

They worked in tandem then, his hand making magic between her thighs while she stroked him root to tip, her tiny hand gliding along his cock.

"You gonna come with me, Lauren?" He felt the need for release rising higher, his body and bear demanding he come and cover her with his cum. If he couldn't claim her from within, he'd make sure she was coated with his scent.

"Uh-huh." Passion glazed eyes met his.

Her pussy milked him rhythmically, but it was her hand he was more concerned with. Like the way she gave a small twist on the up-stroke and a harder squeeze as she went down. Or the way she rubbed the slit on the head.

"Fuck, baby." She pressed against that small split right then. "Gonna make me blow."

"Do it," she panted. "Come. Make me yours. Claim me."

He would have been able to resist her if she'd stopped at "do it," but she'd continued, teasing and tormenting with what he desired most.

He increased his pace, overjoyed when she did the same. But then... then he was lost to her ministrations. His balls hardened and tightened, pulling against his body as the pleasure amassed. His body pulsed with the impending bliss, the coming release.

He pushed her harder, gave her more, demanding she feel as wondrous as him. And her body answered. Her muscles spasmed, a look of pure bliss coating her features.

"Come for me, Lauren." He growled the words, his beast overtaking him.

"Van!" She screamed his name, body stiffening, and he scented the pure pleasure that flowed through her.

His bear reacted, his orgasm rushing through him in a tidal wave of joy while his fangs elongated fully. Her shoulder was there, bared and naked for him, and he took advantage. Before his name died on her lips, he struck.

He shot forward and sank his teeth into her flesh, breaking through her skin without hesitation as he sought to tie them together. She screamed with another release and his inner-beast roared in response. Even more, his body answered as well. His cock pulsed and throbbed, twitching for a moment before the bliss of his orgasm coursed through him.

He snarled against her flesh as the heat of his cum bathed them both, coated their bodies in his primal scent.

He sucked on her flesh, the coppery fluid bathing his tongue as he swallowed her blood. With every pull, he felt their connection solidifying, firming and shifting into place. The rough edges of his bear's temper slowly smoothed, the knowledge that she was theirs finally soothing him.

Shudders wracked them both, his body trembling with the force of his release combined with the fresh mating between them. Lauren clung to him, holding him close and digging her nails into his flesh. At some point she'd released his cock and merely squeezed him.

Slowly he eased the suction, his bear accepting they were now tied. With care, he disengaged his teeth and willed the bear's fangs away. He didn't need them any longer.

Van lapped at the wound, shuddering as the last droplets of her blood slithered over his taste buds. She belonged to him now, his and his alone. No one could steal her from him, no one could touch her. His.

His bear puffed up, growling and roaring a warning to one and all that Lauren was theirs. Eventually he'd slide deep into her pussy and claim her fully. His bear grumbled at the delay, but was satisfied with the knowledge they were now bound for life.

He slid his hand free of her moist heat and, beneath her gaze, he lapped at the digits. Just as he'd imagined—salty sweetness with a hint of what made Lauren, Lauren.

"Delicious, baby."

The sated need in her gaze rekindled, desire flaring to life once again.

Of course his cock twitched in response. Even as his cum coated them, his dick was ready to go again.

He rolled to his back, pulling her along with him, fitting her abundant curves to his body. She cushioned and welcomed him with her lush form. He'd never tire of tasting her, losing himself inside her. His cum slowly cooled against their skin, but screw it. He wanted to simply hold her.

She shuddered and whimpered against him, nuzzling his chest. He reached over and yanked at the bedspread, tugging it until it folded across them. His cock ached once again, throbbing with the need to come, but he brushed aside his desire. Nothing mattered but Lauren. His renewed needs could wait. Regardless of her rekindled desire, she wasn't prepared to give him what he craved most. Some day. But not today.

Like a kitten, she rubbed against him, wiggling and shifting until she found a comfortable spot. She settled in with a deep sigh and a low moan.

"Van? Mmm…"

"I've got you, baby." He pressed a kiss to her temple, drawing in more of her flavors. Happiness and sexual satisfaction coated her from head to toe. Good.

"Uh-huh. You're hard again. We could…"

"I've got everything I want right now," he murmured against her skin. "When you're ready for more, we'll do more. Until them, I'm happy holding you."

His cock protested, but when she released a soft, relief-tinged sigh, he knew he'd said the right thing. His cock wanted Lauren for the short term, but Van was playing a long-term game.

He could wait.

His dick jerked in protest.

He just hoped he wouldn't have to wait too long.

chapter thirteen

Lauren touched the healing wound on her shoulder, fingers brushing the red, scabbed flesh. It was mending a hell of a lot faster than a normal injury, but it still lingered after two days.

Another thing remained, floating between them like the big, neon green, we haven't banged elephant in the room.

Hand jobs? Check.

Oral sex? Check. Check, like, *a lot*. What the man could do with his tongue...

Penis in vagina sex? No check.

She still hadn't figured out if that was a good or bad thing just yet. Part of her yearned for him, begged her to go to him and sacrifice herself at the altar of sexy. They'd touched and tasted and explored each other's bodies. It was like her head was totally fine with exposing herself, but that last step was off-limits for a while. She couldn't explain it, even to herself.

She wanted him, but then she remembered she'd *just* met Van. They barely knew anything about each other.

Okay, they did cover a lot of ground over the last couple of days, but...

But, but, but…

But she did know the scars on his chest were from a recent battle with the hyenas in Boyne Falls. First, hyenas? Wow. Second, a battle? That part of the story had her trembling in fear.

They were animals at heart, she needed to remember that fact. They fought. They were bloody. They had strong opinions and their bears backed them up.

He told her about sharing the now hyena-free town of Boyne Falls with the Redby wolves. Also about the fact the wolf she'd seen was a shapeshifter, he just didn't know who it was.

"Ready?" His deep voice slithered over her nerves, carrying arousal in its wake.

He stood in the bathroom doorway, his uniform snug on his body and outlining every muscle.

The bathroom… She refused to let her gaze skitter to the shower. The blood was gone, washed away by that first shower Van took before he saved her from Charles. But the door was still missing. They'd gotten used to splatters of water decorating the tile floor after they bathed.

"Lauren?"

She jerked her attention to him, tearing herself from the memories. "Sorry, what?"

"You ready to go?"

Go? Wait. He was in his uniform. Right. They had plans for the day.

Drop her at the diner where she worked as a waitress while he did his shift. Before her shift, though, she had to walk to her place and see if she could break her lease and still get her deposit back. He didn't exactly know about that part.

They'd agreed she should move into Van's house since they were mated now. Mated. Like married, but more permanent. God, her life had changed a ton in the last handful of days.

Anyway. Work, but not work. Then real work. Then moving into Vans after real work.

Somewhere in there Anna and Martin would go to Anna's and pack up some of *her* stuff to take to Mia and Ty's. Her friend refused to live with Martin until she was free of Bryson and she also refused to "shove herself" onto Lauren and Van since they'd recently mated.

Plus, Anna, apparently, didn't want to hear them partake of sexytimes.

Lauren refused to remind Anna about the time they'd shared an apartment before Anna married Bryson. Yeah, Lauren had to listen to *a lot* coming from Anna's room.

Van stared at her expectantly, eyebrows raised in question. "You don't have to go, baby. You know I make enough…"

She shook her head. They'd had this conversation, too. He made enough to support her, but she never wanted to be forced to depend on a man. She didn't make a lot at the diner, but *she* earned the money. "No, I'm good."

She smoothed her hands over her uniform, thankful that Van sent Keen to her apartment for clothes. She didn't particularly care that he dug through her panty drawer, but at least she was dressed. She was also thankful that Keen agreed to keep the condition of her place to himself. She'd reasoned with him, assured him that since she was never going back, no one needed to know that she was poorer than a church mouse.

Van didn't look convinced when she assured him she was fine, and he opened his mouth to speak.

Lauren plastered a smile on her face. "I promise. My shoulder only hurts a little and we can't stay holed up in the house much longer. Besides, the Itan needs you at work."

The Itan. She'd had a hard time calling him Ty after she and Van mated. It seemed... disrespectful in a way.

Van rolled his eyes. "*Ty* could get along fine without me. He just doesn't want us to starve. If he makes us leave our den, he can also make sure we eat."

That was another thing she'd had to get used to. Van didn't want *anyone* coming near the house, near his mate.

Comforting yet creepy.

She rubbed her stomach. "I'm good with that plan. I'm wasting away to nothing. Then again," she frowned at her body. "I could probably lose—"

One second he was across the room and then he was there before her, finger on his lips. "If you say one word about this body needing to be anything but what it is right now, I *will* spank you." He wound his arms around her and palmed her butt. "Love this ass, love these tits." He used his grip to lift her and she automatically wrapped her legs around his hips. "Love every inch of you." He nuzzled her neck and pushed at the top of her button-up shirt with his nose. "Love mine."

A spark of arousal formed deep within her and she moaned, enjoying the low glow of need.

"All mine."

What she wouldn't give for another half hour so he could prove how "his" she truly was.

Instead, she nudged at his shoulders, denying them both what they craved. "We don't have time, Van." He growled. "I mean it."

He scraped is teeth around her mark and her pussy clenched in response. Jerk. He knew that was a hot button for her. Cheating asshole.

160

The heavy pounding of someone at the front door had him wrenching away with a curse. "Damn it."

He palmed his cock, pressing against the bulge, and then he flicked it, causing her to giggle. Which, in turn, earned her a glare.

"I told you we didn't have time."

The glare didn't leave. "You don't have to laugh about it, though. Do you know how hard it is to sit with a hard cock?"

She returned his narrow-eyed stare. "Sitting around in wet panties ain't no picnic."

That got him groaning and he slumped into her, his head resting on her shoulder. "Baby, you can't talk about wet panties. Drives me crazy."

"Well, you can be driven crazy tonight. For now, we've got work." She nudged his head, forcing him to back up.

His gaze suddenly went serious, his features settled into a worried frown. "You'll be careful? Today? I won't be with you, and Bryson…"

Bryson was being watched, and he hadn't done anything or met with anyone they considered suspicious. He was the model citizen. That scared her more than anything and she knew it worried Van as well.

"I'll be fine." She stroked his cheek. "I'll never be alone with him. You'll drop me off and then come back at seven to pick me up. Don't worry."

Van's nostrils flared and she held her breath, wondering what his magic nose would find. "You're—"

Another hammering of the door. "C'mon, babe, we gotta go."

He tilted his head, staring at her as if she was a puzzle he needed to decipher. That wasn't good.

She darted forward and pressed a quick kiss to his lips, then she wiggled around him. "The Itan isn't going to wait forever!"

Van grumbled in response, but his heavy tread behind her told her he followed her through the house. Good.

At the front door, she opened it wide, smiling at Ty. "Hi, Itan."

Ty rolled his eyes. "Unless I'm growling at you, it's Ty, Lauren."

She nodded. "Okay, lemme grab my shoes."

She wasn't going to listen. He did so much for the clan, had done so much to protect it from Parker's uncle. The least she could do was show the proper respect for what he'd endured.

"She's not going to listen." Ty sighed.

"Nope." Van agreed and she heard the smile in his voice.

"Damn it." The Itan's curse was low, but apparently, not low enough. Especially when a hollered "language" reached them.

Sliding on her right shoe, Lauren stood and shook her head at Ty and Van, then noticed Mia peeking her head in the doorway. "Really, Ty? Really? Do you want this child born cursing his hair off?"

Ty reached behind himself and snared Mia, dragging her into the house. "It'll be born without hair, so I think we're safe."

"You," Mia poked him, "are a great big cornnut."

The Itan—a big, growly man who inspired fear in all bears—grinned wide, a dopey look on his face. "I still don't know what that means, but I love you."

Lauren watched the exchange with a mixture of desire and hope. She met Van's gaze and saw similar emotions flitting across his features. They both wanted that, wanted what the Itan and Itana had. Given a little more time, she had no doubt they'd get there. Considering the need, the physical pull that drew her to Van, she hoped it was really, really soon.

Lauren tore her gaze from Van's, unwilling to entertain ideas of "soon" when they had to get the show on the road. "Van, Itan, you ready?"

That drew Mia's gaze and the Itana focused on her. "Oh! I'm coming, too. I'm going to keep you company for a little while and then Ty's going to take me baby shopping."

"Great." On the outside, she smiled. On the inside, she cursed. *Fuck.*

Grinning, Mia snuck out of Ty's hold and padded toward her, sliding her arms around Lauren's right arm. She leaned close and whispered a single word. "Language."

Damn it.

"Times two."

Lauren quit while she was ahead. Or rather, behind.

* * *

Van couldn't settle, couldn't sit still as he and Ty waited for Morgan, the Redby Beta, to arrive for their appointment. Reid, the Alpha, was coming along this time, as well. Even after a month of trying to work together, he and Morgan were busting heads. Still.

Van kicked back in his chair, pushing it until he balanced on two legs. If it wasn't for the bullshit in Boyne Falls and the asshole Morgan, he'd be home with Lauren. With her curves and her kisses and her luscious as—

"Van!" Ty snapped at him and he fell forward, front legs of the chair thumping against the aged carpet.

"What?" He hadn't done anything in the last five minutes. How could he be in trouble?

"I get that you're missing your mate, but can you refrain from thinking about her in my office? Right before Reid and Morgan arrive? I really don't want to smell that Lauren gets you hot and bothered."

Internally, he groaned, but externally he rolled his eyes at his brother. "Fine, fine." He checked the wall clock. "What time are they supposed to be here?"

"Ten." One word, short and clipped.

Van understood his brother's anger considering it was ten fifteen.

Another five minutes passed and Van wondered if the Alpha and Beta would even show. Shit, he didn't want to be involved in some dominant shifter pissing match. Sometimes he hated shifter politics more than he hated humans.

Then again, he didn't really hate humans that much anymore, did he? Slowly, he and his bear were coming around to the fact not all humans enjoyed kidnapping little boys and shooting...

He forced himself to forget that snippet of his past.

"How much longer are we gonna wait for them?" Van wanted to maybe swing by the diner and check on Lauren.

Ty opened his mouth to respond, but his desk phone buzzed. A call from the front receptionist. His brother snatched up the receiver and pressed it to his ear. "Yes. Uh-huh. Have them wait." Ty dropped it back into its cradle.

"That them?"

"Yup," another one word answer from Ty.

"How long are we making them wait?" Maybe the politics side could be interesting.

"As long as it takes me to finish this report." His brother kept writing on the form before him, filling out appropriate boxes. Van didn't envy Ty's position as Grayslake Sheriff. Between kissing babies, bullshit paperwork, and then acting as Itan on top of it all… No, he didn't envy the man.

Van kept his gaze locked on the clock, watching the second hand tick its way around the face. One minute became two, became five, and then his brother dropped his pen. "Go get them."

"Me?" He pointed at himself. "That's…" An insult.

"Yup. A five minute wait and being fetched by the Enforcer is a good start."

Most humans would get pissed at being thought of as less than the best, but shifters were realists. They could meet others and know in an instant if they were either stronger or weaker than the animal before them.

Van knew he was weaker than Ty, but also stronger than Morgan. Reid, the Alpha, bypassed Van and probably squeaked by Ty as well. The man was… Well, he didn't want to call the wolf scary, but he would admit to carrying a dose of respectful wariness around the Alpha.

"All right then." Van rose from his chair. "Gimme a sec."

He left his brother's office and wove his way through the building. He turned this way and that, dodging other officers and county personnel. It didn't take long for him to arrive in the lobby. There he found a very large, very angry wolf shifter standing in the room.

Reid planted himself dead center in the space, his arms across his chest and feet shoulder width apart. Every human in the room kept at least ten feet between their bodies as they made their way this way and that. The scent of his anger permeated the area and a hard look at the man's eyes revealed their yellow hue. Oh, he wore thick sunglasses to mask his animal's appearance, but Van saw the lightened, amber color.

Fuck it. Who cared? Ty was pissed too.

165

He looked around for Morgan, knowing the Alpha wouldn't venture into another's territory without his Beta. Agreement to work together or not, it was still dangerous.

It took a moment, but he spotted the man leaning against the wall that led to the administration wing. County Government and the Sheriff's office shared the building. It wasn't an ideal situation, but Grayslake was a small town. No sense in building two smaller buildings when one big one worked just as well.

Van took a deep breath, tasting the air, and he filtered through the flavors. Reid's rage hammered him, but below it lurked… satisfaction.

Morgan's gaze remained steady on the hallway, eyes focused on the distance beyond the lobby, which gave him a chance to observe the wolf.

They'd left Reid and Morgan to cool their heels for five minutes. Shifters who, due to their position, never waited for anything. He understood Reid's anger, but Morgan… wasn't pissed at all. No, the satisfaction was joined by a little bit of happiness and he wondered what was going through the wolf's head.

A large form traveled down the administration main hallway, the height and build coupled with the man's gate told Van who approached.

The mayor—fucking Bryson Davies—and he smiled at Morgan.

And Morgan smiled back, tipping his head in acknowledgement.

Great, something else to keep an eye on.

With a shake of his head, he stepped into sight, drawing the Alpha's attention as well as the Beta's. Reid's eyes flared bright when they landed on Van while Morgan's easy going attitude melted away to feigned anger.

Definitely feigned. He should be filled with rage at the slight Ty delivered. Instead, he seemed mildly agitated.

"Mister Bennett, if you'll follow me." Van tilted his head ever so slightly to the side, exposing a hint of his neck. Not enough to represent submission, but merely a recognition of Reid's power and position.

Reid grunted and it rolled into a growl.

The fucker is not—

Then he noticed the reason for the sound. Morgan sidled up to his Alpha, feigned expression still in place.

All wasn't happy in wolf-land.

Without commenting, he spun on his heel, presenting his back to the two wolves. Dangerous if he hadn't been in a public setting, but at least a dozen bears were in the direct vicinity and another dozen deeper in the building. Humans had no idea how many predators lurked nearby.

Van retraced his steps, following the same path he'd taken, and led the Alpha and Beta to Ty's office. It didn't take as long as before. The shifters in the building must have caught the scent of Reid's rage and were steering clear. Smart.

He rapped his knuckles on Ty's office door and waited for his brother to grant them entrance.

"Enter." The average person probably wouldn't have recognized Ty's anger, but Van surely did.

He didn't envy the wolves.

Van snared the knob and twisted it before nudging the door open. Reid strode through first, followed immediately by Morgan and Van brought up the rear.

The flavors of Ty's rage ballooned in the room, responding to Reid's sudden presence. At the same time, he was close enough to catch a hint of Morgan's giddy happiness.

Van pushed the door closed and rushed to speak before the two shifter leaders began their verbal, and possibly physical, sparring. He retained his position near the office door, slightly behind the two wolves, so he saw only a little of their profile and their backs.

"Itan, if I may?" He presented the perfect picture of respect. He may rag on his brother in private, but he'd never shame his Itan.

"Yes?" Ty glared at him.

"There's one other question regarding our business earlier." He flicked his gaze to the clock before continuing, hoping his brother would follow the path he led. "Who answered the call?"

Ty furrowed his brow. "What?"

Van repeated the move, urging Ty to get it already. They'd been bitching about the clock, about the wolves being late. So, who did Ty speak with when setting their appointment? Because Van had his own suspicions. Ones that said Reid wasn't late on purpose and it was Morgan who'd picked up the phone. Morgan who'd intentionally created this drama.

"Who answered the call, Itan?"

"Good point." Ty's gaze strayed to the clock, not saying another word. He then focused on Reid. "Reid, I think we have a few things to discuss. Alone."

Morgan was the first to object, to jump into the fray and add tension to an already volatile situation. "I won't leave my Alpha to face a bear alone. Who knows what will happen to him."

"You question my honor?" Ty raised a brow and Van had to fight back a chuckle at his brother's overacting. Well, the haughty tone was a bit much, but the anger simmering inside Ty was anything but fake.

"You're a bear. You—"

"Enough, Morgan." Reid cut off his Beta, the full weight of the Alpha's power whipping through the room. Van almost felt the need to bare his throat. Almost.

"Alpha, he's insulted you. Left you waiting—"

On the sideline, he saw Reid gaze at Ty and the two men shared a look. "Enough. I'll meet with the Grayslake Itan alone. He and I will hammer out the details. We've left too many things, too many rules, rather fluid in their interpretation. I don't need you."

Fuckin' A they had.

Another family disappeared yesterday. The grandfather was still recovering from open heart surgery, so Van gave the rest of them permission to remain until he could be moved.

Overnight, they were gone.

Van knew neither he nor his bears helped the group move which left…

Morgan released a low growl, his body tense, gray fur sprouting along his arms. As Van watched, the male's chest widened and fingers began their transformation to wolf-like paws.

Oh, anger at the slight was one thing, but this seemed like some pent up, bottled rage about to boil over. And his Itan was on the other side of the room.

Van tensed, ready to dive onto the wolf's back, take him down if necessary. The man was already close to breaking one of their laws. If a human walked through the door while Morgan was half-shifted…

The bear inside him stilled, power at the ready, waiting to be released. It was annoyed with Morgan. No, more than annoyed. It hated the wolf. They knew, *knew*, he'd done something to those hyenas. No, he hadn't officially broken the law. There were certain guidelines when a purge was ordered, one of which said violators

169

could be eliminated. Not should or would, but *could*. Grayslake leaned toward the less brutal method of dealing with the hyenas.

Morgan did not.

The low crack and snap of bone echoed off the office walls and Morgan's mouth shifted, changing into a bastardized version of his wolf's snout.

Mother fucker. If he went after Ty…

His bear stood at the ready, waiting for the signal, more than prepared to rip past Van's human skin and then rip through Morgan. It wanted the asshole's blood on its fangs.

More hair sprouted, growing from the wolf's skin and Van unclenched his fists, wiggling his fingers in preparation of his shift. The man had to transition fully and then Van could respond. He wouldn't be breaking any laws if it was in reaction to another and in the protection of his Itan.

C'mon, c'mon, c'mon.

The wolf Alpha stepped up to the snarling Morgan as if he didn't have a care in the world. Reid's power swirled in the room, ghosting over everything, passing over his skin before focusing on Morgan. Damn, that was strong. Different, but strong as hell. Thank god the bear couldn't give a fuck about the wolf's dominance.

"Stop." One word. Morgan's transformation halted in its tracks, bones that hadn't even solidified in their new shapes remained broken and unattached. "Shift back."

That was all it took. Oh, the rage Morgan felt still burned hot, but it was impotent against the Alpha. More of the wolf's tumultuous emotions assaulted Van's senses, but the Beta continued to heed his Alpha's instructions. In moments Morgan was human-shaped once again, his chest heaving as he panted and fought for air.

Reid leaned into the gasping male and whispered low, "And that is why you shall never be Alpha." The fury that whipped from Morgan toward Reid burned Van's skin, singeing him with its intensity. And the Alpha… laughed. Just chuckled and smiled as if it were nothing. "Leave us. I expect you in my office when I return."

Van waited for Morgan to strike out, claw his Alpha in retaliation. The male had already proven—in Van's opinion—to be unworthy. Except, rather than attack his leader, he spun on his heel and stomped toward the office door. He wrenched it open and slammed it shut behind him with such force the wall shook.

Reid's attention fixed on the door for a moment and then flicked to Van before turning on Ty. "Titan, it seems there are things we need to discuss."

chapter fourteen

Lauren nibbled her lower lip, her attention alternating between the Itana drinking coffee in the back of the diner and her customers in her section. Crapity crap.

Listen to her. She'd stopped cursing because of the small pregnant woman.

She poured yet another mug of coffee, smiling as she swept away empty plates into her other hand. "I'll have your check in one second."

Balancing the dishes on her arm, she wound her way toward the counter and slid behind it, placing the carafe on the hot plate as she passed. The injury to her shoulder burned and pulled the skin, making itself known as she moved. At the rate it was healing, she'd be fine come morning. It was the getting there that caused her problems.

Ducking into the kitchen, she slid the plates and utensils into the sink, emptying her arms.

Now she had to do it all over again. Sometimes waitressing seemed to be more effort than it was worth. But she knew when she got her tips every evening and her paycheck on Friday, she'd earned every damned dollar.

Lauren paused by the cash register and pulled up table eighteen's ticket. The push of a few buttons had the bill printing. She reached down and stretched to snatch the thermal paper from the printer. The move tugged on the bite and she hissed out a breath when the pain zinged through her. Groaning, she grabbed the slip and stood, rubbing her shoulder, and wishing away the ache.

"You okay, doll?" Nellie's concerned voice came from her right and she turned to face the older woman. She'd owned and operated the diner for as long as Lauren could remember and she looked to her as a surrogate mother of sorts.

"Fine. Just a little…" Bear bite? "thing," she finished lamely.

Nellie snaked her arm around Lauren's and tugged her toward the kitchen. "C'mon now."

"Nellie, I've got table eighteen waiting—"

The woman snatched the slip from her and shoved it at one of the other waitresses. She didn't even pause in their travels. Steal and shove and it was done.

Dang it.

They kept moving past the kitchen and into the back office. The small space was cluttered, almost claustrophobic once they occupied the tiny area.

"All right now, let's see what we've got." Nellie tugged on Lauren's top and bared her shoulder before she could voice a protest.

Now rhinos dressed as butterflies took up residence in her stomach. "It's… it's not… The thing is…"

"The boy got a little excited, hmm?"

"I have no idea what you're talking about. I tripped and fell." She was proud of herself for that lie. Even if it was a lie and her wound was so blatantly a bite.

174

"Uh-huh." Nellie raised a single brow. "Honey, there are some things I don't know, but I know a claiming bite when I see it." The air in Lauren's lungs froze, chest refusing to move. "Breathe, honey. Just breathe." The older woman took a slow, deep breath, encouraging Lauren to do the same. Ha! Easier than it looked.

"How…? I didn't… You *can't tell*."

Nellie rolled her eyes. "Honey, I'm just human enough to slink under the radar and just enough bear to be friends with the Abrams brothers' granddaddy." She held up her hand, holding her thumb and forefinger a hairsbreadth apart. "Was *this close* to mating the old coot, but he had ideas about a fated mate, and I had ideas about college." She shrugged. "Broke my heart for a little while, but then I met my Edward." She released Lauren's top and clapped her hands together. "C'mon then, let's doctor this a little and get some over-the-counter pain medication in you and you'll be as good to go as you can be."

"Nellie…"

"Oh, hush. Van's a good man, better bear. He's like his granddaddy. Out of all of them, he's the one. He had more than a little trouble with humans when he was young, that whole family did, bless their hearts. Now he's the Enforcer and they see and do the worst. Make's 'em biased. Van more than most."

"What—"

"Order up!" Edward yelled from the kitchen. It broke their little moment and sent Nellie into action, bustling around the small space, gathering what they needed. In minutes, Lauren was patched up.

The second she passed into the dining room, she was on automatic, smiling as she refilled glasses and passed out checks. After a little while, the throbbing ache lessened to a dull pulse. Annoying, but not debilitating.

Before long, the breakfast rush was gone, only a few customers lingering at the counter. And then there was Mia, the Itana, munching on toast in the back.

175

Damn it. She needed the woman gone so she could head over to her old apartment and argue with the greasy landlord. The last thing she wanted was Mia to see where she lived, see that her brother-in-law was mated to some trashy, dirt poor woman. Money didn't make her, didn't substantiate her worth, but there were a lot of people who thought differently. Those who looked at someone who survived paycheck to paycheck as something less than them.

Lauren didn't want to be seen that way. Least of all by her mate's family. Or worse, her mate. She wanted to get in, grab her stuff, deal with the landlord, and then get out again. All before Van caught her.

Mia had to ruin her plans by tagging along.

Smiling, she approached Mia's table, coffee carafe in one hand. "Hey, Ita—" She cut herself off before she outed Mia. "Hey, Mia, can I get you more coffee? Breakfast?" She checked her watch. "It's nearing the lunch shift. Did you want a sandwich? Grilled cheese?"

"Grilled cheese?" Mia looked so hopeful. "With real, full fat mayo and bad-for-me cheese?"

"Um, sure?" Lauren wasn't sure what kind of answer the Itana was looking for.

The pregnant woman wiggled out of the booth and wrapped her arms around Lauren in a tight hug. "Thank you, thank you, thank you. Ty keeps throwing away all the good food and is making me eat vegetables and low-fat everything and… *granola*. What do I want with granola?"

"I'm sure he wants you to be healthy through your pregnancy."

Mia snorted. "Happy pregnant women make healthy pregnant women. I should get sick or really fat to spite him."

She smiled and shook her head. "For now we'll stick with grilled cheese."

"And greasy potato chips."

176

"And greasy potato chips," Lauren confirmed. "It should be out in ten minutes or so."

That bought her ten minutes, plus she could get Nellie to deliver it and maybe chat up Mia a little. All in all, she could probably squeeze out a half hour to disappear and then return. The furniture wasn't even hers. So a handful of bags with her few belongings and she was free.

"Yum." Mia clapped her hands and practically bounced.

All righty then.

Lauren headed back to the kitchen, heart rate increasing with every step. In and out, in and out. She kept reminding herself of the plan as she slipped into the kitchen. Not wanting to bother with the computer system, she wrote up an order ticket and popped it in front of Edward at the grill so he could whip up Mia's lunch.

The man simply nodded in acceptance, so Lauren went hunting for Nellie. She found the woman leaning against the counter, chatting up one of the regulars.

"Hey, Nellie?"

The older woman turned toward her. "What's up, honey?"

"I'm gonna take my break real quick. Mia's got an order in. Do you think you could take it over when it's ready?" She leaned closer to whisper in Nellie's ear. "And maybe stall her for a little while?"

She pushed away from the counter and propped her hands on her hips. "What are you up to?"

Lauren did her best to appear innocent. "I don't know what you're talking about."

"Uh-huh." Nellie stared, waiting her out.

Damn it.

"I wanna pack up my stuff. Talk to the landlord. I don't…" She squeezed her eyes shut. "I don't want her seeing that, or him knowing about it, Nellie. Thirty minutes."

She was still so thankful that Keen had agreed to keep her living conditions a secret.

"Honey, you know—"

"*Please.*"

Nellie sighed. "Hurry and don't think I won't rat you out if you're not back in half an hour."

Lauren dropped a kiss on the older woman's cheek. "You're the best."

"Uh-huh."

Not wanting to be around in case Nellie changed her mind, Lauren darted through the kitchen door and toward the back entry. She snagged her purse on the way. Now she had to bolt around the building, ducking down so she couldn't be seen through the walls of windows, and hit the sidewalk. Her apartment was only two blocks down. A quick jog there and back. Easy peasy, no harm, no foul.

Less than a minute later she realized there was no peasy that went with easy.

Damn it.

Mia leaned against the corner of the building, smile wide and one hand protectively cupping her belly. "Language."

Lauren resisted the urge to growl. "Mia, fancy meeting you here."

"Yup. To think, I'm sitting there, waiting for a luscious grilled cheese sandwich with greasy chips, when I hear *someone* chatting about leaving and doing something or other and all that other stuff. I admit, I stopped listening after that person got to the 'leaving' portion of the plan." She pushed away from the wall and closed the distance between them. "Especially considering that person promised Van she'd stay at work. Interesting, isn't it?"

She couldn't help it, she whined, "*Mia,* you don't understand."

The Itana stopped beside her and wrapped an arm around Lauren's waist before urging her toward the sidewalk. "I know what I heard and, while I disagree with everything you told Nellie, I do understand. It's going to take time for you to trust Van. Your mating is maybe a minute old, so you're worried. As for how the family will feel…" Mia rested her head on Lauren's shoulder. "The family is so, so happy that Van found his mate. You could have two heads and they wouldn't care. Your parents could be ax murderers and the trait passed down from generation to generation and they wouldn't bat an eye." She huffed. "So what we're gonna do is go to your apartment and pack things up."

"But…"

"And then we're going to come back here. Ty and Van will be none the wiser. You can't outright lie, you can, however, tell them we had assistance in getting your belongings to the diner." The Itana grinned. "I assisted you and you assisted me."

"Okay then." Lauren wasn't going to argue too much.

It wasn't a lie, but it wasn't the truth. But it still *wasn't* a lie.

"We need to go right at the sidewalk."

"Right it is!" Mia's joy was infectious. "And then it's back for that moan-worthy grilled cheese."

Shaking her head, Lauren led the Itana toward her apartment. Nerves clawed at her belly, but bringing Mia was better than being followed by Van.

It didn't take long to reach her place, Mia's chatter making the trip seem shorter. Then again, that could have been from the rising tension insider her.

The Itana's babbling didn't increase or slow, merely remained steady as they climbed the rickety stairs, gripping the railing around the fourth step and then clutching the wall at the eighth. Mostly because the rail was sorta… gone there.

Her prattle continued as they gathered her few keepsakes, tossing them into a few duffels she dug out of the closet. When all was said and done, she had three bags and one black garbage bag containing the rest of her clothes.

Her life fit in four bags.

How pathetic did that make her?

A lot.

Shaking her head, she pasted a smile on her face. "That's it."

Mia looked down at the pile at their feet. "Yeah?"

When the Itana looked at her again, she ignored the pity in her gaze. Lauren didn't need pity. She'd long ago grown out of pity parties. She wasn't about to have one today.

"Yup." She grabbed the three duffels and held out the bag of clothes. Honestly, it probably weighed all of five pounds considering Keen had snared most of her outfits and whatnot when he'd swung by.

Again she thanked god he'd kept his mouth shut about her shithole apartment.

Lauren tromped down the steps first, taking her time and making sure she braced herself with each one. If Mia slipped and fell, she'd be there to catch her. The last thing she needed was a pregnant Itana breaking her neck on the stairs.

Before long they were on solid ground and toward the sidewalk.

"Lauren? What about the landlord?"

She groaned. After showing Mia her apartment, she really didn't want her meeting the asshole landlord of Pine Place. She shook her head. "My landlord? Brubaker?" She waved her hand pretending to not care when inside, she really, really did. "Naw, I'll call him."

"You sure? We could—"

"What do you think you're doing? Skipping out on me? Rent's late!" The man's raspy voice grated her nerves and Lauren gritted her teeth before turning to face him. The man was tall, fit, and would probably be attractive if he showered and shaved. Ever.

As it was, she held her breath as he approached.

"I asked a question," Brubaker, Bru, barked at her.

Squaring her shoulders, she answered him, careful not to show any weakness. She'd been at his mercy when she barely scraped together enough to afford the place. Now she was Van's mate and she lived in a gorgeous house. She still didn't make a lot, but she wasn't poor any longer. She wasn't alone any longer.

She wasn't alone...

The thought struck home, reverberated deep inside her. She wasn't alone. She had someone to lean on. She had someone who'd always be at her back.

She had Van. She had a family.

Fuck this jerk.

Mia leaned into her. "Language."

Smiling, she stuck out her tongue at the Itana. "I'm moving out. You get half my deposit because I didn't give you notice." She dug into her pocket and tugged out the slip of paper she'd written on that morning. She'd jotted down Van's address, knowing she'd need it for Bru. "You can forward the other half here."

"Deposit?" Brubaker spit on the ground, narrowly missing her feet. He wanted to intimidate her. She wanted Van to come over and beat him to a pulp. "I think there's some damages that'll cost you the rest of that deposit. Those nail holes in the wall and such."

Dick. Prick. Fucker.

Mia leaned in again. "Langua—"

"I get it, I get it." Lauren huffed and wondered how the woman managed to *know*. "Look, Brubaker…" Her voice trailed off as Mia stepped forward, drawing the landlord's attention.

The Itana wiggled her nose and breathed deep, repeating the process twice more before finally releasing the air in a heavy whoosh.

Then she adopted the mantle of authority Lauren had yet to see. "I believe in adhering to any contracts signed, don't you? Now, Brubaker, is there a reason you missed the gathering last week?"

Huh?

"Look, lady—"

"Itana." Mia quietly corrected him and then it hit Lauren between the eyes.

The landlord was one of them, er, her or something. She was a bear, but wasn't a bear, to the clan and she still hadn't figured out how to refer to bear-bears and human-bears.

The change in the male was instant. The cocky, asshole attitude shifted to one of deference, respect, and a hint of fear. Lauren really liked the fear aspect.

"Itana." He tilted his head to the side. "Lauren will get her full deposit. Mailed directly to this address."

"Good. And you weren't at the gathering because…"

Brubaker gulped. "Well…"

182

"The Itan will see you this evening. We can all discuss this little building you're running and your place in the clan. Am I clear?" Mia's voice was hard and firm, the smiling woman she'd been with moments ago now gone beneath the power of her position.

"Yes, Itana."

Mia jerked her head in a quick nod. "Good. I'll see you this evening."

With that proclamation, the Itana spun and stomped down the walkway to the sidewalk. Lauren hurried to keep pace, the woman's strides eating up the ground as she headed back to the diner.

When she finally caught up with Mia, she said the only thing that came to mind. "Holy shit that was awesome."

"Language." The woman shot her a grin. "And yes, it was." Then, the big, bad ass woman bounced. "Totally awesome."

Then things got quite a bit less awesome. Like, holy shit that's bad.

The squeal of tires washed over her moments before a dark blue SUV caught her attention. It roared toward them, front bumper aimed in their direction and its speed increased with every passing second.

Lauren froze, heart beating a frantic rhythm and terror overtook her, invading her body in a tsunami of panic. As if time stood still, she looked to Mia, noted her wide-eyed stare and fear overpowering her features. The Itana clutched her belly, hand resting protectively over the tiny bump, and Lauren did the only thing she could.

Gathering every ounce of strength inside her, she shoved Mia, slamming her body against the Itana's until the woman stumbled aside. That left Lauren in the path of the vehicle, her feet tangled among dropped bags, leaving her a target for the driver. She locked eyes with the man behind the wheel, noted the yellow of his irises and the long canines that extended past his lip.

The SUV was ten feet away.

183

She hoped it was quick. Hoped she wouldn't suffer.

Five feet.

Then… A heavy weight slammed against her, forcing the air from her lungs as she collided with the concrete, the massive bulk holding her firmly against the ground. The roar of the SUV's engine filled her ears, but the true, agonizing pain she expected didn't come. Instead, aches from her smash into the concrete traveled through her.

"Damn it, Lauren." Van's trembling growl filled her ears and she'd never been so happy to be yelled at in her entire life.

chapter fifteen

Van almost lost her. Feet. Inches. That SUV's bumper rushed Lauren and he pulled every ounce of strength his bear possessed to get to her. Even then, it'd been a narrow escape.

Two hours later and his animal still hadn't calmed. It'd pause for a moment, soothed by his attempts at reasoning with the bear, only to have the beast get riled once again.

Fuck. He couldn't stop replaying the moments in his mind. His frustration over Lauren leaving the diner with Mia. Anger that she'd left the safety of her job and trekked to her old apartment.

Then he'd somehow missed her at the apartment. Instead of finding Lauren and Mia, he'd found a dirty bear begging for forgiveness and would the Enforcer put in a good word with the Itan on his behalf. At that point, Van would have agreed to anything if it meant getting to Lauren a second quicker.

After that, he'd taken off at a slow jog, anxious to be at her side.

He came around the corner in time to see her shove Mia to the ground. She froze directly in the path of the SUV, centered between the vehicle's headlights as it barreled toward her. He'd never been so scared in his life, never ran so hard, or demanded so much of his bear.

The shakes attacked him again, vibrating his veins and rattling his heart. He'd almost lost her. The thought kept repeating. It didn't matter that he could reach out and touch her and run his fingers over her bruised skin.

Each recitation of the events scared him a little more, put him more on edge and nearer to losing control. A yellow-eyed man behind the wheel, but she couldn't describe him. The eyes kept her attention. Blue SUV. Van hadn't bothered to check for a license plate when it fled the scene, he'd been too focused on Lauren and Mia.

"Van?" He looked to his mate. "Are you ever going to talk to me?" She squirmed and her worry reached him, but it wasn't enough to override the terror plaguing him.

He wanted to open his mouth, tell her how much she meant to him, how his fucking heart stopped when he didn't think he'd reach her in time.

Ty saved his ass for the two hundredth time in the last couple of hours. "Give him time, Lauren."

His brother cuddled his own mate close, keeping Mia snuggled in his lap.

Van wanted to do that with Lauren, but with his emotions spinning out of control, he wasn't sure he could resist squeezing her to reaffirm she was okay; that she was alive. Would he hold her too tight though? Hurt her in his attempts to confirm she still breathed.

Couldn't risk it.

The heavy stench of pain, emotional pain, reached out to him, wrapped its wicked arms around his chest and clutched him. Her pain. He was hurting her. Hurting her without touching her.

"Okay. Okay, sure." Her voice was so small. So tiny compared to her usual confidence and attitude. Had he done that? Or the accident?

A fleck of blood clung to her cheek, evidence of a scrape. How many more were there? That internal question brought her other injuries to mind. Ones hidden by clothing and obscured from his gaze.

The bear perked up at that, the angry roars turning into concerned huffs and chuffs. They hadn't done very well taking care of her, had they? They'd nearly lost her and now they hadn't bothered getting her cleaned up.

Mia had suffered a few scratches, but her bear blood had them nearly healed. Lauren… Lauren didn't have any hint of animal to help her.

Making a decision and damn his Itan for asking them to stick around, Van pushed to his feet. "I'm taking Lauren to the den."

"Van, we need to let our officers do their jobs. You know as well as I do, who was behind that wheel. Even if we don't have proof." He hated it when Ty was logical.

Bastard.

Lauren shifted in her seat, and he noted the wince she tried to hide.

"No," he shook his head. "She's hurt and I'm taking her home."

His home. His den. The bear purred at the idea. They could protect her on their lands. The number of guards were increased after the interloper. They'd never identified the intruder beyond the fact he was a wolf shifter. They hadn't conclusively recognized the animal as Morgan. Damn it.

A soft knock against Ty's office door preceded a werebear cop's entrance and the newcomer waved a handful of pages in Ty's direction. "Itan, I have news for you."

"One moment." Ty focused on Van once again. "It'd be best if you two stayed here."

"She's human, Ty. She needs rest. I'll take her home, get her cleaned up, and—"

187

The other officer cut him off. "I can take her to the human hospital down the street. Police escort and all. I don't have a problem with humans."

Van slowly turned to look at the interfering male and noticed the waggling of his eyebrows. The man had a death wish.

Carefully, moving leisurely toward the door, he lessened the distance between him and the cop. With equal care, he slid the pages from the man's hands and then he did his own bit of grasping. He wrapped his fist around the man's shirtfront, grabbing and twisting the fabric to strangle him. Then he lifted and pinned the male to the wall with a snarl.

"Mine." The cop gasped and Van shook him. "Say it. Mine."

"Y-y-y—"

Another jiggle. "Mine."

"Y-y-y—"

"He can't answer if you're choking him," Ty drawled.

True.

He lowered the man until the tips of his shoes touched, giving a tiny bit of leeway. "Now. Mine."

"Van." Lauren's soft whisper of his name cut through his focus like nothing before. The single syllable, pleading and exhausted, called to his bear. "Put him down." He growled. He didn't want to listen. Wanted to make the other bear say the word. "Van?"

He huffed and let the man stand. He didn't let him go, though. Instead, he jostled the guy a little more. "Say it."

"Yours, Enforcer. Yours."

Van glared at him a little longer, curling his lip in an additional threat.

"*Van.*" Lauren's anger snapped at him and he released the officer, pushing him toward Ty's desk.

"Now that Van has finished pissing all over the floor," Ty sighed, "what news?"

"The mayor reported a vehicle missing." His brother sighed and pinched the bridge of his nose, the hand stroking Mia's back stilling. "And?"

"And it's a 2012 blue SUV."

Fuck. That just cast more suspicion on the mayor and Morgan both. That nod they'd shared in the lobby… A missing SUV and a wolf behind the wheel… It wasn't looking good for Bryson Davies. Van hoped he'd get to visit a little clan justice on the human male and wolf.

"Great." His brother sighed. "Leave the mayor be for now. Spread the word amongst the neighboring shifters. Let them know the make, model, and year."

"Yes, Itan." The man eased back into the hallway, his attention flitting between Van and Ty, though Van noticed it lingered on him a hair longer.

Good, the man should be afraid of him.

The moment the door clicked shut, he turned to his brother. Plans had changed. "I'll get Lauren to my den and safe, and then I'll kill the mayor. I should be home for dinner."

It wouldn't take long to handle, and then the threat to Lauren and her friend, Anna, would disappear in one swoop. Nice and tidy. Then he'd deal with Morgan. If he hadn't been the one behind the wheel, he'd know who'd been driving.

"No." At Ty's single word, his smile fell.

"What d'ya mean no? He tried to kill Lauren. Again." Anger stretched his skin, the bear pushing the emotion outward.

"We don't know that. Not for sure. Dealing with humans is delicate, Van, humans are different."

"*Humans.*" He spat the word, the syllables rotting on his tongue. He'd met those types of humans. Before Bryson Davies crossed his path. Back when he looked at the world through innocent eyes.

And then remembered who sat feet from him. He winced and the bear snarled inside his head. He was a dumbass. "Lauren…"

Shock coated her features, eyes wide and mouth slightly open. "Van?" She shook her head. "Is that how you really feel? I mean, the way you said 'humans'… Is that…?" She gulped and pushed herself standing. Her arms trembled, legs shaking, as she stood before him. "That's why Martin and Keen were so surprised, isn't it? You," she drew in a sharp breath, pressing a hand to her chest. "You hate them, us, don't you?"

"Not you, Lauren. Never you."

She didn't believe him. He saw it in every broken line of her expression, in the way she held her body stiff and wrapped her arms around herself. Pain, betrayal, heartache. All of it was plain to see.

Lauren tore her gaze from him and turned to Ty. "I'd like to go home, please."

Pity filled Ty's features. "I can't let you go back to your apartment."

She looked at Van. "I don't even know how you mated me. Why you mated me. If you hate us so much…" She focused back on Ty. "I can't stay with Van." Her voice was filled with steel even if her body shook with the effort of standing.

His heart broke with those words, pieces falling and crumbling inside him. The bear whined, and it took everything in him to keep that sound within. He wanted to plead and beg, but now wasn't the time. He had to convince her to come home with him, to return to his den. She wouldn't be safe in that decrepit building.

Mia leaned over and whispered something to his brother, the words so low he couldn't hear them. Finally, his brother brushed a kiss across his mate's forehead and turned back to Lauren.

"You can stay with Mia and me."

"Thank you."

No. The word lingered on the tip of his tongue, but he held it back. The last thing he wanted to do was alienate her further. She'd be safe.

Not in his den, but still safe.

* * *

Dinner had been quiet and quick. Ty scarfed his food, Parker played with most of his, and Lauren picked at hers. It wasn't that the food was terrible. It was because she didn't have Van with her.

She didn't feel safe.

Even after Ty introduced her to the half-dozen guards surrounding the house for the night, she still felt vulnerable.

Six guards on the immediate perimeter and another six in the forest. All of them shifted, all of them waiting for a wolf or a human to try something. They'd received the same veiled order; bear maulings seem to be on the rise, imagine that. Well, that was the "suggestion" for humans. Wolves were simply to be killed on sight. Apparently, the Redby Alpha was on board with that order.

After dinner, Lauren retreated to her assigned room. At first, she'd been surprised to find her belongings in there, all neatly folded and put away.

Keen again.

She forced herself into loose pajamas, refusing to look at the new bruise on her side. She definitely didn't look at the nearly healed mating bite.

191

Mating. Heh. Van mated to a human. Apparently Van's aversion to "skins" was only a surprise to Lauren. She shook her head and eased beneath the sheets. She wondered if there was a way to break the mating. If there was some magical way to make it disappear. There had to be something that made them shifters, right?

She hoped she could free him from a life of being mated to someone like her. Someone human. Hell, she'd been so worried about being two steps above trash when she should have been concerned with the fact she didn't grow fur.

Tears stung her eyes and she blinked them back. She wasn't gonna cry. Nope. Lauren Evans wasn't a crier, she was a doer. She didn't let shit get her down. She got down on shit.

Okay, gross.

But she knew what she meant. She'd shovel her way out of a bad situation. She'd done it before, she'd do it again. How many times had she eaten Ramen for dinner or gone without electricity? How many nights had she and Anna huddled together for warmth because it was insanely cold?

Anna. She hadn't seen Anna in a couple of days, though at least she'd spoken with her best friend. She was deliriously happy with Martin, couldn't wait for her new life to start, and had begun divorce proceedings. Ty also assured her Martin was notified of recent events and he definitely *was not* a human hater.

He'd then gone on to try and talk to her about Van, about how he'd changed since Ty mated Mia, but she'd brushed him off.

Sometimes a leopard couldn't change its spots and a bear couldn't suddenly sprout neon pink fur.

Ty told her not to be so sure about either.

She snorted and wiggled deeper into the bed, snuggling the pillow and tugging a free one to her chest. She may not have had sex with Van, but she had become used to sleeping in his arms.

192

She'd miss that the most.

No, his kisses. She'd miss those more than anything. She sighed.

But then there was the way he…

Lauren tore her thoughts from heading in *that* direction.

For now, and the foreseeable future, a pillow would have to do.

She raised her head and glanced at the digital clock on the end table. It neared midnight. She was on hiatus from her job while Ty and the police figured out Bryson's end game. They also hunted the wolf who'd driven the SUV. But that didn't mean she couldn't get up and help in some way. Gigi, the den house's cook, made breakfast for all of the guards, incoming and those going off their shift.

The least Lauren could do was help out.

She reached over and fiddled with the alarm, setting it for seven since shift change was at nine. That'd give her two hours to wake up and also assist the older woman.

Plan in place, she relaxed against the soft mattress with a gentle sigh. A few hours of sleep and everything would be better in the morning.

Except…

The snap of a twig echoed off the walls, slicing through the silence. Her eyes snapped open and she stared into the darkness. There were bears outside, guarding the house. Was it one of them? Of course it was. No one would take on six shifted bears. The men were massive, heavily muscled, and dangerous as hell. No, she was safe. Safe.

A scrape along the outside of the home reached her, a long, dragging sound that seemed to also dig into her spine.

Lauren gulped. Safe.

It was one of the bears. Had to be.

She stared at the room's window, gaze fully centered on the rectangles of glass, the one portal to the outside world. She strained to see into the darkness, see if one of the guards lingered nearby. And yet all she found was a big old nothing. No moon shone in the sky to cast a glow over the land or make a hint of a shadow visible.

A grumbling growl reached out to her.

Oh god, it sounded so close.

She should race for Ty. But that subconscious part of her, the bit that never made a bit of sense, yet held her childlike ideas, told to stay put. Bad things couldn't break through blankets. As long as she was covered on the bed, she was safe.

Right. Totally a kid throwback.

But the fear… the fear held her immobile.

She was so kicking her own ass in the morning. Especially if it was all in her mind.

Another scratch right outside her window, and then a wet nose pressed against the glass, leaving a slimy trail in its wake.

"*Fuck.*" She hissed at the guard. "*What the fuck are you doing? Peeping asshole!*"

The bear huffed, blowing warm air across the barrier, fogging it up with moisture.

"*Dick. I'm so telling Ty.*" She did her best to yell and whisper at the same time.

Now the fear was replaced with all out anger.

The familiar snap of bone reached her, and she strained to watch the impending shift. It'd be even better if she had a name to place on the dickhead who'd scared her.

The bear's face slowly transformed into his human shape, fur receding, skull reshaping, and teeth sliding away. With each crack, more of the man's true self emerged.

Brown eyes, light brown hair, that small bump along the ridge of his nose, and hints of the scars he'd endured during his fight with the hyenas…

Asshole.

"Van." She glared at the man and stomped to the window.

He flashed her a smile the moment his shift was complete, the grin growing the nearer she came to him. He could save it, his sexy smirk did nothing for her.

She reached up and snared the curtains, yanking them closed in one heave. He could keep his Peeping Tom ass out there and keep his eyes to himself. She didn't need him. Ever.

Lauren squeezed her eyes shut and wondered if she'd ever believe the lie.

The screech of the bedroom window being slid open tore her attention to the hidden portal once again.

No.

Hell no.

Undoing her work, she jerked them open to reveal a nude Van crawling through the opening.

"No." She snapped her fingers. "You are not coming in here."

He eased the rest of the way in and rose to his full height. "Too late."

She shook her head and stepped back, putting space between her and a deliciously naked Van. Damn it, why did she still want him?

Oh. Right. They weren't separated because *she* didn't want *him*. It was the other way around. He was a human hater. A speciest is what Ty called it. And then, once again, he assured her Van wasn't that way anymore. He had his reasons, but he really was working hard to let them go. Every one of the Abrams brothers had negative feelings toward humans when they were younger, when they'd been exposed to the worst the species had to offer. They got over it, but Van… He reminded her once again, Van wasn't like that anymore.

Lauren focused on "anymore."

Could she make a life with a man who'd dislike her best friend because she wasn't able to shift? Or their children? Sure, if she and Van were fated mates, their kids could shift. But what if they *weren't* fated mates? What if the kids were "skins?"

She wasn't sure when the hatred would lash out and when it wouldn't.

That, more than anything, worried her.

"Van, you need to leave." She held out a hand to halt his approach.

It didn't work. "No." He shook his head. "You're here, so I'm here."

"Van…" She kept backing up, kept easing toward the bedroom door over a dozen feet away.

"Lauren, baby, five minutes. Just gimme five minutes."

She shook her head. Nope, because then he'd convince her she hadn't seen hate on his face or heard it in his tone. It was something else. "Not happening. Just stay back."

"Lauren," he sighed, running a hand through his short hair. She focused on his head, on his face, on anything but his nude body.

Then again, she knew what she'd see. The pale scars, the carved muscle, the dusting of hair on his chest and the bit surrounding his cock. It was thick, heavy, and firm in her hand when she stroked

196

him. The memory brought forward others. The way he tasted her, slipped his fingers inside her, begged her to come for him.

Despite her anger, a hint of arousal blossomed inside her, desire unfurling and stretching its ethereal muscles. Parts of her still wanted him, craved him.

Idiot parts. Those bits of her were "too stupid to live."

Van breathed deeply and somehow her gaze wandered to his wide chest, to the way it expanded when he inhaled. "Lauren, love."

She shook her head. No, there was no love. Not between them. Lots of like and a fuckton of lust, but that was it. Okay, the "like" was two fucktons, but she wouldn't say it aloud. Not after the way he reacted in Ty's office.

"No, look," she huffed. "This was a mistake." Van growled, but she continued. It wasn't like he was gonna hurt her. "And I'm sorry we got tied together because of your laws. As soon as we can figure out how, we'll break our mating and—"

Lauren didn't get a chance to finish. He went from near the window to before her in a giant leap. She was alone and then suddenly in his hold, arms wrapped around her like steel bands.

"No. You're mine. *Mine.*"

He should have sounded like a possessive asshole.

Should have, but didn't. Because to her heart, it was the sweetest thing anyone had ever said. No one had ever wanted her, claimed her, and refused to let her go.

She decided to hit where it'd hurt. "Even if I'm human?"

Van grimaced. "That was… the wrong thing to say at the time."

Lauren pushed against his chest. "And there's a right time to say something like that? To spew your hate." She shoved again. "One word and I felt your disgust to my bones, Van."

"Damn it, Lauren, stop struggling. Gimme a minute."

She'd give him something.

He changed his hold, scooping her into his arms and then tossing her onto the bed. He came down atop her, blanketing her with his body.

"Hell no, we are not having sexytimes in the middle of an argument."

Van flashed one of those panty-wetting grins and shook his head. "No, love, that's for after." He gave her more of his weight. "Holding you like this means you can't run."

He was right, so she glared at him.

He propped his upper body on his elbows, his face inches from hers. He couldn't hide from her like this, couldn't turn away or mask his emotions. She wasn't sure if she liked that, or hated it. What would she see? Did she *want* to see?

"In any world, human or shifter, there are preconceived notions."

"Prejudices." She glared at him.

Van gritted his teeth, jaw twitching. "Prejudices. For humans—"

"Like me."

"Yes, like you. Are you going to let me finish?"

Lauren rolled her eyes. "Yes, sorry."

"For humans, you have hatred and prejudices within your own kind. Different religions hate this sect or another, skin color can define the way people are treated, and countries despise other countries." Van twined a lock of her hair between two fingers. "For shifters… We have problems and ideas about different species. Hyenas breed indiscriminately and are the bottom of the barrel when it comes to how they treat their own. Wolves are callous bastards. The Alpha's word is law. No negotiation." He sighed. "That's what makes this thing with Redby so important. Wolves and bears don't mix and that they want peace with us…"

Van shook his head. "Anyway. We have certain ideas like any other group except our prejudices extend to humans as well."

Thanks for that Captain Obvious.

"I've seen things, experienced things…" He turned his head away, gaze unfocused, and Lauren took advantage of his inattention.

He'd been right, they needed to talk, but she didn't have to be held down to listen. She sensed the pain growing in him like a lead ball. It increased in size the closer he got to revealing the truth and maybe, just maybe, he needed to be held and comforted a little too.

She should have known his "dislike" wasn't unreasonable. That something lurked behind the emotions.

She nudged him, surprising him, and he fell to his side. He grasped her forearm, pulling her close, and she twitched out of the way, twining their fingers together instead. Holding tight, she lay her head on one of the bed pillows, showing him without words that she wasn't disappearing. She couldn't read him, read the situation, if he remained hidden from her.

"Tell me."

chapter sixteen

Van didn't want to tell her a fucking thing. Not one word. Not one syllable.

But he didn't want to lose her, either.

So, he allowed the locks on his memories to fall away, allowed the pain to surge forward. He started with the worst, began with the hardest part that hurt to his marrow. There was more pain and hate accumulated through the years, but this was where it started.

"I've always been the Enforcer just as Ty has always been the Itan." He saw the confusion on her face and explained a little more. "The firstborn of an Itan, as long as he's a shifting cub, will inherit the position." At her nod, he continued. "I was born with a protective streak a mile wide and a firm grasp of right and wrong. So, Dad thought I'd be a good Enforcer, Ty's right hand, when I got older. I began training with my father's Enforcer, my uncle, at a young age. I learned fighting techniques, worked on the speed of my shift."

Using his hold on her hand, he eased her closer, gently pulled until she lay snuggled against him. He held her close, not capturing her, but using her presence for comfort as the memories rushed forward.

"It wasn't as if Uncle Bren acted like a drill sergeant. He'd take me out on patrols, hunt with me in the forest, that kind of thing. Every cub got a little of that type of training. I just got more and earlier than others."

Van enjoyed those memories. The ones when he and Uncle Bren would slip into their fur and spend a weekend tracking and hunting. His uncle teaching him how to creep through the forest. The man was a half-ton of bear and managed to not make a sound.

Too bad he wasn't talking to her about the good stuff.

"We spent every Sunday in the forest. It started in the woods surrounding Grayslake, but as I got older, we ventured beyond town limits. The last time…"

Memories roared in, taking over, shoving him back to that day.

Young shifted Van bounded through the bushes and pounced on a small squirrel, catching it with his paws. He didn't hurt or kill it though, that was only allowed if he was hungry and they were hunting. It was a *rule*. Enforcers, bears, didn't harm anything or anyone unless they had a good reason. Not something like Bobby Green taking his pudding cup. It had to be *bad*.

Uncle Bren told him that over and over.

The little squirrel squeaked at him, struggling beneath his paws, and Van leaned down, sniffing the tiny animal. He fought hard to memorize the scent, put it in his brain so he'd always have it there. Remembering was important in case he really was hunting for food. He lowered his nose, intent on taking in his prey's scent, when the stupid-head squirrel bit his snout.

Van whined and jerked back, releasing the animal, and he rubbed his nose with a paw. He didn't wanna smell the dumb thing anyway.

A low rumbling chuff grabbed his attention, his Uncle Bren fussing at him to pay attention. He responded with his own rolling grumble and backed out of the bush, wiggling until he was free of the sticks and leaves. One big shake got rid of the bits that stuck to his fur and then he smiled at his uncle, letting his tongue hang out.

Uncle Bren couldn't stay mad if he made the cute cub face. Even his dad had a hard time resisting that expression.

When his uncle just rolled his eyes, Van knew he wasn't in trouble. Not waiting a second, he bounded toward the other bear, hopping like a rabbit instead of a cub. But it was fun and Uncle Bren didn't huff at him, so he kept going. He jumped from one leg to another, first balance on his right paws and then popping to his left.

Dead leaves and twigs cracked and crunched under his weight. Van's dad said he was big for a cub, super strong too. He said it was part of what would make him a good Enforcer. His brother would be the strongest and bestest, but Van would be almost as good.

Van made sure he kept Uncle Bren in sight. He was supposed to keep up with him, but sometimes he liked to poke around without his uncle. Plus, Uncle Bren wouldn't let anything happen to him.

But then… a new scent teased Van's nose. It was… He pulled it in, drawing it all the way into his toes like his uncle taught him. It wasn't *really* to his toes, but it had to fill his lungs. Van's bear couldn't figure out the source of a scent unless it had a lot of a lot of it.

So, he spread his chest and sucked in as much as he could until he felt like a party balloon. It kinda smelled like deer and a little bit of human. The scent of humans he knew, he lived in Grayslake and the town had lots of them. Not a lot of deer this time of year though. He pulled in more and it was the same, deer and human.

Weird.

Van looked down the path and whined. He couldn't see Uncle Bren anymore. Oh man, his uncle was gonna be *so* mad.

Forgetting about the scent, he trotted toward where he'd last seen the other bear. If he managed to find Uncle Bren before he noticed Van was missing, he wouldn't get in trouble.

More of that human-y scent surrounded him and he picked up his pace. He didn't want to be caught by humans. He tended to shift back into his human shape when he got scared and he didn't wanna do that because then Uncle Bran would have to "deal with" the people who saw him transform. Van wasn't sure what "deal with" meant, but he knew it made Uncle Bren sad when he talked about it, so he never asked.

The rustling of bushes to his left scared Van so bad he stumbled to the right and slid across the leaves. The snap of a tree branch reached him and then he heard a big someone stomping on the ground. Then there were whispers.

Oh man, he was in so much trouble.

"…ready?"

"George says one hundred feet."

He didn't know how far one hundred feet was, but it didn't sound like a super long way away.

"Everyone loaded?"

"Quiet now."

Another break. Another step. Another rub of cloth against cloth.

They were real, real close. He heard four voices and he wondered if there were more. Van listened a little harder, letting his bear take over some more and he shuddered. They were way very near.

Careful now, trying very, very hard to be quiet, Van crept through the forest. He eased off the path him and Uncle Bren were on and eased around some bushes. He needed to be quiet and fast because he knew the humans were up to no good. They'd tried to cover up their scents with deer smelly stuff. Probably to get a real bear to come to them, but werebears were smarter than that.

Van still heard them talking about guns and stuff, but they sounded farther away now. Good, he could get to Uncle Bren and get out of the forest. He didn't wanna play Enforcer anymore. He wanted to go home and eat his mom's cookies already.

A bush to Van's left rustled and he skittered away. Had they found him? He hoped not. It didn't sound like they wanted to do anything good to any bears they caught. He stumbled a little, tripping over a broken branch, and then hands were on him. Big hands. Strange hands.

The scent of deer wrapped around him and he knew he'd been caught by one of those nasty humans. Panic hit him, tearing through him, and he released the loudest roar ever. He opened his mouth wide and screamed into the air, hoping his Uncle Bren would hear him.

The whole time he yelled, he wiggle and squirmed, making sure his claws were out. He slashed at anything he could reach. Sometimes it was air and once or twice it was the guy's arm or leg.

"What the fuck? Little shit."

A new guy stood in front of him, his arms out like he was gonna grab Van and he snapped his teeth at the man. He wasn't big enough to hurt a grown up bear, but he could hurt a human. They didn't have fur, claws, or fangs to protect them.

"Grab his fucking feet and tie them already."

Van couldn't let that happen, so he fought harder. He wiggled and wormed, scraping anything he could touch while he roared even more. Uncle Bren could save him. Uncle Bren could hurt them and make them go away.

"What the hell are you gonna do with him?" Another voice. That meant there were three. Where was the other one? There were four.

"Sell him to a circus. He's young." Van scraped the man's leg and fought to turn around, to bite his arm. "They'll buy a baby bear."

"You know his momma's gotta be around here somewhere."

There was the fourth voice. All four of them wanna sell him to a *circus*. No.

And he did have a momma. As soon as she found out what they'd done to her baby boy she'd hurt them so fast…

Finally, one of the men caught his back paws in one hand. In the other he had a piece of rope. No, he couldn't get tied up. He'd never get away then.

Van released another roar, begging his uncle to find him.

The third man held a looped piece of twine in his hand and his attention was on Van's mouth. He couldn't let that happen either. If he couldn't roar, how would a grown up find him?

He fought harder, squirming and growling and fighting and...

A real roar, a grown up roar, hit Van right in the heart. His Uncle Bren was coming back. He let himself relax a little. He wasn't gonna end up in some circus and his uncle would take care of everything.

"Fuck, fuck, fuck. Told you his momma would come looking. Fucking assholes." That was from the guy Van couldn't see, the one who *wasn't* trying to tie him up. "Get the damn guns."

The man trying to tie his feet let go and ran away and then came back with a really big gun in his hands. "Just let the cub go. Send it back to its momma."

The smell coming from them wasn't just deer and regular human anymore. Now it was kinda rotted and hurt his nose.

"Idiot. He's covered in our scent now. You think she won't hunt our asses down? We gotta kill her."

Kill? No, they couldn't kill his Uncle Bran. They couldn't. Van opened his mouth and released a warning roar. At least, he hoped it was. He prayed it was.

Then his snout was snapped shut and the man with the twine tied his jaws together. He shook his head, trying to dislodge the rope, but it wouldn't go anywhere. It was on tight, and he thought he smelled a little blood, and...

Van saw his Uncle Bren destroying forest as he ran toward them. Trees broke and collapsed, his uncle pushing them aside like they were nothing. He was saved. These men wouldn't sell him to some circus and his uncle would make them pay for hurting him. It was just his nose, but they scared him so bad.

But then… the man who'd gone for the big gun brought it up and braced it against his shoulder. A loud, deafening crack filled the forest and rang in his ears. He couldn't hardly hear, but one thing that did reach him was his uncle's roar. His uncle wasn't slowing down. He was still coming at them, his feet pounding on the leaf strewn ground.

The man holding him moved, stumbled a little, and Van wiggled in his hold. They were shooting at his uncle, but if Van got away, they could just run from these mean humans.

The guy who captured him threw him to the ground and he heard a weird popping sound. Pain blew up in his right front paw, forcing a whine from his tied snout. It hurt real, real bad, but Van shuffled away from the men who'd grabbed him. His uncle always told him that he needed to keep out of the way of fighting bears. They were mean and deadly and they might hurt him.

So he hobbled back until he managed to get most of his body behind a tree, but he could still watch what was going on. He was waiting for his uncle to hurt those mean men. He'd bite one or two and run them off and then they could go home because his leg was hurting more and he wanted a cookie.

The man with the gun did something with it and then pressed it to his shoulder again. Then another one of those loud booms bounced around in his head.

Van's uncle roared and stumbled, and he realized that his uncle's shoulder was real dark and wet. They'd shot him. They *shot* his uncle.

Then his uncle got up and roared some more, rushed forward again.

The man who tied up Van's snout had a gun now. He brought it up and fired it and he saw exactly where it hit Uncle Bren. Right in his chest. But his uncle kept coming. He didn't let something like bullets slow him down.

"It's not fucking going down!" The guy who'd captured him first raised his hand and he had a smaller gun.

Pop. Pop. Pop.

Three more holes in his uncle and Uncle Bren stumbled real hard then. Kinda falling to the side, but then he got up again. His lips curled back, showing off his big teeth.

"Shit."

Pop. Pop.

No! They had to stop hurting Uncle Bren! Van didn't care about his hurt leg. He ran as fast as he could on three legs and he went for that man with the small gun. He couldn't bite him, but he still had claws. Not as big as Uncle Bren's, but big enough. He slid to a stop, falling back on his butt, and took a swipe at the evil man. He cut through his pants and the scent of his blood filled Van's nose. It stank and now he was glad he couldn't bite him. It would have tasted gross.

His uncle gave a different kind of roar. One that told Van to get back and hide. But he was saving his uncle… wasn't he?

"What the fuck?" The man he hurt spun around and then that gun was pointed at Van, aimed for his head.

Now he was running, fighting to get away, and scrambling and slipping on the leaves. The man's aim didn't move and remained on him. He saw him tighten his hand, pulling the trigger, and Van knew a big boom would come and then he'd be bleeding like Uncle Bren.

Then Uncle Bren was there, his uncle coated in blood, his fur dark and stained. He batted at the bad man, slicing him with his big claws. The man fell to the side, but the boom came anyway, immediately followed by pain in his right shoulder. The human shot him and it hurt, and he wanted to cry and scream, but his snout was tied.

Then Uncle Bren looked at him with his black eyes and Van knew he was hurt, knew all the way to his heart that his uncle was in a lot of pain. His uncle roared at him then, the sound nearly breaking his ears and rattling in his head.

He knew what the sound meant—knew what he was supposed to do—but he couldn't. He just *couldn't*.

Except Uncle Bren made that sound again. The one said that he had to run as fast as he could and find a grown up bear. That's what it meant. Go now. Go fast. Go far.

And don't… He did moan then because he didn't like the next part of the rule.

Don't look back.

Van's eyes burned, tears making them hurt and he wanted to whine and tell Uncle Bren "no," that he could stay and help. But then the human with the small gun looked at him, lifted his arm and was ready to shoot Van again. His uncle snarled and growled, reaching out for the bad human and he sent the man slamming to the ground. The human collapsed in a bloody heap and Uncle Bren looked at him, stared at him and gave that roar and Van knew he had to listen. He *had to*.

But he didn't want to, not now, not ever.

Another one of the bad men aimed at Van, his super big gun pointed at him, while the second and third guy focused on Uncle Bren.

And Uncle Bren… He whined, he begged Van with his eyes and his low chuff, he pleaded with Van to run, so he ran and ran and he didn't look back when he heard the first shot, or the second, or the third. He didn't look back when his uncle roared or one of the humans screamed. He didn't…

He stumbled to a stop, tripping over a fallen branch and he landed on his hurt paw. He wanted to cry out, wanted to whine for his mom to come make it better, but there was no one there to help him. No one but him and Uncle Bren, and Uncle Bren was…

209

A low, guttural moan reached Van, the sound deep and filled with sadness and he knew, *knew* it was Uncle Bren. Uncle Bren wasn't dead. He was alive, and Van would go as fast as he could, faster than any cub ever, and get help. He'd…

"How many rounds you got left in that pistol?"

Pop. Pop. Pop.

There weren't any sounds anymore. His uncle didn't call to him and then the humans started talking about getting that one guy an ambulance before he died and maybe one of the medics could take a picture…

The soft touch of delicate fingers ghosting over his skin drew him from the past and back into the present. Drew him back to Lauren's room, and Lauren's bed, and sweet Lauren resting across from him. Her hand slid across his collarbone and then pet the scar that marred his right shoulder. Lauren's voice was barely a whisper, her touch no more than a ghostly caress. "This isn't from the fight with the hyenas."

Van shook his head and cleared his throat, pushing past the lump that'd formed in his chest. "No."

She leaned back further and stroked his arm until she got to his wrist. Her fingers traced the uneven bone, the knot on the left side of his right wrist. "And this…"

"When I was thrown." His heart hammered and fought to burst free of his chest. Emotions overwhelmed him, crashed and slammed into him from all sides. "It was dislocated. It'd mostly healed by the time I found help and I…" He coughed. "I didn't want to ever forget. I wouldn't let them fix it."

"Van." So much emotion, he could read so much in the way she whispered his name. "God, *Van.*"

"It's fine. I'm fine. It was a long time ago."

A bit over twenty years. Twenty two, but he didn't want to count. Didn't want to remember. Sometimes he tried to forget. Tried to remember the good times before... *Before*. He fought to hold onto the times when he'd laugh and play with his uncle, except the hatred refused to be brushed aside.

Lauren shook her head. "No, it's really not."

"It's—"

She propped herself on an elbow and glared down at him, her eyes sparkling with the anger. "It's not. You were what, four? Five? What you had to witness, what you had to experience and then you ran..." She sobbed and he reached for her, his heart breaking that she was so upset by what he'd shared. She batted his hand away. "You were a baby, Van."

"I'm fine now."

"You're not." She shook her head. "You've got so much hate and God knows it's justified. I just wish..."

He tugged her close then and she allowed it, her body sinking into his embrace and collapsing against him. She was what he needed. She was the reason that hate wasn't quite so sharp and deadly any longer. Just having her close healed him. Every second, every minute, blunted the rage a little more.

"I can forget for a while sometimes and then others... Then it's right there in front of me. The roars, the blood, the guns." He traced a pattern on her skin, gliding his finger along her arm. He sighed, more details coming forward.

"I waited, you know. Stuck around until they realized the one man was dead. Stayed close enough to see forest rangers come down and hold the camera while he took pictures of the other three men as they posed with Uncle Bren's body. The ranger was one of us and he..." He swallowed against the bile rising in his throat. "He took the guns away and for the first time in my life, I realized what 'dealt with' meant."

He'd never ever forget those screams or the way they made him feel. For a little while, for the few minutes that the men screamed and fought a full grown grizzly, he'd been happy. It was the first time he'd lusted for blood.

A warm wetness slid over his bare chest, evidence of his mate's tears and pain. For him, all for him.

"That's why…" She didn't finish her sentence, but she didn't need to.

"That's why I have a problem with humans."

"Hate them." Her voice trembled, but remained fairly steady.

"The bear doesn't. Not entirely. It still feels pain over Uncle Bren's loss and a hint of loathing because we couldn't help him. But the second he saw you, it was done. You belonged to us."

"But the human part of you?"

"Still has trouble in certain situations. Except," he rushed to add, "when it comes to you. You are mine, Lauren. I'll still get pissed at humans and may even curse them, I can't lie about that. After my uncle… I have problems. I've been working on them for a long, long time. I'll probably fight them until the day I die. But I promise to give other shifter groups an equal amount of insults."

She got quiet, eyes trained on his chest and her fingers slid over him, tracing the scars that neared his neck. Those few had been close—deep—and the poison in the hyena's claws had nearly done him in.

"I can't even imagine the pain, what you endured that day, but I don't want you to regret choosing me, Van. In a year, five years, ten years, I don't want you to look at me and think for a single instant: *'Human.'*" He hated to see the heartbreak and pain in her features. "I don't want you to look at our children—"

"Cubs." He couldn't withhold the correction. Especially when talk of the future gave him hope. "Shifting or not, they're cubs."

212

"Will you hate them if they don't shift? If they're more human than bear?"

"Love," his heart broke for her and the bear cursed him for the turmoil he'd rained on her. "Never. They'd be ours. Shifter or not, they'd be ours."

"I won't have children raised in a house of prejudice, Van."

He covered her hand with one of his. "I can't promise there won't be the occasional wolf or hyena joke. But I promise you, love, there won't ever be anything negative about humans taught to our children by anyone in our family." He lifted her delicate hand and pressed a kiss to the center of her palm. "And if all else fails, I'll have you there to keep me in line."

"What about the rest of the clan?" A new tension thrummed through her.

"*Our* clan won't say a word. If I can conquer my pain after everything." He took a deep, calming breath. "Then they can do the same. They don't have a right to feel the way they do. They weren't there. They didn't witness…" The ranger's attack had been brutal, bloody. He'd tortured those men, destroyed them, pulled them inside out. And when it was done, he'd cut the twine holding Van's snout shut and carried him to the station. "They didn't see it all. They don't have the right to those emotions. That doesn't mean they won't try, that they won't say things, but they'll only utter the words once." He pictured the Southeast Itan's second-in-command, Malcom in front of him. That asshole had a lot to say about Ty mating Mia. He wouldn't mind punching him a time or two.

"Van, you can't beat up every prejudiced person."

"Nope," he shrugged. "Just the ones who come here or are near you and our cubs."

Lauren sighed.

When she didn't say a word, he spoke up. "Are we okay?"

213

"I just… I can't even imagine… How can you even…?" She nuzzled his chest, kisses traveling to his shoulder and brushing the evidence of that day. "We're not *not* okay."

"But that's not okay-okay?" The memories still clouded his mind, making his thoughts muddled and twisted. Van the man was as confused as his bear. Then again, his bear was confused and very, very annoyed at him. Van's big mouth had gotten them in trouble and he'd had to crawl through a damned window. Then he'd ripped his heart out of his chest and laid it on a platter for Lauren, spread himself to her gaze and relived the past.

"That's…" she growled and his dick twitched. He couldn't help it. They weren't not okay which was halfway to okay and all he knew was he wasn't in the doghouse any longer. *That* meant—hopefully—cock hardening wouldn't earn him a slap.

Lots, hopefully.

He wanted to wash away the pain, shove it back into its hell hole, and revel in life for a while. His uncle had died for Van and he wanted to embrace what he'd been given.

"Van?" She shifted against him, her fabric-covered thigh sliding along his. "Go to sleep."

"Here?"

Another growl. "Yes. We'll talk more in the morning. I understand better and I get that you weren't snarling at *me*, but I've got to work through things and—"

"Naked? Work through them naked?"

Lauren stilled. "Are you fucking kidding me?"

Damn, that was very close to a shout. "Love, what I meant was…"

The bedroom door opened, letting hallway light into the space and revealing them to the interloper.

214

Van jerked up, intent on protecting Lauren from whomever interrupted them, but he froze at Ty's voice. "First, language. The kid is down the hall and if my mate can't scream 'fuck me harder,' you can't say a regular old fuck."

"More than I needed to know about your sex life, Ty."

"And," his brother growled, "Lauren, forgive him. This right here, this is the best version of Van you're ever gonna get. He's an ass, says stupid things, but he's really sorry already. And that shit," his brother coughed and cleared his throat, and Van pretended not to see the light sheen in his eyes. "It just… Give him another chance."

With that, his brother eased back through the door, tugging on the wood panel.

Van called out to him before he disappeared. "Hey, Ty." His brother stuck his head back in, eyebrows raised. "How'd you know I was here?"

Ty snorted. "Did you think the coverage outside Lauren's window was magically light? Or the window was left unlocked accidentally?" His brother stepped into the hallway and the door shut with a low thunk. Though, one chuckled word did reach him. "Sucker."

When it came to Lauren, he really was willing to believe anything if it meant he could be with her.

Gathering her close, he laid back, dragging her along with him. "So…"

"So." She nuzzled him.

"Forgive me for being an ass and a total dick?"

"Have to. The Itan said so." She grinned at him, but his heart became ice.

"Lauren, I don't want—"

215

She nipped him. "I'm not forgiving you because of Ty. I'm forgiving you because you helped me understand where you're coming from." She stroked his chest again and he was beginning to like her fingers tracing his scars. It was oddly soothing, her acceptance of his past warming his soul.

"I'm cautiously optimistic about our relationship." Her words were soft, almost a whisper.

He stroked her, hands sliding over her clothed body. He wished she was naked, bare for him. He'd lick and taste her, glory in her flavors. Slide deep into her.

Damn, he loved her. Right, wrong, or indifferent. He loved Lauren Evans. Even if it was way too early and fast.

Fuck it, he'd push his luck. "How about cautiously, optimistically in love with me, too?"

Lauren growled, but he sensed the playfulness in the sound. He also scented the heat that filled the air, the hint of joy riding on its wings and the edge of uncertainty that trailed in its wake.

She took a deep, slow breath and stared into his eyes, her unwavering gaze locked on his. "Maybe."

"I can work with maybe." His lips spread into a wide, goofy grin. He knew enough about women to recognize that her "maybe" meant yes. She just wasn't ready to tell him her feelings, and he was okay with that. "And just in case you're wondering," he let his bear free and let the full weight of his emotions fill his features. He wanted her to see, to know, he spoke the truth. "I'm cautiously, certainly in love with you."

chapter seventeen

It was the weirdest declaration of love Lauren had ever witnessed, but it was perfect. Perfectly perfect and better than any movie, and she didn't care if it was lame and early and they barely knew each other and…

…*cautiously certainly*…

"Yeah?" She swallowed past the dry lump in her throat.

"Yeah." He jerked his head in a nod and laid back, his chest deflating with a giant sigh.

…*cautiously certainly*…

He was hers. Right then, right there, she realized that for all his faults, for all *her* faults, he belonged to her and her alone. He'd experienced and endured things in his life that altered his perception and ideals. Things no one should ever suffer, child or adult. And now he was attempting to work through his horrific past.

It was time for her to get beyond her own. Being poor, enduring stares as if she was nothing better than the dirt on someone's shoe was nothing compared to Van's life. Her first step would be giving herself to him. Completely.

She thought about the occupants in the house, of the bears who had insanely good hearing and Parker's little ears down the hallway.

"Van?" She fought to keep her voice steady and low, unwilling for anyone inside, or outside, the house to hear her.

"Baby?" The words were husky and deep.

"Take me home."

He stiffened, his muscles going taut. "Lauren, we talked about the danger. You can't—"

She reached up and placed two fingers over his lips. "No, our home."

A new tautness thrummed through him and his cock hardened against her hip, filling and stiffening. "Lauren?"

"Take me to our home, Van. Take me there and make me," she swallowed past the nervousness building inside her, "make me truly yours."

"You want…?"

She reached down, sliding her fingertips over his skin, the familiar textures meeting her touch, and finally stopped when she got to his cock. She encircled his length and stroked him. He shuddered, his body trembling as his dick pulsed against her palm. "I want you. Completely."

"It's not good to tease a bear, baby." He growled low and she smiled.

Pressing her cheek to his chest, she nuzzled him. "I've been telling you that unless you're pushed, you're all roar and no bite." She nibbled his chest, scraping her teeth over his flesh. "Am I pushing you?"

She gathered his skin between her teeth and bit down. Not enough to break the skin, but enough for him to feel it. He jerked and twitched beneath her, his shaft throbbing against her hip.

"*Lauren…*"

"Van, unless you get me snug in our den in the next sixty seconds, everyone in this house, and every single guard lurking outside the window, are gonna hear me scream your name as I come."

That got him moving. He immediately wrapped his arms around her and manhandled her from the bed until her feet were firmly planted on the ground. He snared her wrist and tugged her toward the window.

"I'm not crawling out of a window when there's a perfectly good door—"

"Faster," he growled at her.

"Van—"

He whipped his head toward her and she noticed the flatness of his forehead and the slight protrusion of his jaw. A low growl rolled through the room, vibrating her from within. "Mine."

The bear was making its desires known. And that didn't scare her a bit. "Okay, you win. Out the window it is."

The growl softened into a soft chuff and the sounds of pleasure brought a smile to her lips. "Mine."

Lauren rolled her eyes. "Yeah, yeah, big guy."

If he wasn't so sexy, the whole "mine" thing would be annoying.

Van released her when he got to the window so he could shove it open once again. He stuck his head out, attention shifting side to side and then he was finally satisfied. Geesh.

He crawled through, landing on the solid ground with a grunt. He held out his arms, hands beckoning her to follow him. Groaning, she bent down and slung one leg through the portal, straddling the window sill.

"You know, this seemed like a good idea." But she wasn't that flexible. And her ass was big. Big butted women who weren't flexible did not belong in open windows. "But the door might be better." Van, predictably, growled. "I'm moving. But if I break something, it means no happy-fun-times for you."

He laughed. The jerk.

He assisted her, his massive, occasionally deadly, hands gripped her and gently helped her through the window and carefully placed her on the ground. She took a moment to grin at him, the giddy excitement of sneaking out filling her. She'd never been one to creep from the house after curfew and now she was sneaking out with a *boy*.

That smile died a quick death.

Because suddenly she was head down, ass up, over Van's shoulder. He swung her up in one fluid movement and then turned around. He stomped, naked as the day he was born, toward his house at the bottom of the hill. Ty and Mia's home grew smaller in her vision as they eased farther away. She spied some of the guards in the shadows, their beary faces giving her beary smiles and she wanted to hit them for laughing at her expense.

Instead, she growled and bared her very human, very non-threatening teeth.

That didn't change their expressions, but it did cause Van to halt his progress. "Lauren?"

"Your guys are laughing at me and I don't have claws to make them shut up." Petulant child, party of one.

"Really." His voice was too soft, too even, and she should have expected an outburst. But she didn't, and her eardrums cursed her for it.

Van slowly turned, his arm across the back of her knees, keeping her in place. Once he fully faced Ty's home, a bone-shaking, earthquake-causing roar erupted from his chest. It reverberated and bounced within her, making her teeth chatter. The birds nesting in the trees for the night burst from their perches and took to the air. Immediately following the sound, silence descended, blanketing them in quiet.

He remained in place as the sound drifted away and then just as slowly as before, turned back to his path.

The sight revealed once he faced his home tugged a giggle from her. Every bear who'd been smiling and laughing at her now cowered on the ground, their massive paws covering their ears.

And not a bear-smile in sight.

Ha!

Van stomped over the grass, each of his ground-eating steps jarring her as she bounced against his shoulder. "Ow, ow, ow, ow…" A sharp smack cut through the night, the sound reaching her ears before the pain blossomed in her ass. "Hey!"

He popped her ass again. "You're fine."

"I am not—" Another pop, his hand colliding with her ass in a speedy swat. "Ouch!"

The jerk did it again, only… only it wasn't hurting too-too much anymore. No, those hints of pain blossomed and unfurled with shades of pleasure.

Of course, she would never, ever, admit that getting spanked got her off.

But then Van inhaled, drew in a deep breath and released it with a rumbling purr. "You like that."

"Nu-uh." She shook her head to reinforce her denial and she pretended her ass wasn't wiggling and begging for another swat.

Van listened to her ass and not her mouth because he spanked her again, his bare palm whacking her pajama clad ass and the strike echoed into the night.

Her pussy clenched and released some of her cream, dampening her panties with her juices. Her clit throbbed, and the heat from his strikes surrounded her.

"Yeah, you do." He stroked her abused butt, sliding his hand over her heated flesh and soothing her. "But I like it, too, baby."

She opened her mouth, ready to tell him where he could take his liking and his *babys* and… And then Van clomped up his porch steps and slowly bent at the waist, allowing her to finally put her feet on solid ground.

The second she was settled, she pulled back her arm and let her fist fly. She punched him right in the arm as hard as she could.

"Ouch! What the fu—?" Lauren cut herself off before she could get herself in trouble with Mia. She did not want the Itana getting on her case right that second. As soon as she kicked Van's ass, she was going to boink him.

Van gathered her close, tugging her against him. "Hush." One of his hands drifted down her back, sending a shiver of desire through her body. "You liked it. There's nothing wrong with that. Someday, I'll bend you over." He leaned down, his warm breath fanning her face as he whispered into her ear. "And I'll spank your pretty ass until it glows for me." Oh god, that sounded wonderfully naughty. Her pussy tightened, aching and pulsing with desire. "And then," he scraped his teeth along her neck. "Then I'll fuck you until you scream my name."

Lauren whimpered. That was all. She couldn't think beyond the low sound.

"You like that." He patted her ass and a jolt of pleasure careened through her. "C'mon, baby. Lemme make you feel good. My cock needs to make friends with your pussy."

Lauren snorted. She couldn't help it. Right then, it was the most unsexy thing in the world and yet. "Your rooster is gonna make friends with my cat?"

She tried to stifle the next one, but it didn't happen. Nope. No way.

Van narrowed his eyes at her and snared her wrist, dragging her into the house with a continuous growl. She kept giggling, he kept growling, and they kept moving around furniture and down the hall until they came to his bedroom. Their bedroom.

He released her once they crossed the threshold and nudged her toward the bed. "Okay, baby, let's see what we can do about those giggles."

Still laughing, she turned to face him and… damn. Just *damn*. During the trek she'd forgotten her mate was nude, bare from head to toe. And aroused. Holy shit, her mouth watered at the sight before her. Van was long, thick, and more than ready to get the job done.

Yes, he wanted her.

All thoughts of roosters and cats fled her mind as she watched him reach down and encircle his shaft, stroked his dick from root to tip and back again. A droplet of pre-cum formed at the tip, a small bit of pearly fluid that she wanted to lap up. Salty? Or sweet? Both?

"Lauren?"

"Huh." She blinked and tore her gaze from his dick. She didn't really want to. Not when it was so close and practically begging for her mouth. She'd lick and suck him in that sweet spot below the head and— "What?"

Van grinned at her, the one that said he knew exactly what she'd been thinking and he knew she was a naughty, naughty girl. "If you like those pajamas, you should start taking them off. The bear and I have been waiting for this, baby."

She focused on him through the dim light of the room and saw what he meant. Van's brown eyes were pure black, his animal barely hiding behind his skin. While it should have scared her, it encouraged her. It was so close because of her. *Her.*

"Then come and get me," she taunted and stepped away.

Slowly she eased her thin top up, sliding it over the curve of her stomach and along her rib cage. With each step, it went higher, exposing more of her. She continued to put space between them until the initial four feet became five, then six, then seven...

She rounded the edge of the bed and lifted the fabric past her breasts. She whipped it over her head and reveled in Van's need. His skin darkened in a slow ripple only to lighten back to the tanned hue she was used to. Yes, the bear liked her topless.

"Lauren?"

Lauren let the top drift from her fingers and fall to the bed. "Hmm?"

She turned her back on him, making way to the other side of the bed. She wanted the piece of furniture to separate them. As she moved, she hooked her thumbs into the waist of her pajama bottoms. The long pants were baggy and comfortable. It wouldn't take much for them to fall from her body.

"Lauren?" More than a little of his beast lurked in his voice.

She glanced at him over her shoulder and wiggled her ass, pushing at the cloth until it barely clung to her hips. "Yeah?"

"You should..."

She jiggled her butt and the pants fell, sliding over the final flare of her hips to pool on the ground. "I should...?"

Stepping out of the pajama bottoms, she faced him. Gaze trained on him, watching the shift in his expressions, she cupped first one breast and then the other. She kneaded them, rubbing her thumbs over her nipples as he usually did. It was nothing like his touch, but it sent another bear-tinged shudder through his body.

Lauren placed one knee and then the other on the mattress before falling onto her hands. She crawled across the familiar soft surface. They'd spent night after night in this bed making love without taking that last step. Now, here, she realized how stupid she'd been. From the moment she'd agreed to let Van court her, she belonged to him. Period.

"Van?" He tore his attention from her swinging breasts to focus on her face. Her mate was such a sucker for tits. Well, those and her ass. Finally, in the middle of the bed, she pushed back until she knelt once again. Slowly, she turned her body, shifting until he could see her backside. "Is my ass still red from your hand?"

His gaze flicked to her ass and back again. "Lauren…" the big man whimpered.

"C'mere, Van. Come see. Come feel how hot I am for you and then you're going to claim me fully. Nothing's stopping us now. Not even me." Heated indecision coated his features, the man and bear parts of him fighting and struggling with her words. She'd created this in him with her lack of commitment and it made her sick. "Van, I want you." She was going for the jugular. "Claim me before I find someone else."

Not that she would. Ever. But it got her the desired result.

The size of his body increased, muscles bulging, and chest expanding ever so slightly. "Mine."

"Prove it." She couldn't help but taunt him.

*

Prove it.

Van had never been so fucking hard in his entire life.

Prove it.

Two words that made his bear crazy and his dick throb with the need to be buried deep inside his mate. He let his gaze wander her body, take in the lush curves of her frame and… damn… the red hand prints that covered her perfectly plump ass. The globes were bright red, glowing in the room like a kinky beacon.

She'd enjoyed the spanking even if she wouldn't admit it. The first spank had been a surprise, but by the third, her pussy was so sweet and wet for him. He didn't need to touch her to know that. Her scent surrounded him.

Now, she waited, taunted him, and stared at him expectantly.

He wasn't about to disappoint. They'd been working up to the point for days. Now she had his permanent mark on her shoulder and his handprints on her ass, and she was his.

Without waiting another moment, he pounced. Cats didn't have a monopoly on the move and Van took advantage, tackling her, and forcing a squeal from her lungs. He took her down to the bed and rolled until he straddled his mate's hips. He stared down into her flushed, smiling face and saw nothing but love filled her features. Her scent told him she wanted him, but her expression, her open gaze filled with pure truth, revealed the real story. Despite their problems, she truly desired him as her mate.

Fuck if that realization didn't make his heart hurt and his cock harder than steel.

"I think we've got things a little backward." She wiggled beneath him, his balls sliding over her stomach.

"Maybe," he smirked and mentally ran through all of the wicked things he wanted to do to her body. "Maybe not."

Her gaze strayed to his cock and she licked her lips, her tiny pink tongue coming out to play. That move reminded him about how wonderful it'd been to slip past those plump lips and into his mouth. And *that* had his cock throbbing with the desire for a repeat performance. His balls, snug and warm against her stomach, tightened and hardened, more than ready to come. Now.

"Van?" Her arms twitched, drawing his attention, and he noticed she clutched the blanket as if fighting herself. Again she licked those lips. "Van?" she whimpered.

"Yeah, baby?" He palmed his cock, stroking his dick, and even more pre-cum escaped. "What d'ya need?" A whine came from her and he smiled. "Gotta say it." Even if he knew what she desired. Even if he wanted it as much as her.

Lauren nibbled her lower lip, her attention never slipping away from his hand's travels. "I want to…" She drew in a long, slow breath, her breasts jiggling with the move. "I want to suck your cock."

"Uh-huh?" He pinched below the head, squeezing a hint too hard so that a spike of pain joined his arousal. Fuck, it hurt so damned good. "How, baby?"

Indecision and unease sprinted across her features and he was quick to take the lead. He'd gotten her to this point, he had her in his bed and asking for what she desired, he could help her with the rest.

"Do you want me to scoot up and feed you my dick?" Her arousal dimmed at that question as he knew it would. Maybe someday they'd do that, when they'd built a firmer foundation of trust between them. "Or do you want me on my back and at your mercy?" That brought her need flaring back to life.

Without a word, he rolled to his side and flopped onto his back. He stretched out, hands behind his head much like the first time they'd become intimate. Except this time, he spread his legs wide, giving her room to settle between his legs.

"I'm all yours, baby."

All hesitation fled her, his sweet mate immediately crawling between his thighs, her gaze on her prize.

Lauren scraped his legs with her small nails, digging them into his skin as she traveled along his shins to his knees. From there, she scratched her way along his thighs, leaving a pleasurable burn to follow in her wake. Finally, she circled his cock, those abrasive fingernails easing near his shaft, but not touching. Though, God knew he wanted her touch.

Her nails teased the very edge of his dick, the very base of his shaft. It caused a pleasurable ache within him, and he fought between the need to pull away and the desire for more. Damn it, he was a little like her. He didn't mind a bit of an ache if it meant getting off. Was this how it was when he spanked her moments ago?

"Lauren…" he growled a warning and his mate laughed. The pain in the ass laughed.

But then she delivered. She wrapped her small hand around his girth while lowering her face, mouth open. Oh, fuck, fuck, fuck, he couldn't come before he even got inside her. He couldn't shoot like some teenage bear. But he wanted to. His cock pulsed with the need to release, his pleasure rising with each breath and each second she touched him. He'd come, then recover, then fuck her unconscious. It seemed like a good plan.

Except then her plump lips wrapped around the head of his cock and wet warmth enveloped him. Her tongue tapped against the slit in his cockhead, sliding along that tiny length and he shuddered. "Fuck. S'good, Lauren."

She hummed around him, taking him deeper, only to rise along his shaft once again.

Shit, that sound against his dick. Van fisted the blanket, fighting to keep his hips still and his hands to himself.

But she scraped a nail along his cock as she took him deep and he couldn't take it. He sifted his fingers through her strands and fisted them, holding her tight. Then, when she went down, he flexed his hips the tiniest bit, slipping deeper into her mouth.

A new wave of her scent bowled him over, bathing him in her musky aroma. Yes, his mate liked him taking that bit of control. So he continued, gently pushing her down as he rose up, softly fucking her perfect lips.

Her hand worked in time with her mouth, caressing him with every rise and fall as she sucked. Her spit slicked him, allowing him to move easily in the circle of her hand. She hummed around him again, sending a spear of pleasure through him. His cock throbbed deep within the cavern of her mouth, begging to be thrust in and out of her juicy cunt.

"Fuck. Baby. Like that."

His dick was rock hard and ready to blow, his balls waiting for him to loosen his control for even a second. One moment of relaxation meant he'd spend himself in her mouth and he fucking refused to let that happen. He wanted her pussy, wanted to sink into her, and join with her completely.

He'd stop her in a minute.

She swirled her tongue around the tip and scraped a tooth along the spongy head.

Maybe two minutes.

Lauren sucked him deep then, falling along his length until he met the back of her throat and then—fuck!—she swallowed around him, taking him to the base. His lungs heaved, body aching to respond to the erotic sight before him.

His Lauren, his mate, had taken all of him and gave him a look of pure want, pure need, pure desire. He tensed, fighting his orgasm and the bear at the same time. Their shared body craved release, but he reminded himself for the millionth time it'd be better in her pussy.

He hoped that happened. Soon.

Slowly she eased along his cock, revealing his wet shaft to the room's cool air. Her cheeks were flushed pink, lips swollen and red, but there was no denying the pure sexual craving in her gaze. She got to the tip and released him, running her tongue along the mushroom shaped head.

Their gazes remained locked as she made love to his dick, her tongue dancing over the flesh, tormenting and teasing him. He wasn't sure which was better—feeling or seeing?

Thank god he got both.

"Van?" she whispered against his cock, her warm breath teasing him.

"Mmm hmm?" He hoped she didn't start quizzing him on something other than his cock being in her mouth. He didn't think he could talk about anything else.

"Are you ready to be inside me?"

Okay, *that* he could talk about.

"Fuck, yes." At least, that's what he thought he said, but the bear rode him hard, urged him to flip her over, take her, claim her fully, and fill her with his cub already. The animal knew if they got her barefoot and pregnant, she'd never be able to leave.

The human part of Van figured they could at least keep her in shoes.

The bear did not get the joke.

Lauren suckled the tip of his cock once again, taking in an inch or two only to release him and lap at his slit. "Van?"

What's with the talking?

"Yeah?" He was ninety percent sure that sounded human.

She lifted her head and placed a soft, delicate kiss to his dick before whispering two words against his wet flesh. "Take me."

*

Lauren poked the bear. Poked it super, really, holy crap hard. Now she waited to see how he'd respond. Her heart thundered, pounding out an erratic beat inside her, and she held her breath. She wanted

Van, craved him more than her next breath, and now she awaited his reaction to his taunt.

She didn't have to wait long. In one fluid move she went from crouched between his legs, that beautiful cock filling her vision, to flat on her back.

Van knelt between her thighs, his tension-filled body bathed in the dim moonlight. Each of his muscles were highlighted by the low glow, showing her the restrained strength of her mate.

He took a deep breath, chest expanding a little and expanding further still when his beast pushed past the barrier. Muscles bulged and stretched his skin for a brief moment before he pushed the bear back once again.

He gave her a look... One of apology? Shame? A hint of fear?

"Is he anxious?" She kept her voice low, tone smooth with no hint of fear or worry.

His expression turned wary and Lauren pushed on. She was fully expecting Van *and* his bear. Not one or the other.

She pushed to her elbows, fighting not to cover her plump rolls with her hands while she spoke to him. "Your bear. Is he anxious for me? For you two to claim me?"

Van swallowed hard, his Adam's apple bobbing along his neck, and then he nodded.

She reached for him, snaring his hand and then tugging. "You're a bear and a man, Van. I understand that. So both of you make me yours."

He hovered over her, his heat bathing her with his nearness. He flopped forward, pulling from her hold and placing his palms flat against the mattress. "Lauren. God."

She scraped her nails along his arms, reveling in the responses she lured from him. So she apparently liked her ass spanked. Well, Van liked getting scratched. After that first time together, she'd discovered he liked a tiny hint of pain as well as a small memento. Unfortunately—or fortunately—she couldn't scar him permanently like he'd done to her.

She scratched his shoulders, dragging her fingers along his skin, and she didn't stop until she was able to twine her digits behind his neck. With one tug, his lips were within reach and she captured them with her own. She shoved her tongue deep into his mouth, tasting him.

Van growled against her and joined in the kiss, tangling with her, tasting and being tasted. His heat and dark natural flavors rolled over her tongue and she realized she'd never tire of kissing the man she lov—

Right.

Instead of letting her thoughts wander in that direction, she pulled her lips from his, and smiled against his lips. "Hey."

He grinned. "Hey, back."

"Hey," she leaned up and nipped his jaw. "Why don't you do that thing we talked about?"

"Thing?" He raised his eyebrows, feigning confusion, but she knew that *he knew* what she was talking about.

She dropped her voice to a husky whisper. "That thing where you take your cock…"

He moved one of his hands and she imagined him grasping the base of his dick. The next moment, the blunt tip brushed her wet pussy, sliding through the cream. "This cock?"

"Uh-huh." That was all she could get out because he was rubbing the head along her slit, caressing her entrance and then rising to nudge her clit. "Yeah." He repeated the caress and she fought to keep her eyes open when all she wanted was to let them drift closed as she floated on the pleasure. "That one."

Each touch brought forth another tremor tinged with pleasure. It raced through her blood and crept into every part of her.

"And what am I doing with it?"

Right now what he was doing felt pretty damn good. He nudged her clit, pressing and rubbing the small bundle of nerves. She rode his touch, rocked against his dick in an effort to pick up a gentle rhythm.

"Lauren?" He eased his pressure and she whined as the rising pleasure inside her lessened. "What am I doing with it?"

She glared at him, glared at his midnight eyes, and pointier than normal teeth.

He grinned.

Well, two could play that game.

Lauren ran her hands over him, scratching him here and there, while she also slid her foot along his calf. She hooked one leg, and then the other, around his hips. Using the muscles in her thighs, she squeezed and lifted herself while also rocking her hips. It took barely any effort to close the distance between his hard cock and her slick pussy. She rubbed against him, sliding over his length and the move tore a growl from his chest.

"We can wrestle all night, bear-boy." She tensed and slid over his silken skin. "Or you can give me what we both want."

Van gritted his teeth, the muscles of his neck straining. "What's that?"

Pain in the ass, man.

"You." She relaxed her legs and nipped his chin once again. "In me." She licked away any sting she might have caused. "Or are you not bear enough to fuck me."

There. Gauntlet thrown.

And Van was quick to snap up the challenge. In one move, he went from defiant to aggressive. He shifted his hips, pressed the head of his cock against her slick opening and thrust. He filled and stretched her, spreading her wide with his invasion and Lauren released a pleasure-filled scream.

The bliss of his possession singed her nerves, stoked her arousal with a mixture of ecstasy and a hint of pain. He pushed forward until his hips were snug against hers, his balls resting on the curve of her ass. There, he was inside her. They were one.

She never wanted him to leave her again. If they could somehow live their lives with his cock constantly inside her, she would. A moan at the idea had Van tensing, stilling above her.

"Lauren." Unease and regret slid over his features.

"It's so good, Van. Mate." She rocked her hips, enjoying the feel of him in her pussy.

Some of those negative feelings fled. "Yeah?"

"Uh-huh. Want more."

"This?" He withdrew a little and pressed back in, his balls slapping against her skin.

Lauren gasped with the retreat and advance, the rough thrust dumping a bucket of pleasure into her body. "Oh god, yes."

"What else do you like? What do you love?"

She answered both questions truthfully, she simply couldn't admit it totally, explicitly out loud yet. "You."

A dusting of brown fur slid into sight and then disappeared. "Fuck."

She giggled. "I thought that's what we were doing."

Van shook his head as if to clear it. "Baby, need to do something different." Each word was filled with his bear's growl.

234

"Van?" He didn't respond to her question. He simply rolled to his side, dragging her with him in the sudden shift of positions. She went from huddled beneath him to astride his hips in one move. Now she was the one in control—the fucker, instead of the fuckee. She had to admit she liked the idea.

"He's too close, baby. Don't wanna hurt you." He fisted the sheets and she saw a hint of claw.

"Neither of you would hurt me." She knew that like she knew her name.

Van shook his head. "Ride me. Use me. Love me, baby."

It was there, plain to see, his emotions written across his features. His message was a combination of raunchy and touching, and she decided to give in to his desires. If he was worried about the bear, she wouldn't push him.

Instead, she did as he begged and as her body demanded. Slowly, enjoying the gentle caress of his cock against her inner-walls, she rose. His dick teased all of those delicious nerve endings, tugging a groan from her as she moved.

"Yes," she hissed and the word was answered with a moan from Van.

She then slid down, taking him deep once again. That was her pace, slow and gentle, an easy glide up and then down again. She continued, keeping the rhythm, the sounds of their breathing and the soft meeting of their bodies the only sounds in the room. It wasn't a race, a rush to the end. No, their lovemaking was a slowly kindling fire.

"That's it, baby. So good. So sexy." Van's hands shifted from mattress to her thighs, sliding along her legs until he rested his palms on her hips. "So mine."

He gripped her, tightening his hold until she was forced to move at his pace. The soft rise and fall transformed into small, rocking thrusts and retreats and each meeting of their hips caressed her clit.

"Van!"

"Cup your breasts and lean down for me. Let me suck on one of your pretty nipples." The words said in that gravelly deep voice had her pussy rippling around him, pleasuring them both. "C'mon, gimme what I want."

Thankfully, she wanted it, too.

Lauren let him set their pace, the depth and force of their meetings while she leaned forward and propped herself on her hands. Her breasts hung heavy from her body, swinging gently with each meeting of their hips.

"Lower, baby."

She whimpered and did as he asked, going nearer and turning her body slightly so he could capture one tip between his lips. He hummed against her flesh as he pulled her deep, sucking her in. Each draw went straight to her clit, strumming the bundle, and shooting her desire higher.

Van nibbled the nub, scraping it with his teeth, then flicked it with his tongue. He tormented her breast while his cock teased her pussy.

His hips guided her into a quicker rhythm, a stronger collision of their bodies. Now the meeting of their hips, the slap of skin on skin, joined their heavy panting and delicious moans. She rode him hard, reveling in the pleasure of their lovemaking. No matter how rough and tumble, it'd always be love making.

Lauren gave herself to the pleasure, allowed him to direct their bodies, to take and give whatever bliss he could. His cock stroked those deep nerve endings while his mouth tormented her breasts. She watched him, watched him shift from one nipple to the other. His eyes remained locked on her, the bear peeking out from behind Van's brown irises.

She took and accepted them both. The bear was Van and Van was the bear. One in the same in his human-shaped body.

He scraped her nipple again, sharp tooth grazing the sensitive flesh only for him to soothe the ache with his tongue.

All the while, their hips moved, followed the age-old rhythm that drew pleasure along her nerves in waves of bliss.

"Van…"

He growled and released her breast as he tightened his hold on her hips. "Yes," he hissed.

Her pussy clenched around him, milking his shaft in pre-cursor to her orgasm. She'd come soon, come on his cock, and he'd fill her with his cum. She'd never gone there before, never experienced that level of intimacy, but he was Van. Her mate.

The pace altered, angle adjusted tiniest bit and then the connection was deeper, harsher, and so, so much better. Her clit was slapped with every thrust, tearing a scream from her with each meeting.

"Good. God. Van. Gonna."

He growled again, snarling at her, baring his teeth, and she knew it wasn't in anger, but in need. "Come."

This time it was her who fisted the sheets, he fought to retain control as she was overridden by desire. He pumped in and out of her pussy, fucking her hard and deep as her pleasure rose higher and higher.

The peak was in sight, so close she could almost grab the ball of bliss and hold it tight. Instead, she let Van shove her to the edge, push her nearer and nearer to release.

"Come," he snarled.

And she couldn't deny him. Lauren's body seized, muscles tightening for an unending second and then… then pleasure consumed her. It

237

seared her, burned her from inside out as it overwhelmed her senses. Her mind was overcome by the ecstasy of their lovemaking. It rolled through her in wave after wave of pure joy that seemed endless.

Distantly, she heard Van roar, the sound shaking their home, and a new heat filled her as his cock pulsed within her sheath. That warmth shoved her orgasm higher, forcing her release to resurge before it'd drifted away.

Her cunt continued to spasm around him, milk him of every ounce of his cum. Her body trembled, overwhelmed by their shared passion. She sobbed and cried, slumping against him as the shards of pleasure pierced her over and over.

At some point his hips stilled, and then his warm hands slid along her spine, soothing her as the pleasure waned and eased into a dull, blissful throb. Tremors caused her to twitch, a new ripple of desire attempting to slither forward.

Eventually, she was merely a boneless heap atop Van, allowing her mate—in every sense of the word—hold her weight.

Van continued to run his hands along her hips, down her spine to settle on the curve of her ass. She wiggled and pressed into his touch, enjoying the feel of his hands on her skin while he was still inside her. She knew she'd have to move eventually, let him slip from her body at some point, but she wanted to wait as long as possible. She enjoyed this intimate connection, the proof of the trust they now shared.

She sighed and nuzzled his neck, wishing she never had to move again.

Then he was a dick and smacked her ass.

chapter eighteen

Things had been quiet for days. *Days*. And Lauren was getting bored.

Well, bored-ish. Van kept her busy at night. Very busy. But he had to work during the day, which left her at loose ends.

Not that she didn't enjoy spending time with Mia, Parker (when he was well supervised), and Gigi. No, that wasn't the problem. Her problem stemmed from being useless. She was used to working, used to earning her keep. Hiding on clan lands while Ty and Van hunted up a connection between Morgan and Bryson while also doing their everyday jobs left her nothing to do. She couldn't contribute.

If something non-bad, yet interesting, didn't happen soon she'd go insane.

She'd even tried to cajole Van into taking her to work with him.

"I could answer phones."

"No." He tugged on his shirt.

"Or file. I could file." She knew the alphabet, damn it.

"No."

"What about in the lobby? That woman just sits there and—"

Van spun on her then, gripping her shoulders, and giving her a gentle squeeze. "Davies works in that building. I will not now, or ever, have you close to him again." He tightened his hold for a brief moment. "We know what happens when one of my bears is threatened, we know how I react." His gaze darkened, eyes blackening to midnight. "What do you think will happen if you get hurt? If he harms you in some way? If Morgan gets near you?"

"I'll be fine… We don't know Morgan is involved." She refused to address his question.

"In your gut, you know. In Ty's gut, in my gut, we know. Somehow the two of them are working together. For some reason, Morgan sent wolves into our territory." He tugged her close, hugging her tight. "I would destroy the town to get to anyone who hurt you and the bear and I wouldn't care who got in the way. So, please, stay safe. For me and for them."

She had a hard time arguing with him when he got logical. And now logical had her sitting on her ass watching soap operas and talk shows.

Ugh.

She pushed a button on the remote, flicking from one channel to another. Flick, flick, flickity flick. He hadn't even left the password for the pay per view service. The least he could have done was given her a way to rent a movie. Anything was better than what she had before her.

Another ugh.

Lauren tossed the remote on the end table and sighed. At this point, being mauled by Parker seemed fun.

A knock on the front drew her attention and she shoved herself from the couch with a frown. She hadn't had visitors at Van's with the exception of the weird guy, Charles. Any other time she saw someone, it was at the Itan and Itana's home.

Another knock came as she reached for the knob. She half turned it and then froze. What if someone snuck onto clan lands? What if someone—? Then she remembered where she was and snorted. Clan lands. Who wanted to deal with bears? There were at least a good two dozen wandering the forests. Plus, all the single males knew she'd mated Van. They weren't going to bother her.

Regardless, she peeked through the peephole and then let out a loud squeal as she yanked the door open.

"Anna!" She bounced in place and then reached for her best friend, hugging her close. "Oh my god," she pushed her friend back, taking a moment to inspect the woman. The swelling in her face was gone, the purple nearly vanished as well. "You look great!" Better than great. She glowed, happiness radiated from her and practically shined through her skin. "How are you?" She hooked her arm around Anna's, dragging her into the house. "How'd you get here? Did Martin come? How are you feeling?"

Lauren couldn't help but fire off the questions, one after another. She'd spent days joyously in Van's company, but there was nothing like girl talk.

Anna laughed, the sound high and pure and Lauren froze, halting their progress. She felt tears forming behind her eyes, stinging her as they grew.

"Lauren?" Her friend's brow was furrowed, concern filling her gaze.

"It's been a really long time since you laughed. That's all." She wiped her eyes, pretending tears weren't trailing down her cheeks. "Never mind, I'm an idiot."

Anna stepped forward, wrapping her arms around Lauren and she clung to her friend. "No, you're not. It's been a long time since I wanted to laugh, but Martin…"

She giggled and squeezed Anna a hint tighter as a smile blossomed on her lips. "Yeah, Van, too." She released her best friend and grabbed Anna's hand, tugging her deeper into the house. "C'mon. We can dish and munch on food with way too many calories."

241

Anna's smile was blinding in its intensity and Lauren realized this was her friend of years ago, before Bryson Davies got his abusive clutches in her. "Deal."

They padded into the kitchen and dug through the cabinets, gathering anything full of fat and filled with comfort. In fifteen minutes they had their carbfest setup in the living room and had successfully weaseled the pay per view pin out of Van.

Life was good.

Until two hours later, when it went from good to oh-fuck-you're-fucking-kidding-me.

A low thud from the direction of the bedrooms snared Lauren's attention and she turned her head to stare at the dim hallway. Then another came, softer, but still audible.

"What the hell's that?" Anna sounded confused and Lauren felt a little of the same, but there was something else she had going on too.

Fear.

"No idea." She handed the remote to her friend. "Lemme check."

She moved to rise, but Anna wrapped her fingers around Lauren's wrist. "No, wait. In the movies, the girl who investigates the weird sounds first *always* dies. I'll go check."

Lauren glared at Anna. "So you can die first? How fair is that?"

"What, you wanna go?"

"Well, I don't wanna die, but I don't see the connection between a thump in the back of my house and an idiot girl in the movies." She rolled her eyes.

"Your house? So you're staying?" Anna grinned and Lauren answered with one of her own.

Then rolled her eyes because they were getting off track. "I still need to see where the hell that sound came from. For all we know, Parker's trying to wiggle in through the window and got stuck."

Anna raised her eyebrows. "That's happened."

"Yeah," she sighed. "He feels bad and has been trying to bring me breakfast in bed to apologize. His pop does that for his mim when she gets mad at him, though he does admit he doesn't know why they make weird noises after that." Lauren snickered and remembered the Itana's bright red face when the little cub admitted that aloud. "Anyway, lemme go."

Anna sighed. "Fine, I tried to warn you. You shall be yet another too stupid to live casualty of the film industry."

"I'll be the best idiot on the screen." She rolled her eyes and turned back to the hallway and froze. "Shit."

"What?" Anna peeked around her, her friend pressed against her back. "Oh, shit."

Panic built inside her, boiling and bubbling in her stomach and radiating through her body. How odd was it that she was so used to bears now, used to the animals that weighed over a ton, but she freaked out over a simple hunk of metal?

Well, a hunk of metal held by a man. Okay, not a man in the literal sense, but a man-shaped bear. Fuck it, her ex-landlord was in her damn house with a fucking gun and he looked extremely pissed.

Lauren gulped, staring at the man while she tried to keep the panic at bay. "Wh-what are you doing here, Brubaker?" She clutched Anna's arm and eased her friend behind her. "How'd you get in?"

Brubaker smiled, exposing near rotted teeth. "Got a little help getting in. As for why…" He waved his gun. "You and me got some business. It just happens to go along with those other guy's." He strode forward, a swagger in his steps as he eased closer. "You got the Itan after me. Wanting me to clean up my act. Fining me for not coming to gatherings and shit."

Lauren nudged Anna back, trying to put more space between them and Bru. "Look, it wasn't me. I just wanted my shit. Having the Itana with me was an accident. I didn't know you're a bear."

He shrugged. "Doesn't change anything. I still gotta deal with the Itan's shit until he's taken care of and the man still wants you gone."

"Taken care of?" She needed to stall him. There had to be a nearby bear who'd recognize the strange scent, right? Bru had apparently been absent from the clan for a while. He wasn't familiar to the members. What was the point of having the super sniffers if they didn't use them? "What's gonna happen?"

Anna tripped on a piece of furniture, stumbling a little and bringing Bru's attention on her. "I got you, and I got another pretty, huh?" Brubaker leered at Anna. "They didn't say what I should do with an extra."

"What's gonna happen to Ty? What are you supposed to do to me, Bru?" Lauren's heart was gonna burst from her chest, explode right then and there.

He shrugged. "Kill you. The Itan is someone else's problem. Something about that Alpha and causing a dumb assed blood war."

So simple. Two words strung together like any other. "How?"

She'd address the issue with Ty and the Alpha once she got out of this mess alive. She shuffled along the wall, drawing him with her. The massive glass doors were ahead. She hoped if she could lure him in front of them, someone would see the male.

"Who told you? Did they say how? Are you their puppet?"

"Brubaker Jones isn't a puppet! Especially not to some mamby-pamby high and mighty mayor." The man growled, his shoulders widening as more of his bear came out to play.

Goody. Well, at least she knew who wanted her dead. Not that it was a surprise or anything.

Anna whimpered and shrunk against Lauren. She wanted to do the same thing, but somebody had to be in front. Instead of cowering, she kept them moving, dodging furniture while weaving their way across the room.

"Quitcha moving. I'm not supposed to touch anything. You keep moving and I'll hit something and then the plans for shit." Bru growled then, his free hand forming a fist.

"Sorry. Don't want to ruin your plan to kill me." She dropped as much sarcasm as she dared into the sentence.

"You're an uppity bitch, aintcha?" He waved the gun, muzzle encompassing her body as it swung. "I know why the high and mighty asshole wants ya dead. What about the other guy? What's so special 'bout you?"

"The other?" Good god, did she really piss off that many people that they wanted her dead? Right, he'd said "other guy's." Apparently she had pissed off at least two men.

"The wolf. Why'd he want you—?"

A shower of glass hit Lauren, the doors shattering as a massive form flew through the barrier. The furred body destroyed the panels, smashing them into a million pieces as it bulldozed its way into Van's home. It knocked over furniture when it slid to a stop before her, the bulk shielding her and Anna from Bru.

A handful of low pops filled the room and the bear roared, the sound bouncing off the wooden walls. It rose to its hind legs, stretching to its full height.

She finally realized why the ceiling was so high. Huh.

The snap of bone reached her, telling her Brubaker initiated his own change, but the newcomer was already on him, his teeth and claws going after Bru with intent focus. Brubaker tried to dodge the bear, tried to move around the furniture cluttering the living room, but couldn't escape.

245

Blood coated the shined floors, both Brubaker's and the stranger's, dyeing the wood red. Dark patches covered their savior, the telling spots letting her know just how hurt the bear was.

Bru shot again, three muzzle flashes followed by the pop and thump when the bullets found home. The asshole. The asshole was shooting at the man who'd saved them.

Lauren shoved Anna toward the kitchen, pushing her through the doorway. "Call for help."

Then she turned back to the battle.

Bru was still working through his shift, pieces of him transformed into his bear while others remained human. Their savior wasn't giving the man time to concentrate, to truly call on his animal.

Good.

The bear fought to keep up with the mostly human Bru, pushing and shoving his way past the larger pieces of furniture that marred his path.

And Bru… Well, he was focused on the bear.

Which meant he didn't notice Lauren grab a fire poker. He didn't realize she stood behind him. And he definitely hadn't expected her to nail him in the head with the rod.

She brought it down as hard as possible, intent on knocking his half-furry ass out. The metal collided with his skull with a dull, reverberating thunk, sending painful vibrations up her arms. Brubaker turned toward her, shock filling his gaze for a brief moment before his eyes rolled up, exposing only the whites. He fell in a boneless heap, body collapsing into a pile of bloodied arms and legs.

The bear snarled at her, baring his fangs, and he dug his claws into the wood. She was sure bloodlust still rode the man hard, it was one thing Van warned her about when it came time for hunts and gatherings. Werebears were always a little more bear than man when a lot of blood was involved.

"Nice bear." She slowly lowered the fire poker, easing it to the ground with great care. "You don't wanna eat me, right? I'm so totally not tasty. Very fatty. Not worth the trouble or anything."

The bear glared at her a moment and then huffed what almost sounded like a laugh. Then the slow, agonizing process of his shift began. Fur receded to expose torn flesh, holes peppering his shoulders and arms as well as one in his side. She kept hunting for others as his transformation continued, but she stopped her exploration when she got to his junk. He could tell her about any injuries farther south.

One thing she did notice about the male that surprised her more than anything was the identity of her savior.

"Charles."

The man groaned, stumbling a tiny bit, and Lauren rushed forward to help him. She forced him to lean into her, dragging one of his arms across her shoulders. He was a hell of a lot taller than her, but they made it work as she eased him toward the dining room. It was the one place that hadn't been destroyed by the battle.

"Anna!" No sooner had her friend's name left her lips before she came running into the room, phone in hand.

"I called the house, they're on their way."

Lauren nodded. "Good. Tell them Charles is hurt and grab some towels from beneath the sink." In the meantime, she ripped her own shirt up and off, anxious to press it against his wounds.

"Your mate is gonna finish the job that asshole started if he comes in here and sees you topless." He hissed when she shoved the fabric against the largest of the wounds. "Especially after…"

"Good thing he's at work, then."

"Sorry 'bout that, by the way."

Nice of him to be sorry for being a total freak. Then again, he'd saved their ass and Lauren figured she could forgive a lot. She just wouldn't be around the guy alone. Like, ever.

Voices and the pounding of the heavy males running through the house reached her, and she let a little of the tension inside her ease. Help. They had help now. Which meant she could freak out.

Soon, even.

As soon as she took care of one last thing. "Charles?"

He grunted when she shifted the cloth. "Yeah?"

"Make sure they ask Bru about a wolf and Ty. The mayor wanted me dead, but wolves are doing something to mess up things between the clan and pack."

"Why don't you?"

She swallowed hard, pushing back the nausea and darkness that threatened. She wasn't sure which of the two would win, but one of them would in the next few minutes. So much *blood*. "I'm gonna…" She swayed, head seeming to float above her. "…pass out first."

* * *

Van fought the urge to wipe the smile off Morgan's face. Barely. The asshole had been being a dick since the moment he'd walked through the door.

After the last meeting in Ty's office, it'd been decided that they'd get together on neutral ground and the Itan and Alpha would coordinate get-togethers. Things were too important to be ruined by internal posturing and politics. The two would be able to continue coordinating efforts, but strict guidelines were in place.

Van was a little disappointed considering he'd wanted an excuse to kick Morgan's ass. Deep down, he knew Morgan was behind the lurking wolves and the attempt on Lauren's life.

Instead of gutting the wolf, he got to sit across a table from him in a supposedly neutral home.

Supposedly. Because it smelled a little too wolfy for Van's tastes, a little like the pack's Alpha. He couldn't imagine Reid doing anything to threaten their tentative peace, but the scent simply urged him to remain on guard.

The bear was ready and pacing. It definitely didn't like Morgan.

"My Itan and your Alpha," Van began and ignored Morgan's snort. "Have agreed to a final evacuation plan."

Van opened his folder and pulled out two copies of Ty's notes. He'd taken his brother's chicken scratch and created a bullet pointed list for him and Morgan to review. He also snared his listing of the remaining families to cross reference with the injured and sick in the hospitals.

"First, we need to grade the remaining medical cases and rate them in order of removal." He clicked his pen, ready to take notes. "Justin Montgomery is a quarter shifter and suffers from—"

"Non-issue." Morgan's voice was flat, devoid of emotion. "Taken care of."

He forced himself to take a deep, calming breath and let it out slowly. "Where did you move them?"

He shrugged. "Doesn't matter. They've been gone for over a week. Before your little Itan met with Reid."

He was going to be sick. "Melissa Slade—"

"Non-issue."

His bear roared, clawing and scraping at him. Melissa Slade had a rough pregnancy and had been hospitalized for a list of problems related to her pup. He'd been notified that she gave birth four days ago.

"Since when?" The animal struck him, pushed against him, demanded to be released because it knew the fucking answer to that question already.

"The day of the meeting. The meeting, which I did not attend." The dick didn't look a bit sorry about that fact.

Van took a deep breath and rolled his head, loosening his neck. He needed to relax, stay clear headed through the meeting. He could destroy something later.

"What the fuck is *wrong* with you?" His skin prickled, burning with the stretch and pull of his beast.

"Me?" Morgan rose, placing his fists on the tabletop as he leaned forward and glared at Van. "I'm not some pussy bear. I get shit *done*. I *protect* my pack from pieces of shit like those fucking hyenas. I've got the balls to do what needs doing."

Van stood so fast his chair went flying behind him, skittering over the floor. "You disgusting, sadistic *fuck*." Spittle flew from his mouth as he spoke, fury pulsing through him with every word. "You're nothing but a twisted killer."

"Fuck yeah, I am. The order was a purge, *bear*." Morgan sneered the last word. "What the hell did you think would happen? You and your pussy clan don't have the balls to do their jobs so the wolves took care of it. We fucking took out the hyenas when you needed help. Their blood was on our claws, not yours. Now suddenly you're getting a fucking conscience?"

He flexed his fingers, fighting the need to shift. His digits stretched and knuckles cracked, his bones attempting to lengthen and reform into claws. Van admitted the wolves had been an integral part of the fight against the hyenas, but they'd all fought the twisted, evil parts of the pack. Not pregnant women and teens. "Those weren't our orders and you know it."

"Fuck you. Read between the lines." Morgan pointed at himself. "I protect my pack and I got those hyenas out of here."

"That's not what your Alpha ordered and you know it." Van knew as sure as he breathed. He'd met Reid on many occasions. The man was cold, but he wasn't heartless.

"Sometimes an Alpha doesn't know what's good for him. Sometimes an Alpha is just fucking soft and needs to be taken out." Morgan twisted his neck, popping a line of vertebrae before turning golden eyes on Van. "Sometimes it's time for new blood." The wolf licked a slowly lengthening fang. "I'm going to take yours and then, when the time is right, I'll take his. The plan is in play. Ty's going to fall beneath wolf claws. It'll look like Reid did it, and then I'll challenge my *Alpha* for leadership. Fucking perfect."

The bear was ready for the challenge, ready to tear into the wolf who'd hurt so many, who'd probably killed entire families in the clan's name and who planned on fucking with his brother. "C'mon then."

He stepped away from the table, tearing at his clothes as he fought to hold the change back until he was nude. No sense in ruining his shirt or jeans. He'd need them once he finished slicing and dicing this asshole.

Morgan had no such worries. He let his shift ripple through him, his wolf bursting forward and shredding his clothing in seconds.

Van wasn't worried. He'd trained for things like this. The wolf's change was fast, but Van's was faster. It'd be even quicker since the bear was more than eager to burst free.

His shirt floated from his fingertips, the fabric drifting away, and then he was a bear. Quick and painless. His human body expanded, exploded, and folded in on itself to become the bear. Faster than a blink, he embraced his animal.

251

The speed surprised Morgan, the wolf stilling as he caught sight—or rather didn't—of Van's change. With the man distracted, he batted the table out of the way, giving him a clear shot at the wolf.

He'd tear into him, slice and dice the asshole. He'd done his best to undermine their tenuous peace, intended on wresting the pack from Reid, and had already admitted to killing families in Boyne Falls. How many others suffered the same fate? How many others fell beneath Morgan's claw for no reason other than his enjoyment? Now he wanted Ty?

Those questions enraged his beast even more, and he released a wall-shaking roar. The sound enveloped the home, bouncing and echoing off every surface.

Morgan merely snarled and darted forward, snapping at him without connecting. Testing him. Van didn't care. Let the puny animal try to take him out. Let him try to—

"Stop." The voice was familiar, deep and commanding, and a wash of power rolled over him. It paused around him for a moment, but the bear shrugged it off. It wasn't his Itan's order, so screw it and the shapeshifting horse it rode in on.

It did, however, have an effect on Morgan. The wolf froze, its lips still pulled back and exposing his fangs, growl still rumbling. Yet, he didn't move. He remained immobile as the source of the word stepped into view.

A tall, broad shouldered, and menacing male stepped from the shadows.

Reid Bennett.

Without a care in the world, he sauntered up to Morgan, slowly making his way around the shattered table. He squatted near the wolf, bringing his face eye level with the beast.

"Shift." One word and yet again that dominance radiated from the Alpha.

With a whimper, Morgan did as ordered, his body slowly transforming from wolf to human. What had previously been swift and fluid, was now harsh and rough, and filled with jerky spasms as pieces changed.

The man fought his Alpha's order with every breath in his body. And it didn't work. Reid was too strong and Morgan obviously wasn't in the same league as his Alpha. A few minutes later, a panting, sweat-covered Morgan lay on the ground, his nude body glistening and trembling with exertion.

Finally, Reid stood and looked at him, his wolf's eyes shining. "If you wouldn't mind shifting, Enforcer. Ty is waiting for your call."

He didn't sense a threat from the male. He didn't get the feeling this whole situation was a setup to kill him once he was in his human skin, so he did as asked. The bear reluctantly gave up control, allowing his fur to recede. Unlike Morgan, his shift back took a mere second, leaving him standing nude and strong before the wolf Alpha.

"Alpha." He tipped his head slightly and the wolf did the same.

"Enforcer. Your Itan will give you his apologies for keeping you in the dark, but I will as well." Reid's hard-eyed gaze centered on the prone Morgan. "I knew he wanted to be Alpha, and was undermining our peace, but that's typical for stronger wolves. It doesn't mean they can, but they crave the power. This one," Reid nudged the nude man with his boot, "couldn't hold the position for more than a day even if he wanted to."

A low growl came from the ground and this time, Reid really did kick the man. "What he is, is devious. Sneaky. Fanatically so. He's a planner, always working one step ahead of the rest. Except for me." Reid's gaze centered on him once again and Van saw something darker peer out from behind the wolf's eyes. "What he doesn't understand is I'm the embodiment of the beast. I can't go feral, because I was born that way. That's the trick. Wolves are brutal, evil, constantly fighting to be on top. But me," Reid grinned, exposing his white canines, "I *am* the top."

"So you knew…?"

"I've always known," Reid shrugged. "And while my wolf wants to gorge on the blood of those weaker than him, my human half does have a conscience, albeit a small one. Check your phone when you get to your car. The locations of the missing families can be found there."

"I killed them." Morgan shoved the words past his lips and Reid snarled at the man.

"You left the job to others." The Alpha squatted. "And what you forget is they owe their lives and their loyalty to *me.*" He fisted Morgan's hair and then turned his attention to Van. "It might be a good idea to leave now. Besides, your mate needs you."

"My—" He glared at the wolf struggling in Reid's grip. "What'd he do?"

"It was what he put into motion, who he became involved with. But from all reports, your female is feisty." The feral, lascivious grin that came his way had his bear's hackles rising and a growl forming in his throat. The Alpha waved him away. "I don't want yours. Go take care of your mate while I have a little fun with this one. I'll send you a piece or two once it's done."

Van wanted to assure the Alpha that "a piece or two" of Morgan wasn't necessary, but the Alpha was no longer paying attention to him. No, the male was fully focused on Morgan.

His bear whined, reminding him of their need to get to Lauren. He didn't *not* trust the wolf Alpha, but he wouldn't be at peace until he held her in his arms.

Ignoring the whimpers coming from Morgan, Van gathered his clothing and shoved his legs into his jeans. Fuck putting on the rest, he had to get to Lauren.

"And, Enforcer? Tell the Itan he has a lovely, thoroughly insane gift at the station." Van raised a single brow in question and the Alpha flashed him a purely evil, sadistic grin. "The mayor and I had an enjoyable, claw-tipped conversation."

Van gave the Alpha a jerky nod, but didn't stick around any longer. He carried his clothing in his arms, dumping it on the floorboard as soon as he climbed in. He dug out his keys and started the SUV with ease. The moment he hit the highway, he yanked out his cell phone, giving the piece of equipment verbal instructions to call Ty.

His brother answered on the first ring. "She's fine."

chapter nineteen

Lauren wondered if she'd spend the rest of her life alternating between hurt and bored with sex sprinkled in between.

At the moment, it seemed so.

No, that wasn't even true. She wasn't *really* bored. She was waiting. For Van. For *hours*.

Or fifteen minutes, but who was counting.

The point was, she was left to her own devices for the first time in weeks and all she wanted to do was curl up in Van's lap and snuggle. He'd somehow turned her into a lap cat.

Bastard.

Though, when he called her a lap cat, she did remind him how easy it'd be to turn him into a bearskin rug.

That argument ended in several hours of sexytimes.

She called that a win.

Which contrasted with right now because she was alone and considered it a great big loss.

Lauren glanced at the mantel clock and huffed. She still had another five minutes before he got home. She looked down at her outfit, making sure she wore what he'd requested. He was surprising her with something he promised would be amazing, so the least she could do was dress as he'd asked. Besides, he wanted her in shorts, a tank top, and flip-flops. She wasn't going to argue about comfy-wear.

He'd even told her a bra and panties were optional. Lauren snorted. She was not letting the girls swing free. They were too big for all that.

She released another long sigh that slowly morphed into a groan. She hated waiting. And yes, she knew she acted like a two year old with her mental whining, but that didn't change her mind. She still hated waiting.

The familiar, deep rumble of a truck reached her and she gasped. He hadn't, had he? She bolted for the front door and yanked it open, spilling onto the porch.

Yup, he had, there was Van driving her big assed, ugly as hell truck Betsy. Another bear, Ash, drove Van's SUV and pulled in behind her mate. Lauren only had eyes for her pickup.

"You brought her back!" She smiled wide and bounced down the steps.

Van just rolled his eyes. He shoved the driver's door open and stepped from her baby. "Yeah, yeah. Michael at the shop finally fixed her."

She glared at him, knowing he was lying. They'd been playing this game for weeks. Her begging for her truck and him, repeating over and over that the shop was "waiting for parts."

They were damned brake lines. Not gold-plated spark plugs or a solid platinum ashtray. She figured it was because he wanted to cart her around, make sure she got to her destination safe and sound. Secretly, she liked that.

"So," she grinned and held out her hand palm up. She wiggled her fingers. "Is this my surprise? Hand 'em over. Momma hasn't driven her in a while."

A nearby snort reminded her they weren't alone and she turned her glare on Ash. She'd made friends-ish with the man, but she was reconsidering that decision. She opened her mouth to tell him where to stuff his laugh, but Van took care of it for her. He growled.

It was wrong that she found it so sexy. He was being a big, bad bear and she was getting wet. Sad state of affairs.

"Sorry, Enforcer." Ash gave Van a little half salute. "I'll see you guys later."

With that, he jogged toward the tree line, his lope carrying him farther away. She'd grown used to things like that. The men wouldn't head to the main clan house. They'd simply run into the forest and get furry, using four feet instead of two to get where they needed to be.

The second he disappeared, she remembered she still had her *empty* hand held out toward Van. She wiggled her fingers once again. "My surprise. Can I have her keys now?"

Van grinned at her, the one that said sexy-fun-times were on the horizon.

Not until she got her surprise, damn it. She'd let him score later.

"What will ya give me?"

She narrowed her eyes at him. "That's not how surprises work. You give them for the joy of giving."

"And I'm hoping you'll be so overjoyed," he stepped toward her, keys dangling from his fingers and clanking as he walked, "you'll give me a little more 'joy.'"

More joy? He was obviously talking about sex. The man couldn't keep his hands to himself. "Oh god, you're as big a cornnut as your brother."

Van huffed. "That right there did two things."

"Huh?"

"It killed my boner and told me you're spending too much time with Mia."

Lauren rolled her eyes. "Parker's young and has little ears and—"

"I know." He sighed. "So no extra 'joy'?"

"No. Is the truck my surprise or is there something else?"

He actually pouted and poked out his lower lip. "Are you sure there's no extra 'joy?' Even if there's something else."

"Bribery? Really?" She shook her head. "Then there is no extra 'joy.'"

"Yeah, yeah. C'mon and get in. We're taking a drive."

Lauren perked up. "And I get to drive? I haven't been behind Betsy's wheel—"

"No. Just… no." The massive bear shifter sounded so scared and he actually shuddered.

Lauren glared really, really hard. Clip a guard rail one time…

Van took a step forward and snared a belt loop on her shorts, tugging her toward him. She went easily, falling against him and letting him take her weight. All those muscles reminded her of all the times she'd seen them naked and then they'd done magical naked things and…

"Hey, missed you."

260

She pushed to her tiptoes and rubbed her nose against his. "Missed you, too."

"Yeah?"

She nodded, accepting his slow, gentle kiss. His tongue skated over her lips and she opened for him, granting him access while gently slipping into him as well. His heated flavors slid over her taste buds and she had to admit it was like coming home. Right there, right then, Van was her home. Tomorrow, if he left the toilet seat up, he was very, very anti-home. The antithesis of home. If home were chocolate cake, he'd be dry, fresh broccoli with no ranch dressing in sight.

Van eased the kiss, slowly pulling his lips from hers and she whimpered.

And he laughed.

Way too sexy werebear.

He reached around her and patted her ass. "C'mon, baby. We're gonna be late."

"Late?" Arousal and need still clouded her mind. "Where are we going?"

"That is the surprise." He nudged her away from him and he turned toward the driver's side of her truck once again.

"You're driving?" She shook her head, trying to get rid of the sensual fog he'd thrown over her.

"Yup. I know you missed her, but I need you to keep your eyes shut. The least I can do is let you ride in her. So, get your sexy ass in this truck before I drag you into the house and fuck you stupid."

She squeaked. "Stupid? I have never been—"

"You couldn't talk for three hours the other morning."

Oh, he was not getting sex for a super long time. "I was hoarse. It had nothing to do with you fucking me until I couldn't speak."

He grinned and winked at her so she growled and snapped her teeth at *him*.

"You know that makes my dick hard." He jerked his head toward the truck. "Get in already or I really will toss you over my shoulder and drag you inside."

She wasn't seeing a downside to his threat, but she knew he'd gone to a lot of trouble to organize whatever he was about to show her. He'd been whispering with Ty for days and reminding her over and over that she needed to be available today.

Lauren snorted. "Okay, lemme lock up the house—"

"The house is fine."

"But someone—"

"Baby," she focused on him, her mate, the man with a bear inside him who currently peeked out behind Van's human orbs, "no one is going to go near our house. No man or bear has balls that big."

"But…"

"Lauren?" He held his hand out for her and she went to him, readily walking into his arms.

"Mmm hmm?"

"I'm gonna tell you something and you have to promise not to be afraid of me."

She rolled her eyes. "Van, I'd never—"

"Promise."

The dark gaze, the intent seriousness that filled her features, had the next joke on her lips fleeing. "I promise."

He stared at her, no hint of emotions coursing through him, but she knew… His pulse raced, the rapid throb of the vein in his temple telling her of his unease. She pressed her palm to his chest and felt the heavy, speedy thump of his heart.

"I promise, Van. Nothing you could say or do would ever scare me."

Van remained quiet for a moment, his gaze turning inward and she imagined him rolling through the different ways he could get the words out. That was her Van. Sometimes he spoke before he thought and other times he'd take ten minutes to order a danged cheeseburger.

"Reid took care of Morgan."

Lauren nodded. She knew that. Morgan had conspired against the Alpha and intentionally endangered—tried to kill—another shifter's mate. Then there was the fact he tried to organize Ty's death while framing the Alpha. Reid dispensed a wolf's justice and Morgan had become a "non-issue."

"Davies is in an institution."

Another nod. Reid introduced Bryson to werewolves and a little bit of claw and fang hospitality. Mostly bruises, a few cuts, they told the man would turn him into a werewolf, and a whole lotta terror. The end result was a mentally broken Bryson Davies, ex-mayor of Grayslake and current resident at Whitely Cross Psychiatric Institution. He'd be there for a long, long, forever kind of time.

"And Brubaker…"

Ah, the heart of the matter. "Van," she shook her head. "You don't have to tell me anything."

"I do. At least a little. Some of the bears in the clan might act… differently toward you."

She suppressed her snort. The day after Bru suffered from an unfortunate "bear mauling" they began acting differently. This was not news. "I know."

"No, I—"

"Van," she pushed against his hold and stepped out of the circle of his arms. "Your job is dangerous and bloody and your bear has to be mean sometimes. I get it. So, you telling me that you ripped Bru to shreds and scared the hockey sticks out of the clan, is not a surprise."

He grinned at her, the darkness in his gaze fleeing. "Hockey sticks?"

"The Itana has been all over my ass about cursing. It's demeaning. How's the deliver guy at the diner supposed to take me seriously when I no longer speak fluent fuckyou-ish?" She huffed and propped her hands on her hips.

"Fuckyou-ish?"

"The English dialect of the ancient language 'fuckyou.' Very old. Dignified even." She nodded to punctuate her statement.

"You don't care?"

"I don't care." She shook her head. "I love you, why would I care?"

Shit. There it was. Out there in the world and floating between them. The silence stretched, growing longer and larger with every passing second.

"What kind of love?" Hope shone in his eyes, but he held himself back. They'd never said another word about love after that one time he laid out his feelings.

I'm cautiously, certainly, in love with you.

Lauren licked her lips, nerves taking flight in her stomach and stomping her intestines. Okay, ew, she was thinking about professing her love and… intestines. Gross. She was spending way too much time in the company of little boys.

264

"I'm," she took a deep breath and let it out slowly. "not-so-cautiously, certainly in love with you."

"Yeah?" His smile blossomed, mouth spreading, reaching all the way to his black-hued eyes.

"Yeah." She mirrored his expression.

Van dug into his pocket and tugged his cell phone free. He tossed it to her and she fumbled as she caught the thing. "Call Ty."

"Huh, why am I calling Ty? Aren't we—" Lauren squeaked, her position going from solidly on two feet to tossed over Van's shoulder in a blink.

"Because you need to tell him we're not coming."

"What?" She wiggled her ass and he spanked her. She hated that she liked it. "What about my surprise?"

"I have a surprise in my pants for you."

"You did not… You just… Does it vibrate? Because if it doesn't, I don't want it!" At some point they'd made it inside the house and Van lowered her feet to the ground so she could stand once again. "I mean it!"

"Lauren?"

She narrowed her eyes. He was not getting out of giving her the surprise. "What?"

"I certainly, certainly love you."

Okay, maybe he was.

"We're so lame." Lauren grinned, replaying their oddball declarations.

"I'm a big, bad werebear." He growled, playing along. "I'm never lame."

She backed away from him, tossing the cell phone onto a nearby chair. "You're all growl and no bite, mister."

Van raised single brow. "I thought it was roar?"

"Nah, I like it better when you growl." She teased him, running her hands over her hips and near the juncture of her thighs. "When you press your mouth against me and those vibrations…"

Then he did growl.

He leapt for her, stretching out, and she darted away. Laughing, she skirted the couch, sliding across the repaired, polished floor and on to the other side of the room.

The cell phone rang, vibrating and bouncing on the chair, but she only had eyes for Van. Whoever it was could wait.

Except Van, still smiling at her, reached down and snagged the hunk of cock-blocking-plastic. "Hello?" All hints of his smile fled, and suddenly he was stern and serious, no hint of their playfulness remaining. "I see… yes, I understand. I was a little busy…"

Van moved toward the end table where they kept pens and paper. Lauren was right there, heart hammering in her chest as she dug through a drawer and hunted what he'd need. God, what happened now? Things were so calm. Smooth sailing, steady sails, and every other idiom that meant crap was not blowing up on them.

There'd been more than one occasion he'd been called out for one bear matter or another and each one worried her. Right now, the seriousness in his expression scared her. She hadn't seen him this way before, this intense as he stared at her while speaking.

"Yes, I did have plans. No, this takes precedence." He raised an eyebrow to confirm his statement and she readily nodded.

His bear was out in full force, his eyes pure black and a light dusting of fur covered his cheeks. Whatever had him this upset was definitely more important. They had the rest of their lives. The situation needed him now.

Van cradled the phone between his ear and shoulder, holding out his hands for the pen and paper. She quickly closed the distance between them, handing it over in an instant.

He took the supplies from her and tugged her close, wrapping an arm around her waist, pulling her against him.

That's when she noticed two things—his cock was rock hard and the tension in him had nothing to do with worry.

"Van?"

He dropped the pen and paper then snared the phone and shoved it at her. "Got you." He winked and tossed her over his shoulder once again.

"Damn it, Van!"

"Language!" Mia's yelled at her through the phone.

Van popped her ass.

"What the fuck?"

"Language."

Smack.

This was fucking ridiculous.

"Language!"

"Oh, for the love of… Fuck you very much, Itana. Van, put my fucking, fuckity fuck ass down and quit spanking it or so help me…"

Distantly, she recognized that Mia was yelling "language" a lot, but her attention was solely focused on the hand on her ass and the way his spanks felt oh so good.

Lauren noted that he carried her down the hallway and toward their bedroom, each step bringing them closer and closer to the greatest thing ever—a bed.

"Are you listening to me?" Mia screeched.

She brought the phone to her ear. "Not so much, no. I'm pretty sure some major boinkage is gonna happen so…"

"But… Your surprise…"

"Itana, I need a night with the man I love." Lauren gasped, air suddenly rushing into her lungs as Van tossed her onto the bed. "Whatever it is, it's not more important than three little words."

As she said the words, basically told her Itana to go to hell, Lauren accepted the truth behind the statement. She tossed the phone aside, not caring where it landed or if Mia still listened.

The thing she cherished most in the world stood before her. He stripped, peeling layer after layer from his body and exposing more and more muscle and skin.

There was nothing more important than love—pure, unconditional love.

And growling against her pink bits.

Thankfully, with Van, she got both.

The End

If you enjoyed All Roar and No Bite, please be totally awesomesauce and leave a review so others may discover it as well. Long review or short, your opinion will help other readers make future purchasing decisions. So, go forth and rate my level-o-awesome!

By the way... here's a link to help you hunt up the first book of the Grayslake series:

http://bookbit.ly/noifszon

about celia kyle

Ex-dance teacher, former accountant and erstwhile collectible doll salesperson, New York Times and USA Today bestselling author Celia Kyle now writes paranormal romances for readers who:

1) Like super hunky heroes (they generally get furry)
2) Dig beautiful women (who have a few more curves than the average lady)
3) Love laughing in (and out of) bed.

It goes without saying that there's always a happily-ever-after for her characters, even if there are a few road bumps along the way.

Today she lives in central Florida and writes full-time with the support of her loving husband and two finicky cats.

If you'd like to be notified of new releases, special sales, and get FREE ebooks, subscribe here: http://celiakyle.com/news

You can find Celia online at:
http://celiakyle.com
http://facebook.com/authorceliakyle
http://twitter.com/celiakyle

copyright

Made in the USA
Columbia, SC
21 December 2019

85696947R00167